AGATHA CHR...
BOOK ONE

C000149625

BOOKS BY AGATHA CHRISTIE

The ABC Murders
The Adventure of the
    Christmas Pudding
After the Funeral
And Then There Were None
Appointment with Death
At Bertram's Hotel
The Big Four
The Body in the Library
By the Pricking of My Thumbs
Cards on the Table
A Caribbean Mystery
Cat Among the Pigeons
The Clocks
Crooked House
Curtain: Poirot's Last Case
Dead Man's Folly
Death Comes as the End
Death in the Clouds
Death on the Nile
Destination Unknown
Dumb Witness
Elephants Can Remember
Endless Night
Evil Under the Sun
Five Little Pigs
4.50 from Paddington
Hallowe'en Party
Hercule Poirot's Christmas
Hickory Dickory Dock
The Hollow
The Hound of Death
The Labours of Hercules
The Listerdale Mystery
Lord Edgware Dies
The Man in the Brown Suit
The Mirror Crack'd from Side
    to Side
Miss Marple's Final Cases
The Moving Finger
Mrs McGinty's Dead
The Murder at the Vicarage
Murder in Mesopotamia
Murder in the Mews
A Murder is Announced
Murder is Easy
The Murder of Roger Ackroyd
Murder on the Links
Murder on the Orient Express
The Mysterious Affair at Styles

The Mysterious Mr Quin
The Mystery of the Blue Train
Nemesis
N or M?
One, Two, Buckle My Shoe
Ordeal by Innocence
The Pale Horse
Parker Pyne Investigates
Partners in Crime
Passenger to Frankfurt
Peril at End House
A Pocket Full of Rye
Poirot Investigates
Poirot's Early Cases
Postern of Fate
Problem at Pollensa Bay
Sad Cypress
The Secret Adversary
The Secret of Chimneys
The Seven Dials Mystery
The Sittaford Mystery
Sleeping Murder
Sparkling Cyanide
Taken at the Flood
They Came to Baghdad
They Do It With Mirrors
Third Girl
The Thirteen Problems
Three-Act Tragedy
Towards Zero
Why Didn't They Ask Evans

Novels under the Nom de Plume of
'Mary Westmacott'
Absent in the Spring
The Burden
A Daughter's A Daughter
Giant's Bread
The Rose and the Tew Tree
Unfinished Portrait

Books under the name of
Agatha Christie Mallowan
Come Tell me How You Live
Star Over Bethlehem

Autobiography
Agatha Christie: An
    Autobiography

Agatha Christie's Poirot

BOOK ONE

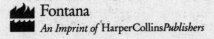

Fontana
An Imprint of HarperCollins*Publishers*

Fontana
An Imprint of HarperCollins*Publishers*
77–85 Fulham Palace Road,
Hammersmith, London W6 8JB

This collection first published by Fontana 1989
under the title Hercule Poirot's Casebook
9 8 7 6 5 4

'The Incredible Theft', 'Murder in the Mews' and 'Triangle at Rhodes'
were first published in *Murder in the Mews*, 1937; 'The Dream' and
'Four and Twenty Blackbirds' were first published in *The Adventure of
the Christmas Pudding*, 1960; and 'Problem at Sea', 'The Third-floor
Flat', 'The Adventure of Johnnie Waverly', 'The King of Clubs' and
'The Adventure of the Clapham Cook' were first published in *Poirot's
Early Cases*, 1947.

ISBN 0 00 647301 6

Set in Plantin

Printed in Great Britain by
HarperCollinsManufacturing Glasgow

CONTENTS

THE INCREDIBLE THEFT

CHAPTER 1

As the butler handed round the soufflé, Lord Mayfield leaned confidentially towards his neighbour on the right, Lady Julia Carrington. Known as a perfect host, Lord Mayfield took trouble to live up to his reputation. Although unmarried, he was always charming to women.

Lady Julia Carrington was a woman of forty, tall, dark and vivacious. She was very thin, but still beautiful. Her hands and feet in particular were exquisite. Her manner was abrupt and restless, that of a woman who lived on her nerves.

About opposite to her at the round table sat her husband, Air Marshal Sir George Carrington. His career had begun in the Navy, and he still retained the bluff breeziness of the ex-Naval man. He was laughing and chaffing the beautiful Mrs Vanderlyn, who was sitting on the other side of her host.

Mrs Vanderlyn was an extremely good-looking blonde. Her voice held a soupçon of American accent, just enough to be pleasant without undue exaggeration.

On the other side of Sir George Carrington sat Mrs Macatta, M.P. Mrs Macatta was a great authority on Housing and Infant Welfare. She barked out short sentences rather than spoke them, and was generally of somewhat alarming aspect. It was perhaps natural that the Air Marshal would find his right-hand neighbour the pleasanter to talk to.

Mrs Macatta, who always talked shop wherever she was, barked out short spates of information on her special subjects to her left-hand neighbour, young Reggie Carrington.

Reggie Carrington was twenty-one, and completely uninterested in Housing, Infant Welfare, and indeed any political subject. He said at intervals, 'How frightful!' and 'I absolutely agree with you,' and his mind was clearly elsewhere. Mr Carlile, Lord Mayfield's private secretary, sat between young Reggie and his mother. A pale young man with pince-nez and an air of intelligent reserve, he talked little, but was always ready to fling himself into any conversational breach. Noticing that Reggie Carrington was struggling with a yawn, he leaned forward and adroitly asked Mrs Macatta a question about her 'Fitness for Children' scheme.

Round the table, moving silently in the subdued amber light, a butler and two footmen offered dishes and filled up wine-glasses. Lord Mayfield paid a very high salary to his chef, and was noted as a connoisseur of wines.

The table was a round one, but there was no mistaking who was the host. Where Lord Mayfield sat was so very decidedly the head of the table. A big man, square-shouldered, with thick silvery hair, a big straight nose and a slightly prominent chin. It was a face that lent itself easily to caricature. As Sir Charles McLaughlin, Lord Mayfield had combined a political career with being the head of a big engineering firm. He was himself a first-class engineer. His peerage had come a year ago, and at the same time he had been created first Minister of Armaments, a new ministry which had only just come into being.

The dessert had been placed on the table. The port had circulated once. Catching Mrs Vanderlyn's eye, Lady Julia rose. The three women left the room.

The port passed once more, and Lord Mayfield referred lightly to pheasants. The conversation for five minutes or so was sporting. Then Sir George said:

'Expect you'd like to join the others in the drawing-room, Reggie, my boy. Lord Mayfield won't mind.'

The boy took the hint easily enough.

'Thanks, Lord Mayfield, I think I will.'

Mr Carlile mumured:

'If you'll excuse me, Lord Mayfield – certain memoranda and other work to get through...'

Lord Mayfield nodded. The two young men left the room.

The servants had retired some time before. The Minister for Armaments and the head of the Air Force were alone.

After a minute or two, Carrington said:

'Well – O.K.?'

'Absolutely! There's nothing to touch this new bomber in any country in Europe.'

'Make rings round 'em, eh? That's what I thought.'

'Supremacy of the air,' said Lord Mayfield decisively.

Sir George Carrington gave a deep sigh.

'About time! You know, Charles, we've been through a ticklish spell. Lots of gunpowder everywhere all over Europe. And we weren't ready, damn it! We've had a narrow squeak. And we're not out of the wood yet, however much we hurry on construction.'

Lord Mayfield murmured:

'Nevertheless, George, there are some advantages in starting late. A lot of the European stuff is out of date already – and they're perilously near bankruptcy.'

'I don't believe that means anything,' said Sir George gloomily. 'One's always hearing this nation and that is bankrupt! But they carry on just the same. You know, finance is an absolute mystery to me.'

Lord Mayfield's eyes twinkled a little. Sir George Carrington was always so very much the old fashioned 'bluff, honest old sea dog'. There were people who said that it was a pose he deliberately adopted.

Changing the subject, Carrington said in a slightly over-casual manner:

'Attractive woman, Mrs Vanderlyn – eh?'

Lord Mayfield said:

'Are you wondering what she's doing here?'

His eyes were amused.

Carrington looked a little confused.

'Not at all – not at all.'

'Oh, yes, you were! Don't be an old humbug, George. You were wondering, in a slightly dismayed fashion, whether I was the latest victim!'

9

Carrington said slowly:

'I'll admit that it *did* seem a trifle odd to me that she should be here – well, this particular weekend.'

Lord Mayfield nodded.

'Where the carcass is, there are the vultures gathered together. We've got a very definite carcass, and Mrs Vanderlyn might be described as Vulture No. 1.'

The Air Marshal said abruptly:

'Know anything about this Vanderlyn woman?'

Lord Mayfield clipped off the end of a cigar, lit it with precision and, throwing his head back, dropped out his words with careful deliberation.

'What do I know about Mrs Vanderlyn? I know that she's an American subject. I know that she's had three husbands, one Italian, one German and one Russian, and that in consequence she has made useful what I think are called "contacts" in three countries. I know that she manages to buy very expensive clothes and live in a very luxurious manner, and that there is some slight uncertainty as to where the income comes from which permits her to do so.'

With a grin, Sir George Carrington murmured:

'Your spies have not been inactive, Charles, I see.'

'I know,' Lord Mayfield continued, 'that in addition to having a seductive type of beauty, Mrs Vanderlyn is also a very good listener, and that she can display a fascinating interest in what we call "shop". That is to say, a man can tell her all about his job and feel that he is being intensely interesting to the lady! Sundry young officers have gone a little too far in their zeal to be interesting, and their careers have suffered in consequence. They have told Mrs Vanderlyn a little more than they should have done. Nearly all the lady's friends are in the Services – but last winter she was hunting in a certain county near one of our largest armament firms, and she formed various friendships not at all sporting in character. To put it briefly, Mrs Vanderlyn is a very useful person to ...' He described a circle in the air with his cigar. 'Perhaps we had better not say to whom!

We will just say to a European power – and perhaps to more than one European power.'

Carrington drew a deep breath.

'You take a great load off my mind, Charles.'

'You thought I had fallen for the siren? My dear George! Mrs Vanderlyn is just a little too obvious in her methods for a wary old bird like me. Besides, she is, as they say, not quite so young as she once was. Your young squadron leaders wouldn't notice that. But I am fifty-six, my boy. In another four years I shall probably be a nasty old man continually haunting the society of unwilling debutantes.'

'I was a fool,' said Carrington apologetically, 'but it seemed a bit odd –'

'It seemed to you odd that she should be here, in a somewhat intimate family party just at the moment when you and I were to hold an unofficial conference over a discovery that will probably revolutionize the whole problem of air defence?'

Sir George Carrington nodded.

Lord Mayfield said, smiling:

'That's exactly it. That's the bait.'

'The bait?'

'You see, George, to use the language of the movies, we've nothing actually "on" the woman. And we want something! She's got away with rather more than she should in the past. But she's been careful – damnably careful. *We* know what she's been up to, but we've got no definite proof of it. We've got to tempt her with something big.'

'Something big being the specification of the new bomber?'

'Exactly. It's got to be something big enough to induce her to take a risk – to come out into the open. And then – *we've got her!*'

Sir George grunted.

'Oh, well,' he said. 'I dare say it's all right. But suppose she won't take the risk?'

'That would be a pity,' said Lord Mayfield. Then he added: 'But I think she will…'

He rose.

'Shall we join the ladies in the drawing-room? We mustn't deprive your wife of her bridge.'

Sir George grunted:

'Julia's a damned sight too fond of her bridge. Drops a packet over it. She can't afford to play as high as she does, and I've told her so. The trouble is, Julia's a born gambler.'

Coming round the table to join his host, he said:

'Well, I hope your plan comes off, Charles.'

CHAPTER 2

In the drawing-room conversation had flagged more than once. Mrs Vanderlyn was usually at a disadvantage when left alone with members of her own sex. That charming sympathetic manner of hers, so much appreciated by members of the male sex, did not for some reason or other commend itself to women. Lady Julia was a woman whose manners were either very good or very bad. On this occasion she disliked Mrs Vanderlyn, and was bored by Mrs Macatta, and made no secret of her feelings. Conversation languished, and might have ceased altogether but for the latter.

Mrs Macatta was a woman of great earnestness of purpose. Mrs Vanderlyn she dismissed immediately as a useless and parasitic type. Lady Julia she tried to interest in a forthcoming charity entertainment which she was organizing. Lady Julia answered vaguely, stifled a yawn or two and retired into her own inner preoccupation. Why didn't Charles and George come? How tiresome men were. Her comments became even more perfunctory as she became absorbed in her own thoughts and worries.

The three women were sitting in silence when the men finally entered the room.

Lord Mayfield thought to himself:

'Julia looks ill tonight. What a mass of nerves the woman is.'

Aloud he said:

'What about a rubber – eh?'

Lady Julia brightened at once. Bridge was as the breath of life to her.

Reggie Carrington entered the room at that minute, and a four was arranged. Lady Julia, Mrs Vanderlyn, Sir George and young Reggie sat down to the card-table. Lord Mayfield devoted himself to the task of entertaining Mrs Macatta.

When two rubbers had been played, Sir George looked ostentatiously at the clock on the mantelpiece.

'Hardly worth while beginning another,' he remarked.

His wife looked annoyed.

'It's only a quarter to eleven. A short one.'

'They never are, my dear,' said Sir George good-temperedly. 'Anyway, Charles and I have some work to do.'

Mrs Vanderlyn murmured:

'How important that sounds! I suppose you clever men who are at the top of things never get a real rest.'

'No forty-eight hour week for us,' said Sir George.

Mrs Vanderlyn murmured:

'You know, I feel rather ashamed of myself as a raw American, but I do get so *thrilled* at meeting people who control the destinies of a country. I expect that seems a very crude point of view to you, Sir George.'

'My dear Mrs Vanderlyn, I should never think of you as "crude" or "raw."'

He smiled into her eyes. There was, perhaps, a hint of irony in the voice which she did not miss. Adroitly she turned to Reggie, smiling sweetly into his eyes.

'I'm sorry we're not continuing our partnership. That was a frightfully clever four no-trump call of yours.'

Flushed and pleased, Reggie mumbled:

'Bit of a fluke that it came off.'

'Oh, no, it was really a clever bit of deduction on your part. You'd deduced from the bidding exactly where the cards must be, and you played accordingly. I thought it was brilliant.'

Lady Julia rose abruptly.

'The woman lays it on with a palette-knife,' she thought disgustedly.

Then her eyes softened as they rested on her son. He believed it all. How pathetically young and pleased he looked. How incredibly naïve he was. No wonder he got into scrapes. He was too trusting. The truth of it was he had too sweet a nature. George didn't understand him in the least. Men were so unsympathetic in their judgments. They forgot that they had even been young themselves. George was much too harsh with Reggie.

Mrs Macatta had risen. Goodnights were said.

The three women went out of the room. Lord Mayfield helped himself to a drink after giving one to Sir George, then he looked up as Mr Carlile appeared at the door.

'Get out the files and all the papers, will you, Carlile? Including the plans and the prints. The Air Marshal and I will be along shortly. We'll just take a turn outside first, eh, George? It's stopped raining.'

Mr Carlile, turning to depart, murmured an apology as he almost collided with Mrs Vanderlyn.

She drifted towards them, murmuring:

'My book, I was reading it before dinner.'

Reggie sprang forward and held up a book.

'Is this it? On the sofa?'

'Oh, yes. Thank you *so* much.'

She smiled sweetly, said goodnight again and went out of the room.

Sir George had opened one of the french windows.

'Beautiful night now,' he announced. 'Good idea of yours to take a turn.'

Reggie said:

'Well, goodnight, sir. I'll be toddling off to bed.'

'Goodnight, my boy,' said Lord Mayfield.

Reggie picked up a detective story which he had begun earlier in the evening and left the room.

Lord Mayfield and Sir George stepped out upon the terrace.

It was a beautiful night, with a clear sky studded with stars.

Sir George drew a deep breath.

'Phew, that woman uses a lot of scent,' he remarked.

Lord Mayfield laughed.

'Anyway, it's not cheap scent. One of the most expensive brands on the market, I should say.'

Sir George gave a grimace.

'I suppose one should be thankful for that.'

'You should, indeed. I think a woman smothered in cheap scent is one of the greatest abominations known to mankind.'

Sir George glanced up at the sky.

'Extraordinary the way it's cleared. I heard the rain beating down when we were at dinner.'

The two men strolled gently along the terrace.

The terrace ran the whole length of the house. Below it the ground sloped gently away, permitting a magnificent view over the Sussex weald.

Sir George lit a cigar.

'About this metal alloy –' he began.

The talk became technical.

As they approached the far end of the terrace for the fifth time, Lord Mayfield said with a sigh:

'Oh, well, I suppose we'd better get down to it.'

'Yes, good bit of work to get through.'

The two men turned, and Lord Mayfield uttered a surprised ejaculation.

'Hallo! See that?'

'See what?' asked Sir George.

'Thought I saw someone slip across the terrace from my study window.'

'Nonsense, old boy. I didn't see anything.'

'Well, I did – or I thought I did.'

'Your eyes are playing tricks on you. I was looking straight down the terrace, and I'd have seen anything there was to be seen. There's precious little *I* don't see – even if I do have to hold a newspaper at arm's length.'

Lord Mayfield chuckled.

'I can put one over on you there, George. I read easily without glasses.'

'But you can't always distinguish the fellow on the other side of the House. Or is that eyeglass of yours sheer intimidation?'

Laughing, the two men entered Lord Mayfield's study, the french window of which was open.

Mr Carlile was busy arranging some papers in a file by the safe.

He looked up as they entered.

'Ha, Carlile, everything ready?'

'Yes, Lord Mayfield, all the papers are on your desk.'

The desk in question was a big important-looking writing-table of mahogany set across a corner by the window. Lord Mayfield went over to it, and began sorting through the various documents laid out.

'Lovely night now,' said Sir George.

Mr Carlile agreed.

'Yes, indeed. Remarkable the way it's cleared up after the rain.'

Putting away his file, Mr Carlile asked:

'Will you want me any more tonight, Lord Mayfield?'

'No, I don't think so, Carlile. I'll put all these away myself. We shall probably be late. You'd better turn in.'

'Thank you. Goodnight, Lord Mayfield. Goodnight, Sir George.'

'Goodnight, Carlile.'

As the secretary was about to leave the room, Lord Mayfield said sharply:

'Just a minute, Carlile. You've forgotten the most important of the lot.'

'I beg your pardon, Lord Mayfield.'

'The actual plans of the bomber, man.'

The secretary stared.

'They're right on the top, sir.'

'They're nothing of the sort.'

'But I've just put them there.'

'Look for yourself, man.'

16

With a bewildered expression, the young man came forward and joined Lord Mayfield at the desk.

Somewhat impatiently the Minister indicated the pile of papers. Carlile sorted through them, his expression of bewilderment growing.

'You see, they're not there.'

The secretary stammered:

'But – but it's incredible. I laid them there not three minutes ago.'

Lord Mayfield said good-humouredly:

'You must have made a mistake, they must be still in the safe.'

'I don't see how – I *know* I put them there!'

Lord Mayfield brushed past him to the open safe. Sir George joined them. A very few minutes sufficed to show that the plans of the bomber were not there.

Dazed and unbelieving, the three men returned to the desk and once more turned over the papers.

'My God!' said Mayfield. 'They're gone!'

Mr Carlile cried:

'But it's impossible!'

'Who's been in this room?' snapped out the Minister.

'No one. No one at all.'

'Look here, Carlile, those plans haven't vanished into thin air. Someone has taken them. Has Mrs Vanderlyn been in here?'

'Mrs Vanderlyn? Oh, no, sir.'

'I'll back that,' said Carrington. He sniffed the air! 'You'd soon smell if she had. That scent of hers.'

'Nobody has been in here,' insisted Carlile. 'I can't understand it.'

'Look here, Carlile,' said Lord Mayfield. 'Pull yourself together. We've got to get to the bottom of this. You're absolutely sure the plans were in the safe?'

'Absolutely.'

'You actually saw them? You didn't just assume they were among the others?'

'No, no, Lord Mayfield. I saw them. I put them on top of the others on the desk.'

'And since then, you say, nobody has been in the room. Have you been out of the room?'

'No – at least – yes.'

'Ah!' cried Sir George. 'Now we're getting at it!'

Lord Mayfield said sharply:

'What on earth –' when Carlile interrupted.

'In the normal course of events, Lord Mayfield, I should not, of course, have dreamt of leaving the room when important papers were lying about, but hearing a woman scream –'

'A woman scream?' ejaculated Lord Mayfield in a surprised voice.

'Yes, Lord Mayfield. It startled me more than I can say. I was just laying the papers on the desk when I heard it, and naturally I ran out into the hall.'

'Who screamed?'

'Mrs Vanderlyn's French maid. She was standing half-way up the stairs, looking very white and upset and shaking all over. She said she had seen a ghost.'

'Seen a ghost?'

'Yes, a tall woman dressed all in white who moved without a sound and floated in the air.'

'What a ridiculous story!'

'Yes, Lord Mayfield, that is what I told her. I must say she seemed rather ashamed of herself. She went off upstairs and I came back in here.'

'How long ago was this?'

'Just a minute or two before you and Sir George came in.'

'And you were out of the room – how long?'

The secretary considered.

'Two minutes – at the most three.'

'Long enough,' groaned Lord Mayfield. Suddenly he clutched his friend's arm.

'George, that shadow I saw – slinking away from this

18

window. That was it! As soon as Carlile left the room, he nipped in, seized the plans and made off.'

'Dirty work,' said Sir George.

Then he seized his friend by the arm.

'Look here, Charles, this is the devil of a business. What the hell are we going to do about it?'

CHAPTER 3

'At any rate give it a trial, Charles.'

It was half an hour later. The two men were in Lord Mayfield's study, and Sir George had been expending a considerable amount of persuasion to induce his friend to adopt a certain course.

Lord Mayfield, at first most unwilling, was gradually becoming less averse to the idea.

Sir George went on:

'Don't be so damned pig-headed, Charles.'

Lord Mayfield said slowly:

'Why drag in a wretched foreigner we know nothing about?'

'But I happen to know a lot about him. The man's a marvel.'

'Humph.'

'Look here, Charles. It's a chance! Discretion is the essence of this business. If it leaks out –'

'*When* it leaks out is what you mean!'

'Not necessarily. This man, Hercule Poirot –'

'Will come down here and produce the plans like a conjurer taking rabbits out of his hat, I suppose?'

'He'll get at the truth. And the truth is what we want. Look here, Charles, I take all responsibility on myself.'

Lord Mayfield said slowly:

'Oh, well, have it your own way, but I don't see what the fellow can do...'

Sir George picked up the phone.

'I'm going to get through to him – now.'

'He'll be in bed.'

'He can get up. Dash it all, Charles, you can't let that woman get away with it.'

'Mrs Vanderlyn, you mean?'

'Yes. You don't doubt, do you, that she's at the bottom of this?'

'No, I don't. She's turned the tables on me with a vengeance. I don't like admitting, George, that a woman's been too clever for us. It goes against the grain. But it's true. We shan't be able to prove anything against her, and yet we both know that she's been the prime mover in the affair.'

'Women are the devil,' said Carrington with feeling.

'Nothing to connect her with it, damn it all! We may believe that she put the girl up to that screaming trick, and that the man lurking outside was her accomplice, but the devil of it is we can't prove it.'

'Perhaps Hercule Poirot can.'

Suddenly Lord Mayfield laughed.

'By the Lord, George, I thought you were too much of an old John Bull to put your trust in a Frenchman, however clever.'

'He's not even a Frenchman, he's a Belgian,' said Sir George in a rather shamefaced manner.

'Well, have your Belgian down. Let him try his wits on this business. I'll bet he can't make more of it than we can.'

Without replying, Sir George stretched a hand to the telephone.

CHAPTER 4

Blinking a little, Hercule Poirot turned his head from one man to the other. Very delicately he smothered a yawn.

20

It was half-past two in the morning. He had been roused from sleep and rushed down through the darkness in a big Rolls Royce. Now he had just finished hearing what the two men had to tell him.

'Those are the facts, M. Poirot,' said Lord Mayfield.

He leaned back in his chair, and slowly fixed his monocle in one eye. Through it a shrewd, pale-blue eye watched Poirot attentively. Besides being shrewd the eye was definitely sceptical. Poirot cast a swift glance at Sir George Carrington.

That gentleman was leaning forward with an expression of almost childlike hopefulness on his face.

Poirot said slowly:

'I have the facts, yes. The maid screams, the secretary goes out, the nameless watcher comes in, the plans are there on top of the desk, he snatches them up and goes. The facts – they are all very convenient.'

Something in the way he uttered the last phrase seemed to attract Lord Mayfield's attention. He sat up a little straighter, his monocle dropped. It was as though a new alertness came to him.

'I beg your pardon, M. Poirot?'

'I said, Lord Mayfield, that the facts were all very convenient – for the thief. By the way, you are sure it was a *man* you saw?'

Lord Mayfield shook his head.

'That I couldn't say. It was just a – shadow. In fact, I was almost doubtful if I had seen anyone.'

Poirot transferred his gaze to the Air Marshal.

'And you, Sir George? Could you say if it was a man or a woman?'

'I didn't see anyone myself.'

Poirot nodded thoughtfully. Then he skipped suddenly to his feet and went over to the writing-table.

'I can assure you that the plans are not there,' said Lord Mayfield. 'We have all three been through those papers half a dozen times.'

'All three? You mean, your secretary also?'

'Yes, Carlile.'

Poirot turned suddenly.

'Tell me, Lord Mayfield, which paper was on top when you went over to the desk?'

Mayfield frowned a little in the effort of remembrance.

'Let me see – yes, it was a rough memorandum of some sort of our air defence positions.'

Deftly, Poirot nipped out a paper and brought it over.

'Is this the one, Lord Mayfield?'

Lord Mayfield took it and glanced over it.

'Yes, that's the one.'

Poirot took it over to Carrington.

'Did you notice this paper on the desk?'

Sir George took it, held it away from him, then slipped on his pince-nez.

'Yes, that's right. I looked through them too, with Carlile and Mayfield. This was on top.'

Poirot nodded thoughtfully. He replaced the paper on the desk. Mayfield looked at him in a slightly puzzled manner.

'If there are any other questions –' he began.

'But yes, certainly there is a question. Carlile. Carlile is the question!'

Lord Mayfield's colour rose a little.

'Carlile, M. Poirot, is quite above suspicion! He has been my confidential secretary for nine years. He has access to all my private papers, and I may point out to you that he could have made a copy of the plans and a tracing of the specifications quite easily without anyone being the wiser.'

'I appreciate your point,' said Poirot. 'If he had been guilty there would be no need for him to stage a clumsy robbery.'

'In any case,' said Lord Mayfield, 'I am sure of Carlile. I will guarantee him.'

'Carlile,' said Carrington gruffly, 'is all right.'

Poirot spread out his hands gracefully.

'And this Mrs Vanderlyn – she is all wrong?'

'She's a wrong 'un all right,' said Sir George.

Lord Mayfield said in more measured tones:

'I think, M. Poirot, that there can be no doubt of Mrs Vanderlyn's – well – activities. The Foreign Office can give you more precious data as to that.'

'And the maid, you take it, is in with her mistress?'

'Not a doubt of it,' said Sir George.

'It seems to me a plausible assumption,' said Lord Mayfield more cautiously.

There was a pause. Poirot sighed, and absent-mindedly re-arranged one or two articles on a table at his right hand. Then he said:

'I take it that these papers represented money? That is, the stolen papers would be definitely worth a large sum in cash.'

'If presented in a certain quarter – yes.'

'Such as?'

Sir George mentioned the names of two European powers. Poirot nodded.

'That fact would be known to anyone, I take it?'

'Mrs Vanderlyn would know it all right.'

'I said to *anyone*?'

'I suppose so, yes.'

'Anyone with a minimum of intelligence would appreciate the cash value of the plans?'

'Yes, but M. Poirot –' Lord Mayfield was looking rather uncomfortable.'

Poirot held up a hand.

'I do what you call explore all the avenues.'

Suddenly he rose again, stepped nimbly out of the window and with a flashlight examined the edge of the grass at the farther side of the terrace.

The two men watched him.

He came in again, sat down and said:

'Tell me, Lord Mayfield, this malefactor, this skulker in the shadows, you do not have him pursued?'

Lord Mayfield shrugged his shoulders.

'At the bottom of the garden he could make his way out to a main road. If he had a car waiting there, he would soon be out of reach –'

23

'But there are the police – the A.A. scouts –'

Sir George interrupted.

'You forget, M. Poirot. *We cannot risk publicity.* If it were to get out that these plans had been stolen, the result would be extremely unfavourable to the Party.'

'Ah, yes,' said Poirot. 'One must remember *La Politique*. The great discretion must be observed. You send instead for me. Ah well, perhaps it is simpler.'

'You are hopeful of success, M. Poirot?' Lord Mayfield sounded a trifle incredulous.

The little man shrugged his shoulders.

'Why not? One has only to reason – to reflect.'

He paused a moment and then said:

'I would like now to speak to Mr Carlile.'

'Certainly.' Lord Mayfield rose. 'I asked him to wait up. He will be somewhere at hand.'

He went out of the room.

Poirot looked at Sir George.

'*Eh bien*,' he said. 'What about this man on the terrace?'

'My dear M. Poirot. Don't ask me! I didn't see him, and I can't describe him.'

Poirot leaned forward.

'So you have already said. But it is a little different from that is it not?'

'What d'you mean?' asked Sir George abruptly.

'How shall I say it? Your disbelief, it is more profound.'

Sir George started to speak, then stopped.

'But yes,' said Poirot encouragingly. 'Tell me. You are both at the end of the terrace. Lord Mayfield sees a shadow slip from the window and across the grass. Why do you not see that shadow?'

Carrington stared at him.

'You've hit it, M. Poirot. I've been worrying about that ever since. You see, I'd swear that no one did leave this window. I though Mayfield had imagined it – branch of a tree waving – something of that kind. And then when we came in here and

24

found there had been a robbery, it seemed as though Mayfield must have been right and I'd been wrong. And yet –'

Poirot smiled.

'And yet you still in your heart of hearts believe in the evidence (the negative evidence) of your own eyes?'

'You're right, M. Poirot, I do.'

Poirot gave a sudden smile.

'How wise you are.'

Sir George said sharply:

'There were no footprints on the grass edge?'

Poirot nodded.

'Exactly. Lord Mayfield, he fancies he sees a shadow. Then there comes the robbery and he is sure – but sure! It is no longer a fancy – he actually *saw* the man. But that is not so. Me, I do not concern myself much with footprints and such things but for what it is worth we have that negative evidence. *There were no footprints on the grass.* It had rained heavily this evening. If a man had crossed the terrace to the grass this evening his footprints would have shown.'

Sir George said, staring: 'But then – but then –'

'It brings us back to the house. To the people in the house.'

He broke off as the door opened and Lord Mayfield entered with Mr Carlile.

Though still looking very pale and worried, the secretary had regained a certain composure of manner. Adjusting his pince-nez he sat down and looked at Poirot inquiringly.

'How long had you been in this room when you heard the scream, monsieur?'

Carlile considered.

'Between five and ten minutes, I should say.'

'And before that there had been no disturbance of any kind?'

'No.'

'I understand that the house-party had been in one room for the greater part of the evening.'

'Yes, the drawing-room.'

Poirot consulted his notebook.

'Sir George Carrington and his wife. Mrs Macatta. Mrs

Vanderlyn. Mr Reggie Carrington. Lord Mayfield and your-self. Is that right?'

'I myself was not in the drawing-room. I was working here the greater part of the evening.'

Poirot turned to Lord Mayfield.

'Who went up to bed first?'

'Lady Julia Carrington, I think. As a matter of fact, the three ladies went out together.'

'And then?'

'Mr Carlile came in and I told him to get out the papers as Sir George and I would be along in a minute.'

'It was then that you decided to take a turn on the terrace?'

'It was.'

'Was anything said in Mrs Vanderlyn's hearing as to your working in the study?'

'The matter was mentioned, yes.'

'But she was not in the room when you instructed Mr Carlile to get out the papers?'

'No.'

'Excuse me, Lord Mayfield,' said Carlile. 'Just after you had said that, I collided with her in the doorway. She had come back for a book.'

'So you think she might have overheard?'

'I think it quite possible, yes.'

'She came back for a book,' mused Poirot. 'Did you find her her book, Lord Mayfield?'

'Yes, Reggie gave it to her.'

'Ah, yes, it is what you call the old gasp – no, pardon, the old wheeze – that – to come back for a book. It is often useful!'

'You think it was deliberate?'

Poirot shrugged his shoulders.

'And after that, you two gentlemen go out on the terrace. And Mrs Vanderlyn?'

'She went off with her book.'

'And the young M. Reggie. He went to bed also?'

'Yes.'

'And Mr Carlile he comes here and sometime between five

and ten minutes later he heard a scream. Continue, M. Carlile. You heard a scream and you went out into the hall. Ah, perhaps it would be simplest if you reproduced exactly your actions.'

Mr Carlile got up a little awkwardly.

'Here I scream,' said Poirot helpfully. He opened his mouth and emitted a shrill bleat. Lord Mayfield turn his head away to hide a smile and Mr Carlile looked extremely uncomfortable.

'*Allez!* Forward! March!' cried Poirot. 'It is your cue that I give you there.'

Mr Carlile walked stiffly to the door, opened it and went out. Poirot followed him. The other two came behind.

'The door, did you close it after you or leave it open?'

'I can't really remember. I think I must have left it open.'

'No matter. Proceed.'

Still with extreme stiffness, Mr Carlile walked to the bottom of the staircase and stood there looking up.

Poirot said:

'The maid, you say, was on the stairs. Whereabouts?'

'About half-way up.'

'And she was looking upset.'

'Definitely so.'

'*Eh bien*, me, I am the maid.' Poirot ran nimbly up the stairs. 'About here?'

'A step or two higher.'

'Like this?'

Poirot struck an attitude.

'Well – er – not quite like that.'

'How then?'

'Well, she had her hands to her head.'

'Ah, her hands to her *head*. That is very interesting. Like this?' Poirot raised his arms, his hands rested on his head just above each ear.

'Yes that's it.'

'Aha! And tell me, M. Carlile, she was a pretty girl – yes?'

'Really, I didn't notice.'

Carlile's voice was repressive.

'Aha, you did not notice? But you are a young man. Does not a young man notice when a girl is pretty?'

'Really, M. Poirot, I can only repeat that *I* did not do so.'

Carlile cast an agonized glance at his employer. Sir George Carrington gave a sudden chuckle.

'M. Poirot seems determined to make you out a gay dog, Carlile,' he remarked.

'Me, I always notice when a girl is pretty,' announced Poirot as he descended the stairs.

The silence with which Mr Carlile greeted this remark was somewhat pointed. Poirot went on:

'And it was then she told this tale of having seen a ghost?'

'Yes.'

'Did you believe the story?'

'Well, hardly, M. Poirot!'

'I do not mean, do you believe in ghosts. I mean, did it strike you that the girl herself really thought she had seen something?'

'Oh, as to that, I couldn't say. She was certainly breathing fast and seemed upset.'

'You did not see or hear anything of her mistress?'

'Yes, as a matter of fact I did. She came out of her room in the gallery above and called, "Leonie."'

'And then?'

'The girl ran up to her and I went back to the study.'

'Whilst you were standing at the foot of the stairs here, could anyone have entered the study by the door you had left open?'

Carlile shook his head.

'Not without passing me. The study door is at the end of the passage, as you see.'

Poirot nodded thoughtfully. Mr Carlile went on in his careful, precise voice.

'I may say that I am very thankful that Lord Mayfield actually saw the thief leaving the window. Otherwise I myself should be in a very unpleasant position.'

'Nonsense, my dear Carlile,' broke in Lord Mayfield impatiently. 'No suspicion could possibly attach to you.'

'It is very kind of you to say so, Lord Mayfield, but facts are facts, and I can quite see that it looks badly for me. In any case I hope that my belongings and myself may be searched.'

'Nonsense, my dear fellow,' said Mayfield.

Poirot murmured:

'You are serious in wishing that?'

'I should infinitely prefer it.'

Poirot looked at him thoughtfully for a minute or two and murmured, 'I see.'

Then he asked:

'Where is Mrs Vanderlyn's room situated in regard to the study?'

'It is directly over it.'

'With a window looking out over the terrace?'

'Yes.'

Again Poirot nodded. Then he said:

'Let us go to the drawing-room.'

Here he wandered round the room, examined the fastenings of the windows, glanced at the scorers on the bridge table and then finally addressed Lord Mayfield.

'This affair,' he said, 'is more complicated than it appears. But one thing is quite certain. The stolen plans have not left this house.'

Lord Mayfield stared at him.

'But, my dear M. Poirot, the man I saw leaving the study –'

'There was no man.'

'But I *saw* him –'

'With the greatest respect, Lord Mayfield, you imagined you saw him. The shadow cast by the branch of a tree deceived you. The fact that a robbery occurred naturally seemed a proof that what you had imagined was true.'

'Really, M. Poirot, the evidence of my own eyes –'

'Back my eyes against yours any day, old boy,' put in Sir George.

'You must permit me, Lord Mayfield, to be very definite on that point. *No one crossed the terrace to the grass.*'

Looking very pale and speaking stiffly, Mr Carlile said:

'In that case, if M. Poirot is correct, suspicion automatically attaches itself to me. I am the only person who could possibly have committed the robbery.'

Lord Mayfield sprang up.

'Nonsense. Whatever M. Poirot thinks about it, I don't agree with him. I am convinced of your innocence, my dear Carlile. In fact, I'm willing to guarantee it.'

Poirot murmured mildly:

'But I have not said that I suspect M. Carlile.'

Carlile answered:

'No, but you've made it perfectly clear that no one else had a chance to commit the robbery.'

'*Du tout! Du tout!*'

'But I have told you nobody passed me in the hall to get to the study door.'

'I agree. But someone might have come in through the study *window.*'

'But that is just what you said did not happen?'

'I said that no one from *outside* could have come and left without leaving marks on the grass. But it could have been managed from *inside* the house. Someone could have gone out from his room by one of these windows, slipped along the terrace, in at the study window, and back again in here.'

Mr Carlile objected:

'But Lord Mayfield and Sir George Carrington were on the terrace.'

'They were on the terrace, yes, but they were *en promenade*. Sir George Carrington's eyes may be of the most reliable' – Poirot made a little bow – 'but he does not keep them in the back of his head! The study window is at the extreme left of the terrace, the windows of this room come next, but the terrace continues to the right past one, two, three, perhaps four rooms?'

'Dining-room, billiard-room, morning room and library,' said Lord Mayfield.

'And you walked up and down the terrace, how many times?'

'At least five or six.'

'You see, it is easy enough, the thief has only to watch for the right moment!'

Carlile said slowly:

'You mean that when I was in the hall, talking to the French girl, the thief was waiting in the drawing-room?'

'That is my suggestion. It is, of course, only a suggestion.'

'It doesn't sound very probable to me,' said Lord Mayfield. 'Too risky.'

The Air Marshall demurred.

'I don't agree with you, Charles. It's perfectly possible. Wonder I hadn't the wits to think of it for myself.'

'So you see,' said Poirot, 'why I believe that the plans are still in the house. The problem now is to find them!'

Sir George snorted.

'That's simple enough. Search everybody.'

Lord Mayfield made a movement of dissent, but Poirot spoke before he could.

'No, no, it is not so simple as that. The person who took those plans will anticipate that a search will be made and will make quite sure that they are not found amongst his or her belongings. They will have been hidden in neutral ground.'

'Do you suggest that we've got to go playing hide and seek all over the bally house?'

Poirot smiled.

'No, no, we need not be so crude as that. We can arrive at the hiding-place (or alternatively at the identify of the guilty person) by reflection. That will simplify matters. In the morning I would like an interview with every person in the house. It would, I think, be unwise to seek those interviews now.'

Lord Mayfield nodded.

'Cause too much comment,' he said, 'if we dragged everybody out of their beds at three in the morning. In any case you'll have to proceed with a good deal of camouflage, M. Poirot. This matter has got to be kept dark.'

Poirot waved an airy hand.

'Leave it to Hercule Poirot. The lies I invent are always most

31

delicate and most convincing. Tomorrow, then, I conduct my investigations. But tonight, I should like to begin by interviewing you, Sir George and you, Lord Mayfield.'

He bowed to them both.

'You mean – alone?'

'That was my meaning.'

Lord Mayfield raised his eyes slightly, then he said:

'Certainly. I'll leave you alone with Sir George. When you want me, you'll find me in my study. Come, Carlile.'

He and the secretary went out, shutting the door behind them.

Sir George sat down, reaching mechanically for a cigarette. He turned a puzzled face to Poirot.

'You know,' he said slowly. 'I don't quite get this.'

'That is very simply explained,' said Poirot with a smile. 'In two words, to be accurate. Mrs Vanderlyn!'

'Oh,' said Carrington. 'I think I see. Mrs Vanderlyn?'

'Precisely. It might be, you see, that it would not be very delicate to ask Lord Mayfield the question I want to ask. *Why* Mrs Vanderlyn? This lady, she is known to be a suspicious character. Why, then, should she be here? I say to myself there are three explanations. One, that Lord Mayfield has a *penchant* for the lady (and that is why I seek to talk to you alone. I do not wish to embarrass him). Two, that Mrs Vanderlyn is perhaps the dear friend of someone else in the house?'

'You can count me out!' said Sir George with a grin.

'Then, if neither of those cases is true, the question returns in redoubled force. *Why Mrs Vanderlyn?* And it seems to me I perceive a shadowy answer. There was a *reason.* Her presence at this particular juncture was definitely desired by Lord Mayfield for a special reason. Am I right?'

Sir George nodded.

'You're quite right,' he said. 'Mayfield is too old a bird to fall for her wiles. He wanted her here for quite another reason. It was like this.'

He retailed the conversation that had taken place at the dinner-table. Poirot listened attentively.

32

'Ah,' he said. 'I comprehend now. Nevertheless, it seems that the lady has turned the tables on you both rather neatly!'

Sir George swore freely.

Poirot watched him with some slight amusement, then he said:

'You do not doubt that this theft is her doing – I mean, that she is responsible for it, whether or no she played an active part?'

Sir George stared.

'Of course not! There isn't any doubt of that. Why, who else would have any interest in stealing those plans?'

'Ah!' said Hercule Poirot. He leaned back and looked at the ceiling. 'And yet, Sir George, we agreed, not a quarter of an hour ago, that these papers represented very definitely money. Not perhaps, in quite so obvious a form as banknotes, or gold, or jewellery, but nevertheless they were potential money. If there were anyone here who was hard up –'

The other interrupted him with a snort.

'Who isn't these days? I suppose I can say it without incriminating myself.'

He smiled and Poirot smiled politely back at him and murmured:

'*Mais oui*, you can say what you like, for you, Sir George, have the one unimpeachable alibi in this affair.'

'But I'm damned hard up myself!'

Poirot shook his head sadly.

'Yes, indeed, a man in your position has heavy living expenses. Then you have a young son at a most expensive age –'

Sir George groaned.

'Education's bad enough, then debts on top of it. Mind you, this lad's not a bad lad.'

Poirot listened sympathetically. He heard a lot of the Air Marshal's accumulated grievances. The lack of grit and stamina in the younger generation, the fantastic way in which mothers spoilt their children and always took their side, the curse of gambling once it got hold of a woman, the folly of playing for higher stakes than you could afford. It was couched

33

in general terms, Sir George did not allude directly to either his wife or his son, but his natural transparency made his generalizations very easy to see through.

He broke off suddenly.

'Sorry, mustn't take up your time with something that's right off the subject, especially at this hour of the night – or rather, morning.'

He stifled a yawn.

'I suggest, Sir George, that you should go to bed. You have been most kind and helpful.'

'Right, think I will turn in. You really think there is a chance of getting the plans back?'

Poirot shrugged his shoulders.

'I mean to try. I do not see why not.'

'Well, I'll be off. Goodnight.'

He left the room.

Poirot remained in his chair staring thoughtfully at the ceiling, then he took out a little notebook and turning to a clean page, he wrote:

> Mrs Vanderlyn?
> Lady Julia Carrington?
> Mrs Macatta?
> Reggie Carrington?
> Mr Carlile?

Underneath he wrote:

> Mrs Vanderlyn and Mr Reggie Carrington?
> Mrs Vanderlyn and Lady Julia?
> Mrs Vanderlyn and Mr Carlile?

He shook his head in a dissatisfed manner, murmuring: '*C'est plus simple que ça.*'

Then he added a few short sentences.

Did Lord Mayfield see a 'shadow'? If not, why did he say he did? Did Sir George see anything? He was positive he had seen nothing AFTER I examined flower-bed. Note: Lord Mayfield is near-sighted, can read without glasses but has to use a monocle to look across a room. Sir George is long-sighted. Therefore, from the far end of the terrace, his sight is more to be depended upon than Lord Mayfield's. Yet Lord Mayfield is very positive that he DID see something and is quite unshaken by his friend's denial.

Can anyone be quite as above suspicion as Mr Carlile appears to be? Lord Mayfield is very emphatic as to his innocence. Too much so. Why? Because he secretly suspects him and is ashamed of his suspicions? Or because he definitely suspects some other person? That is to say, some person OTHER than Mrs Vanderlyn?

He put the notebook away.

Then, getting up, he went along to the study.

CHAPTER 5

Lord Mayfield was seated at his desk when Poirot entered the study. He swung round, laid down his pen, and looked up inquiringly.

'Well, M. Poirot, had your interview with Carrington?'

Poirot smiled and sat down.

'Yes, Lord Mayfield. He cleared up a point that had puzzled me.'

'What was that?'

'The reason for Mrs Vanderlyn's presence here. You comprehend, I thought it possible –'

Mayfield was quick to realize the cause of Poirot's somewhat exaggerated embarrassment.

'You thought I had a weakness for the lady? Not at all. Far from it. Funnily enough, Carrington thought the same.'

'Yes, he has told me of the conversation he held with you on the subject.'

Lord Mayfield looked rather rueful.

'My little scheme didn't come off. Always annoying to have to admit that a woman has got the better of you.'

'Ah, but she has not got the better of you *yet*, Lord Mayfield.'

'You think we may yet win? Well, I'm glad to hear you say so. I'd like to think it was true.'

He sighed.

'I feel I've acted like a complete fool – so pleased with my stratagem for entrapping the lady.'

Hercule Poirot said, as he lit one of his tiny cigarettes:

'What *was* your stratagem exactly, Lord Mayfield?'

'Well,' Lord Mayfield hesitated. 'I hadn't exactly got down to details.'

'You didn't discuss it with anyone?'

'No.'

'Not even with Mr Carlile?'

'No.'

Poirot smiled.

'You prefer to play a lone hand, Lord Mayfield.'

'I have usually found it the best way,' said the other a little grimly.

'Yes, you are wise. *Trust no one*. But you *did* mention the matter to Sir George Carrington?'

'Simply because I realized that the dear fellow was seriously perturbed about me.'

Lord Mayfield smiled at the remembrance.

'He is an old friend of yours?'

'Yes. I have known him for over twenty years.'

'And his wife?'

'I have known his wife also, of course.'

'But (pardon me if I am impertinent) you are not on the same terms of intimacy with her?'

'I don't really see what my personal relationships to people has to do with the matter in hand, M. Poirot.'

'But I think, Lord Mayfield, that they may have a good deal to do with it. You agreed, did you not, that my theory of someone in the drawing-room was a possible one?'

'Yes. In fact, I agree with you that that is what must have happened.'

'We will not say "must." That is too self-confident a word. But if that theory of mine is true, who do you think the person in the drawing-room could have been?'

'Obviously Mrs Vanderlyn. She had been back there once for a book. She could have come back for another book, or a handbag, or a dropped handkerchief – one of a dozen feminine excuses. She arranges with her maid to scream and get Carlile away from the study. Then she slips in and out by the windows as you said.'

'You forget it could not have been Mrs Vanderlyn. Carlile heard her call the maid from *upstairs* while he was talking to the girl.'

Lord Mayfield bit his lip.

'True. I forgot that.' He looked thoroughly annoyed.

'You see,' said Poirot gently. 'We progress. We have first the simple explanation of a thief who comes from *outside* and makes off with the booty. A very convenient theory as I said at the time, too convenient to be readily accepted. We have disposed of that. Then we come to the theory of the foreign agent, Mrs Vanderlyn, and that again seems to fit together beautifully up to a certain point. But now it looks as though that, too, was too easy – too convenient – to be accepted.'

'You'd wash Mrs Vanderlyn out of it altogether?'

'It was not Mrs Vanderlyn in the drawing-room. It may have been an ally of Mrs Vanderlyn's who committed the theft, but it is just possible that it was committed by another person altogether. If so, we have to consider the question of motive.'

'Isn't this rather far-fetched, M. Poirot?'

'I do not think so. Now what motives could there be? There is the motive of money. The papers may have been stolen with the object of turning them into cash. That is the simplest motive to consider. But the motive might possibly be something quite different.'

'Such as –'

Poirot said slowly:

'It might have been done definitely with the idea of damaging someone.'

'Who?'

'Possibly Mr Carlile. He would be the obvious suspect. But there might be more to it than that. The men who control the destiny of a country, Lord Mayfield, are particularly vulnerable to displays of popular feeling.'

'Meaning that the theft was aimed at damaging *me*?'

Poirot nodded.

'I think I am correct in saying, Lord Mayfield, that about five years ago you passed through a somewhat trying time. You were suspected of friendship with a European Power at that time bitterly unpopular with the electorate of this country.'

'Quite true, M. Poirot.'

'A statesman in these days has a difficult task. He has to pursue the policy he deems advantageous to his country, but he has at the same time to recognize the force of popular feeling. Popular feeling is very often sentimental, muddle-headed, and eminently unsound, but it cannot be disregarded for all that.'

'How well you express it! That is exactly the curse of a politician's life. He has to bow to the country's feeling, however dangerous and foolhardy he knows it to be.'

'That was your dilemma, I think. There were rumours that you had concluded an agreement with the country in question. This country and the newspapers were up in arms about it. Fortunately the Prime Minister was able categorically to deny the story, and you repudiated it, though still making no secret of the way your sympathies lay.'

'All this is quite true, M. Poirot, but why rake up past history?'

'Because I consider it possible that an enemy, disappointed in the way you surmounted that crisis, might endeavour to stage a further dilemma. You soon regained public confidence.

Those particular circumstances have passed away, you are now, deservedly, one of the most popular figures in political life. You are spoken of freely as the next Prime Minister when Mr Hunberly retires.'

'You think this is an attempt to discredit me? Nonsense!'

'*Tout de même*, Lord Mayfield, it would not look well if it were known that the plans of Britain's new bomber had been stolen during a weekend when a certain very charming lady had been your guest. Little hints in the newspapers as to your relationship with that lady would create a feeling of distrust in you.'

'Such a thing could not really be taken seriously.'

'My dear Lord Mayfield, you know perfectly well it could! It takes so little to undermine public confidence in a man.'

'Yes, that's true,' said Lord Mayfield. He looked suddenly very worried. 'God! how desperately complicated this business is becoming. Do you really think – but it's impossible – impossible.'

'You know of nobody who is – jealous of you?'

'Absurd!'

'At any rate you will admit that my questions about your personal relationships with the members of this house-party are not totally irrelevant.'

'Oh, perhaps – perhaps. You asked me about Julia Carrington. There's really not very much to say. I've never taken to her very much, and I don't think she cares for me. She's one of these restless, nervy women, recklessly extravagant and mad about cards. She's old-fashioned enough, I think, to despise me as being a self-made man.'

Poirot said:

'I looked you up in *Who's Who* before I came down. You were the head of a famous engineering firm and you are yourself a first-class engineer.'

'There's certainly nothing I don't know about the practical side. I've worked my way up from the bottom.'

Lord Mayfield spoke rather grimly.

'Oh la la!' cried Poirot. 'I have been a fool – but a fool!'

The other stared at him.

'I beg your pardon, M. Poirot?'

'It is that a portion of the puzzle has become clear to me. Something I did not see before ... But it all fits in. Yes – it fits in with beautiful precision.'

Lord Mayfield looked at him in somewhat astonished inquiry.

But with a slight smile Poirot shook his head.

'No, no, not now. I must arrange my ideas a little more clearly.'

He rose.

'Goodnight, Lord Mayfield. I think I know where those plans are.'

Lord Mayfield cried out:

'You know? Then let us get hold of them at once!'

Poirot shook his head.

'No, no, that would not do. Precipitancy would be fatal. But leave it all to Hercule Poirot.'

He went out of the room. Lord Mayfield raised his shoulders in contempt.

'Man's a mountebank,' he muttered. Then, putting away his papers and turning out the lights, he, too, made his way up to bed.

CHAPTER 6

'If there's been a burglary, why the devil doesn't old Mayfield send for the police?' demanded Reggie Carrington.

He pushed his chair slightly back from the breakfast table.

He was the last down. His host, Mrs Macatta and Sir George had finished their breakfasts some time before. His mother and Mrs Vanderlyn were breakfasting in bed.

Sir George, repeating his statement on the lines agreed upon

40

between Lord Mayfield and Hercule Poirot, had a feeling that he was not managing it as well as he might have done.

'To send for a queer foreigner like this seems very odd to me,' said Reggie. 'What has been taken, Father?'

'I don't know exactly, my boy.'

Reggie got up. He looked rather nervy and on edge this morning.

'Nothing – important? No – papers or anything like that?'

'To tell you the truth, Reggie, I can't tell you exactly.'

'Very hush-hush, is it? I see.'

Reggie ran up the stairs, paused for a moment half-way with a frown on his face, and then continued his ascent and tapped on his mother's door. Her voice bade him enter.

Lady Julia was sitting up in bed, scribbling figures on the back of an envelope.

'Good morning, darling.' She looked up, then said sharply: 'Reggie, is anything the matter?'

'Nothing much, but it seems there was a burglary last night.'

'A burglary? What was taken?'

'Oh, I don't know. It's all very hush hush. There's some odd kind of private-inquiry agent downstairs asking everybody questions.'

'How extraordinary!'

'It's rather unpleasant,' said Reggie slowly, 'staying in a house when that kind of thing happens.'

'What did happen exactly?'

'Don't know. It was some time after we all went to bed. Look out, Mother, you'll have that tray off.'

He rescued the breakfast-tray and carried it to a table by the window.

'Was money taken?'

'I tell you I don't know.'

Lady Julia said slowly:

'I suppose this inquiry man is asking everybody questions?'

'I suppose so.'

'Where they were last night? All that kind of thing?'

'Probably. Well, I can't tell him much. I went straight up to bed and was asleep in next to no time.'

Lady Julia did not answer.

'I say, Mother, I suppose you couldn't let me have a spot of cash. I'm absolutely broke.'

'No, I couldn't,' his mother replied decisively. 'I've got the most frightful overdraft myself. I don't know what your father will say when he hears about it.'

There was a tap at the door and Sir George entered.

'Ah, there you are, Reggie. Will you go down to the library? M. Hercule Poirot wants to see you.'

Poirot had just concluded an interview with the redoubtable Mrs Macatta.

A few brief questions had elicited the information that Mrs Macatta had gone up to bed just before eleven, and had heard or seen nothing helpful.

Poirot slid gently from the topic of the burglary to more personal matters. He himself had a great admiration for Lord Mayfield. As a member of the general public he felt that Lord Mayfield was a truly great man. Of course, Mrs Macatta, being in the know, would have a far better means of estimating that than himself.

'Lord Mayfield has brains,' allowed Mrs Macatta. 'And he has carved his career out entirely for himself. He owes nothing to hereditary influence. He has a certain lack of vision, perhaps. In that I find all men sadly alike. They lack the breadth of a woman's imagination. Woman, M. Poirot, is going to be the great force in government in ten years' time.'

Poirot said that he was sure of it.

He slid to the topic of Mrs Vanderlyn. Was it true, as he had heard hinted, that she and Lord Mayfield were very close friends?

'Not in the least. To tell you the truth I was very surprised to meet her here. Very surprised indeed.'

Poirot invited Mrs Macatta's opinion of Mrs Vanderlyn – and got it.

'One of those absolutely *useless* women, M. Poirot. Women

42

that make one despair of one's own sex! A parasite, first and last a parasite.'

'Men admired her?'

'Men!' Mrs Macatta spoke the word with contempt. 'Men are always taken in by those very obvious good looks. That boy, now, young Reggie Carrington, flushing up every time she spoke to him, absurdly flattered by being taken notice of by her. And the silly way she flattered him too. Praising his bridge – which actually was far from brilliant.'

'He is not a good player?'

'He made all sorts of mistakes last night.'

'Lady Julia is a good player, is she not?'

'Much *too* good in my opinion,' said Mrs Macatta. 'It's almost a profession with her. She plays morning, noon, and night.'

'For high stakes?'

'Yes, indeed, much higher than I would care to play. Indeed I shouldn't consider it *right*.'

'She makes a good deal of money at the game?'

Mrs Macatta gave a loud and virtuous snort.

'She reckons on paying her debts that way. But she's been having a run of bad luck lately, so I've heard. She looked last night as though she had something on her mind. The evils of gambling, M. Poirot, are only slightly less than the evils caused by drink. If I had my way this country should be purified –'

Poirot was forced to listen to a somewhat lengthy discussion on the purification of England's morals. Then he closed the conversation adroitly and sent for Reggie Carrington.

He summed the young man up carefully as he entered the room, the weak mouth camouflaged by the rather charming smile, the indecisive chin, the eyes set far apart, the rather narrow head. He thought that he knew Reggie Carrington's type fairly well.

'Mr Reggie Carrington?'

'Yes. Anything I can do?'

'Just tell me what you can about last night?'

43

'Well, let me see, we played bridge – in the drawing-room. After that I went up to bed.'

'That was at what time?'

'Just before eleven. I suppose the robbery took place after that?'

'Yes, after that. You did not hear or see anything?'

Reggie shook his head regretfully.

'I'm afraid not. I went straight to bed and I sleep pretty soundly.'

'You went straight up from the drawing-room to your bedroom and remained there until the morning?'

'That's right.'

'Curious,' said Poirot.

Reggie said sharply:

'What do you mean, curious?'

'You did not, for instance, hear a scream?'

'No, I didn't.'

'Ah, very curious.'

'Look here, I don't know what you mean.'

'You are, perhaps, slightly deaf?'

'Certainly not.'

Poirot's lips moved. It was possible that he was repeating the word curious for the third time. Then he said:

'Well, thank you, Mr Carrington, that is all.'

Reggie got up and stood rather irresolutely.

'You know,' he said, 'now you come to mention it, I believe I did hear something of the kind.'

'Ah, you did hear something?'

'Yes, but you see, I was reading a book – a detective story as a matter of fact – and I – well, I didn't really quite take it in.'

'Ah,' said Poirot, 'a most satisfying explanation.'

His face was quite impassive.

Reggie still hesitated, then he turned and walked slowly to the door. There he paused and asked:

'I say, what was stolen?'

'Something of great value, Mr Carrington. That is all I am at liberty to say.'

'Oh,' said Reggie rather blankly.

He went out.

Poirot nodded his head.

'It fits,' he murmured. 'It fits very nicely.'

He touched a bell and inquired courteously if Mrs Vanderlyn was up yet.

CHAPTER 7

Mrs Vanderlyn swept into the room looking very handsome. She was swearing an artfully-cut russet sports-suit that showed up the warm lights of her hair. She swept to a chair and smiled in a dazzling fashion at the little man in front of her.

For a moment something showed through the smile. It might have been triumph, it might almost have been mockery. It was gone almost immediately, but it had been there. Poirot found the suggestion of it interesting.

'Burglars? Last night? But how dreadful! Why no, I never heard a *thing*. What about the police? Can't they *do* anything?'

Again, just for a moment, the mockery showed in her eyes.

Hercule Poirot thought:

'It is very clear that *you* are not afraid of the police, my lady. You know very well that they are not going to be called in.'

And from that followed – what?

He said soberly:

'You comprehend, madame, it is an affair of the most discreet.'

'Why, naturally, M. – Poirot – isn't it? – I shouldn't dream of breathing a word. I'm much too great an admirer of dear Lord Mayfield's to do anything to cause him the least little bit of worry.'

She crossed her knees. A highly-polished slipper of brown leather dangled on the tip of her silk-shod foot.

She smiled, a warm, compelling smile of perfect health and deep satisfaction.

'Do tell me if there's anything at all I can do?'

'I thank you, madame. You played bridge in the drawing-room last night?'

'Yes.'

'I understand that then all the ladies went up to bed?'

'That is right.'

'But someone came back to fetch a book. That was you, was it not, Mrs Vanderlyn?'

'I was the first one to come back – yes.'

'What do you mean – the *first* one?' said Poirot sharply.

'I came back right away,' explained Mrs Vanderlyn. Then I went up and rang for my maid. She was a long time in coming. I rang again. Then I went out on the landing. I heard her voice and I called her. After she had brushed my hair I sent her away, she was in a nervous, upset state and tangled the brush in my hair once or twice. It was then, just as I sent her away, that I saw Lady Julia coming up the stairs. She told me she had been down again for a book, too. Curious, wasn't it?'

Mrs Vanderlyn smiled as she finished, a wide, rather feline smile. Hercule Poirot thought to himself that Mrs Vanderlyn did not like Lady Julia Carrington.

'As you say, madame. Tell me, did you hear your maid scream?'

'Why, yes, I did hear something of that kind.'

'Did you ask her about it?'

'Yes. She told me she thought she had seen a floating figure in white – such nonsense!'

'What was Lady Julia wearing last night?'

'Oh, you think perhaps – Yes, I see. She *was* wearing a white evening-dress. Of course, that explains it. She must have caught sight of her in the darkness just as a white figure. These girls are so superstitious.'

'Your maid has been with you a long time, madame?'

'Oh, no.' Mrs Vanderlyn opened her eyes rather wide. 'Only about five months.'

'I should like to see her presently, if you do not mind, madame.'

Mrs Vanderlyn raised her eyebrows.

'Oh, certainly,' she said rather coldly.

'I should like, you understand, to question her.'

'Oh, yes.'

Again a flicker of amusement.

Poirot rose and bowed.

'Madame,' he said. 'You have my complete admiration.'

Mrs Vanderlyn for once seemed a trifle taken aback.

'Oh, M. Poirot, how nice of you, but why?'

'You are, madame, so perfectly armoured, so completely sure of yourself.'

Mrs Vanderlyn laughed a little uncertainly.

'Now I wonder,' she said, 'if I am to take that as a compliment?'

Poirot said:

'It is, perhaps, a warning – not to treat life with arrogance.'

Mrs Vanderlyn laughed with more assurance. She got up and held out a hand.

'Dear M. Poirot, I do wish you all success. Thank you for all the charming things you have said to me.'

She went out. Poirot murmured to himself:

'You wish me success, do you? Ah, but you are very sure I am not going to meet with success! Yes, you are very sure indeed. That, it annoys me very much.'

With a certain petulance, he pulled the bell and asked that Mademoiselle Leonie might be sent to him.

His eyes roamed over her appreciatively as she stood hesitating in the doorway, demure in her black dress with her neatly-parted black waves of hair and her modestly-dropped eyelids. He nodded slow approval.

'Come in, Mademoiselle Leonie,' he said. 'Do not be afraid.'

She came in and stood demurely before him.

'Do you know,' said Poirot with a sudden change of tone, 'that I find you very good to look at.'

Leonie responded promptly. She flashed him a glance out of the corner of her eyes and murmured softly:

'Monsieur is very kind.'

'Figure to yourself,' said Poirot. 'I demand of M. Carlile whether you are or not good-looking and he replies that he does not know!'

Leonie cocked her chin up contemptuously.

'That image!'

'That describes him very well.'

'I do not believe he has ever looked at a girl in his life, that one.'

'Probably not. A pity. He has missed a lot. But there are others in this house who are more appreciative, is it not so?'

'Really, I do not know what monsieur means.'

'Oh, yes, Mademoiselle Leonie, you know very well. A pretty history that you recount last night about a ghost that you have seen. As soon as I hear that you are standing there with your hands to your head, I know very well that there is no question of ghosts. If a girl is frightened she clasps her heart, or she raises her hands to her mouth to stifle a cry, but if her hands are on her hair it means something very different. *It means that her hair has been ruffled and that she is hastily getting it into shape again!* Now then, mademoiselle, let us have the truth. Why did you scream on the stairs?'

'But monsieur it is true, I saw a tall figure all in white –'

'Mademoiselle, do not insult my intelligence. That story, it may have been good enough for M. Carlile, but it is not good enough for Hercule Poirot. The truth is that you had just been kissed, is it not so? And I will make a guess that it was M. Reggie Carrington who kissed you.'

Leonie twinkled an unabashed eye at him.

'*Eh bien,*' she demanded, 'after all, what is a kiss?'

'What, indeed?' said Poirot gallantly.

'You see, the young gentleman he came up behind me and caught me round the waist – and so naturally he startled me and I screamed. If I had known – well, then naturally I would not have screamed.'

'Naturally,' agreed Poirot.

'But he came upon me like a cat. Then the study door opened and out came M. le secrétaire and the young gentleman slipped away upstairs and there I was looking like a fool. Naturally I had to say something – especially to –' she broke into French, '*un jeune homme comme ça, tellement comme il faut!*'

'So you invent a ghost?'

'Indeed, monsieur, it was all I could think of. A tall figure all in white, that floated. It is ridiculous but what else could I do?'

'Nothing. So now, all is explained. I had my suspicions from the first.'

Leonie shot him a provocative glance.

'Monsieur is very clever, and very sympathetic.'

'And since I am not going to make you any embarrassments over the affair you will do something for me in return?'

'Most willingly, monsieur.'

'How much do you know of your mistress's affairs?'

The girl shrugged her shoulders.

'Not very much, monsieur. I have my ideas, of course.'

'And those ideas?'

'Well, it does not escape me that the friends of madame are always soldiers or sailors or airmen. And then there are other friends – foreign gentlemen who come to see her very quietly sometimes. Madame is very handsome, though I do not think she will be so much longer. The young men, they find her very attractive. Sometimes I think, they say too much. But it is only my idea, that. Madame does not confide in me.'

'What you would have me to understand is that madame plays a lone hand?'

'That is right, monsieur.'

'In other words, you cannot help me.'

'I fear not, monsieur. I would do if I could.'

'Tell me, your mistress is in a good mood today?

'Decidedly, monsieur.'

'Something has happened to please her?'

'She has been in good spirits ever since she came here.'

'Well, Leonie, you should know.'

The girl answered confidently:

'Yes, monsieur. I could not be mistaken there. I know all madame's moods. She is in high spirits.'

'Positively triumphant?'

'That is exactly the word, monsieur.'

Poirot nodded gloomily.

'I find that – a little hard to bear. Yet I perceive that it is inevitable. Thank you, mademoiselle, that is all.'

Leonie threw him a coquettish glance.

'Thank you, monsieur. If I meet monsieur on the stairs, be well assured that I shall not scream.'

'My child,' said Poirot with dignity. 'I am of advanced years. What have I to do with such frivolities?'

But with a little twitter of laughter, Leonie took herself off.

Poirot paced slowly up and down the room. His face became grave and anxious.

'And now,' he said at last, 'for Lady Julia. What will she say, I wonder?'

Lady Julia came into the room with a quiet air of assurance. She bent her head graciously, accepted the chair that Poirot drew forward and spoke in a low, well-bred voice.

'Lord Mayfield says that you wish to ask me some questions.'

'Yes, madame. It is about last night.'

'About last night, yes?'

'What happened after you had finished your game of bridge?'

'My husband thought it was too late to begin another. I went up to bed.'

'And then?'

'I went to sleep.'

'That is all?'

'Yes. I'm afraid I can't tell you anything of much interest. When did this' – she hesitated – 'burglary occur?'

'Very soon after you went upstairs.'

'I see. And what exactly was taken?'

'Some private papers, madame.'

'Important papers?'

'Very important.'

She frowned a little and then said:

'They were – valuable?'

'Yes, madame, they were worth a good deal of money.'

'I see.'

There was a pause, and then Poirot said:

'What about your book, madame?'

'My book?' She raised bewildered eyes to him.

'Yes, I understand Mrs Vanderlyn to say that some time after you three ladies had retired you went down again to fetch a book.'

'Yes, of course, so I did.'

'So that, as a matter of fact, you did *not* go straight to bed when you went upstairs? You returned to the drawing-room?'

'Yes, that is true. I had forgotten.'

'While you were in the drawing-room, did you hear someone scream?'

'No – yes – I don't think so.'

'Surely, madame. You could not have failed to hear it in the drawing-room.'

Lady Julia flung her head back and said firmly:

'I heard nothing.'

Poirot raised his eyebrows, but did not reply.

The silence grew uncomfortable. Lady Julia asked abruptly:

'What is being done?'

'Being done? I do not understand you, madame.'

'I mean about the robbery. Surely the police must be doing something.'

Poirot shook his head.

'The police have not been called in. I am in charge.'

She stared at him, her restless haggard face sharpened and tense. Her eyes, dark and searching, sought to pierce his impassivity.

They fell at last – defeated.

'You cannot tell me what is being done?'

'I can only assure you, madame, that I am leaving no stone unturned.'

'To catch the thief – or to – recover the papers?'

'The recovery of the papers is the main thing, madame.'

Her manner changed. It became bored, listless.

'Yes,' she said indifferently. 'I suppose it is.'

There was another pause.

'Is there anything else, M. Poirot?'

'No, madame. I will not detain you further.'

'Thank you.'

He opened the door for her. She passed out without glancing at him.

Poirot went back to the fireplace and carefully rearranged the ornaments on the mantelpiece. He was still at it when Lord Mayfield came in through the window.

'Well?' said the latter.

'Very well, I think. Events are shaping themselves as they should.'

Lord Mayfield said, staring at him:

'You are pleased.'

'No, I am not pleased. But I am content.'

'Really, M. Poirot, I cannot make you out.'

'I am not such a charlatan as you think.'

'I never said –'

'No, but you *thought*! No matter. I am not offended. It is sometimes necessary for me to adopt a certain pose.'

Lord Mayfield looked at him doubtfully with a certain amount of distrust. Hercule Poirot was a man he did not understand. He wanted to despise him, but something warned him that this ridiculous little man was not so futile as he appeared. Charles McLaughlin had always been able to recognize capability when he saw it.

'Well,' he said, 'we are in your hands. What do you advise next?'

'Can you get rid of your guests?'

'I think it might be arranged ... I could explain that I have to go to London over this affair. They will then probably offer to leave.'

'Very good. Try and arrange it like that.'

Lord Mayfield hesitated.

'You don't think –?'

'I am quite sure that that would be the wise course to take.'

Lord Mayfield shrugged his shoulders.

'Well, if you say so.'

He went out.

CHAPTER 8

The guests left after lunch. Mrs Vanderlyn and Mrs Macatta went by train, the Carringtons had their car. Poirot was standing in the hall as Mrs Vanderlyn bade her host a charming farewell.

'So terribly sorry for you having this bother and anxiety. I do hope it will turn out all right for you. I shan't breathe a word of anything.'

She pressed his hand and went out to where the Rolls was waiting to take her to the station. Mrs Macatta was already inside. Her adieu had been curt and unsympathetic.

Suddenly Leonie, who had been getting in front with the chauffeur, came running back into the hall.

'The dressing-case of madame, it is not in the car,' she exclaimed.

There was a hurried search. At last Lord Mayfield discovered it where it had been put down in the shadow of an old oak chest. Leonie uttered a glad little cry as she seized the elegant affair of green morocco, and hurried out with it.

Then Mrs Vanderlyn leaned out of the car.

'Lord Mayfield, Lord Mayfield.' She handed him a letter. 'Would you mind putting this in your post-bag? If I keep it meaning to post it in town, I'm sure to forget. Letters just stay in my bag for days.'

Sir George Carrington was fidgeting with his watch, opening and shutting it. He was a maniac for punctuality.

'They're cutting it fine,' he murmured. 'Very fine. Unless they're careful, they'll miss the train –'

His wife said irritably:

'Oh, don't fuss, George. After all, it's their train, not ours!'

He looked at her reproachfully.

The Rolls drove off.

Reggie drew up at the front door in the Carringtons' Morris. 'All ready, Father,' he said.

The servants began bringing out the Carringtons' luggage. Reggie supervised its disposal in the dickey.

Poirot moved out of the front door, watching the proceedings.

Suddenly he felt a hand on his arm. Lady Julia's voice spoke in an agitated whisper.

'M. Poirot. I must speak to you – at once.'

He yielded to her insistent hand. She drew him into a small morning-room and closed the door. She came close to him.

'Is it true what you said – that the discovery of the papers is what matters most to Lord Mayfield?'

Poirot looked at her curiously.

'It is quite true, madame.'

'If – if those papers were returned to you, would you undertake that they should be given back to Lord Mayfield, and no questions asked?'

'I am not sure that I understand you.'

'You must! I am sure that you do! I am suggesting that the – the thief should remain anonymous if the papers are returned.'

Poirot asked:

'How soon would that be, madame?'

'Definitely within twelve hours.'

'You can promise that?'

'I can promise it.'

54

As he did not answer, she repeated urgently:

'Will you guarantee that there will be no publicity?'

He answered then – very gravely:

'Yes, madame, I will guarantee that.'

'Then everything can be arranged.'

She passed abruptly from the room. A moment later Poirot heard the car drive away.

He crossed the hall and went along the passage to the study. Lord Mayfield was there. He looked up as Poirot entered.

'Well?' he said.

Poirot spread out his hands.

'The case is ended, Lord Mayfield.'

'What?'

Poirot repeated word for word the scene between himself and Lady Julia.

Lord Mayfield looked at him with a stupefied expression.

'But what does it mean? I don't understand.'

'It is very clear, is it not? Lady Julia knows who stole the plans.'

'You don't mean she took them herself?'

'Certainly not. Lady Julia may be a gambler. She is not a thief. But if she offers to return the plans, it means that they were taken by her husband or her son. Now Sir George Carrington was out on the terrace with you. That leaves us the son. I think I can reconstruct the happenings of last night fairly accurately. Lady Julia went to her son's room last night and found it empty. She came downstairs to look for him, but did not find him. This morning she hears of the theft, and she also hears that her son declares that he went straight to his room *and never left it*. That, she knows, is not true. And she knows something else about her son. She knows that he is weak, that he is desperately hard-up for money. She has observed his infatuation for Mrs Vanderlyn. The whole thing is clear to her. Mrs Vanderlyn has persuaded Reggie to steal the plans. But she determines to play her part also. She will tackle Reggie, get hold of the papers and return them.'

'But the whole thing is quite impossible,' cried Lord Mayfield.

'Yes, it is impossible, but Lady Julia does not know that. She does not know what I, Hercule Poirot, know, that young Reggie Carrington was not stealing papers last night, but instead was philandering with Mrs Vanderlyn's French maid.'

'The whole thing is a mare's nest!'

'Exactly.'

'And the case is not ended at all!'

'Yes, it is ended. *I, Hercule Poirot, know the truth.* You do not believe me? You did not believe me yesterday when I said I knew where the plans were. But I did know. They were very close at hand.'

'Where?'

'They were in your pocket, my lord.'

There was a pause, then Lord Mayfield said:

'Do you really know what you are saying, M. Poirot?'

'Yes, I know. I know that I am speaking to a very clever man. From the first it worried me that you, who were admittedly short-sighted, should be so positive about the figure you had seen leaving the window. You wanted that solution – the convenient solution – to be accepted. Why? Later, one by one, I eliminated everyone else. Mrs Vanderlyn was upstairs, Sir George was with you on the terrace, Reggie Carrington was with the French girl on the stairs, Mrs Macatta was blamelessly in her bedroom. (It is next to the housekeeper's room, and Mrs Macatta snores!) Lady Julia clearly believed her son guilty. So there remained only two possibilities. Either Carlile did not put the papers on the desk but into his own pocket (and that is not reasonable, because, as you pointed out, he could have taken a tracing of them), or else – or else the plans were there when you walked over to the desk, and the only place they could have gone was into *your* pocket. In that case everything was clear. Your insistence on the figure you had seen, your insistence on Carlile's innocence, your disinclination to have me summoned.

'One thing did puzzle me – the motive. You were, I was convinced, an honest man, a man of integrity. That showed in

56

your anxiety that no innocent person should be suspected. It was also obvious that the theft of the plans might easily affect your career unfavourably. Why, then, this wholly unreasonable theft? And at last the answer came to me. The crisis in your career, some years ago, the assurances given to the world by the Prime Minister that you had had no negotiations with the power in question. Suppose that that was not strictly true, that there remained some record – a letter, perhaps – showing that in actual fact you *had* done what you had publicly denied. Such a denial was necessary in the interests of public policy. But it is doubtful if the man in the street would see it that way. It might mean that at the moment when supreme power might be given into your hands, some stupid echo from the past would undo everything.

'I suspect that that letter has been preserved in the hands of a certain government, that that government offered to trade with you – the letter in exchange for the plans of the new bomber. Some men would have refused. You – did not! You agreed. Mrs Vanderlyn was the agent in the matter. She came here by arrangement to make the exchange. You gave yourself away when you admitted that you had formed no definite stratagem for entrapping her. That admission made your reason for inviting her here incredibly weak.

'You arranged the robbery. Pretended to see the thief on the terrace – thereby clearing Carlile of suspicion. Even if he had not left the room, the desk was so near the window that a thief might have taken the plans while Carlile was busy at the safe with his back turned. You walked over to the desk, took the plans and kept them on your own person until the moment when, by prearranged plan, you slipped them into Mrs Vanderlyn's dressing-case. In return she handed you the fatal letter disguised as an unposted letter of her own.'

Poirot stopped.

Lord Mayfield said:

'Your knowledge is very complete, M. Poirot. You must think me an unutterable skunk.'

Poirot made a quick gesture.

'No, no, Lord Mayfield. I think, as I said, that you are a very clever man. It came to me suddenly as we talked here last night. You are a first-class engineer. There will be, I think, some subtle alterations in the specifications of that bomber, alterations done so skilfully that it will be difficult to grasp why the machine is not the success it ought to be. A certain foreign power will find the type a failure ... It will be a disappointment to them, I am sure...'

Again there was a silence – then Lord Mayfield said:

'You are much too clever, M. Poirot. I will only ask you to believe one thing. I have faith in myself. I believe that I am the man to guide England through the days of crisis that I see coming. If I did not honestly believe that I am needed by my country to steer the ship of state, I would not have done what I have done – made the best of both worlds – saved myself from disaster by a clever trick.'

'My lord,' said Poirot, 'if you could not make the best of both worlds, you could not be a politician!'

MURDER IN THE MEWS

CHAPTER 1

'Penny for the guy, sir?'

A small boy with a grimy face grinned ingratiatingly.

'Certainly not!' said Chief Inspector Japp. 'And, look here, my lad –'

A short homily followed. The dismayed urchin beat a precipitate retreat, remarking briefly and succinctly to his youthful friends:

'Blimey, if it ain't a cop all togged up!'

The band took to its heels, chanting the incantation:

> Remember, remember
> The fifth of November
> Gunpowder treason and plot.
> We see no reason
> Why gunpowder treason
> Should ever be forgot.

The chief inspector's companion, a small, elderly man with an egg-shaped head and large, military-looking moustaches, was smiling to himself.

'*Très bien*, Japp,' he observed. 'You preach the sermon very well! I congratulate you!'

'Rank excuse for begging, that's what Guy Fawkes' Day is!' said Japp.

'An interesting survival,' mused Hercule Poirot. 'The fireworks go up – crack – crack – long after the man they commemorate and his deed are forgotten.'

The Scotland Yard man agreed.

'Don't suppose many of those kids really know who Guy Fawkes was.'

'And soon, doubtless, there will be confusion of thought. Is it in honour or in execration that on the fifth of November the *feu d'artifice* are sent up? To blow up an English Parliament, was it a sin or a noble deed?'

Japp chuckled.

'Some people would say undoubtedly the latter.'

Turning off the main road, the two men passed into the comparative quiet of a mews. They had been dining together and were now taking a short cut to Hercule Poirot's flat.

As they walked along the sound of squibs was still heard periodically. An occasional shower of golden rain illuminated the sky.

'Good night for a murder,' remarked Japp with professional interest. 'Nobody would hear a shot, for instance, on a night like this.'

'It has always seemed odd to me that more criminals do not take advantage of the fact,' said Hercule Poirot.

'Do you know, Poirot, I almost wish sometimes that *you* would commit a murder.'

'*Mon cher!*'

'Yes, I'd like to see just how you'd set about it.'

'My dear Japp, *if* I committed a murder you would not have the least chance of seeing – how I set about it! You would not even be aware, probably, that a murder had been committed.'

Japp laughed good-humouredly and affectionately.

'Cocky little devil, aren't you?' he said indulgently.

At half-past eleven the following morning, Hercule Poirot's telephone rang.

''Allo? 'Allo?'

'Hallo, that you, Poirot?'

'*Oui, c'est moi.*'

'Japp speaking here. Remember we came home last night through Bardsley Gardens Mews?'

'Yes?'

'And that we talked about how easy it would be to shoot a person with all those squibs and crackers and the rest of it going off?'

'Certainly.'

'Well, there was a suicide in that mews. No. 14. A young widow – Mrs Allen. I'm going round there now. Like to come?'

'Excuse me, but does someone of your eminence, my dear friend, usually get sent to a case of suicide?'

'Sharp fellow. No – he doesn't. As a matter of fact our doctor seems to think there's something funny about this. Will you come? I kind of feel you ought to be in on it.'

'Certainly I will come. No. 14, you say?'

'That's right.'

Poirot arrived at No. 14 Bardsley Gardens Mews almost at the same moment as a car drew up containing Japp and three other men.

No. 14 was clearly marked out as the centre of interest. A big circle of people, chauffeurs, their wives, errand boys, loafers, well-dressed passers-by and innumerable children were drawn up all staring at No. 14 with open mouths and a fascinated stare.

A police constable in uniform stood on the step and did his best to keep back the curious. Alert-looking young men with cameras were busy and surged forward as Japp alighted.

'Nothing for you now,' said Japp, brushing them aside. He nodded to Poirot. 'So here you are. Let's get inside.'

They passed in quickly, the door shut behind them and they found themselves squeezed together at the foot of a ladder-like flight of stairs.

A man came to the top of the staircase, recognized Japp and said:

'Up here, sir.'

Japp and Poirot mounted the stairs.

The man at the stairhead opened a door on the left and they found themselves in a small bedroom.

'Thought you'd like me to run over the chief points, sir.'

'Quite right, Jameson,' said Japp. 'What about it?'

Divisional Inspector Jameson took up the tale.

'Deceased's a Mrs Allen, sir. Lived here with a friend – a Miss Plenderleith. Miss Plenderleith was away staying in the country and returned this morning. She let herself in with her key, was surprised to find no one about. A woman usually comes in at nine o'clock to do for them. She went upstairs first into her own room (that's this room) then across the landing to her friend's room. Door was locked on the inside. She rattled the handle, knocked and called, but couldn't get any answer. In the end getting alarmed she rang up the police station. That was at ten forty-five. We came along at once and forced the door open. Mrs Allen was lying in a heap on the ground shot through the head. There was an automatic in her hand – a Webley .25 – and it looked a clear case of suicide.'

'Where is Miss Plenderleith now?'

'She's downstairs in the sitting-room, sir. A very cool, efficient young lady, I should say. Got a head on her.'

'I'll talk to her presently. I'd better see Brett now.'

Accompanied by Poirot he crossed the landing and entered the opposite room. A tall, elderly man looked up and nodded.

'Hallo, Japp, glad you've got here. Funny business, this.'

Japp advanced towards him. Hercule Poirot sent a quick searching glance round the room.

It was much larger than the room they had just quitted. It had a built-out bay window, and whereas the other room had been a bedroom pure and simple, this was emphatically a bedroom disguised as a sitting-room.

The walls were silver and the ceiling emerald green. There were curtains of a modernistic pattern in silver and green. There was a divan covered with a shimmering emerald green silk quilt and numbers of gold and silver cushions. There was a tall antique walnut bureau, a walnut tallboy, and several modern chairs of gleaming chromium. On a low glass table there was a big ashtray full of cigarette stubs.

Delicately Hercule Poirot sniffed the air. Then he joined Japp where the latter stood looking down at the body.

In a heap on the floor, lying as she had fallen from one of the chromium chairs, was the body of a young woman of perhaps twenty-seven. She had fair hair and delicate features. There was very little make-up on the face. It was a pretty, wistful, perhaps slightly stupid face. On the left side of the head was a mass of congealed blood. The fingers of the right hand were clasped round a small pistol. The woman was dressed in a simple frock of dark green high to the neck.

'Well, Brett, what's the trouble?'

Japp was looking down also at the huddled figure.

'Position's all right,' said the doctor. 'If she shot herself she'd probably have slipped from the chair into just that position. The door was locked and the window was fastened on the inside.'

'That's all right, you say. Then what's wrong?'

'Take a look at the pistol. I haven't handled it – waiting for the fingerprint men. But you can see quite well what I mean.'

Together Poirot and Japp knelt down and examined the pistol closely.

'I see what you mean,' said Japp rising. 'It's in the curve of her hand. It *looks* as though she's holding it – but as a matter of fact she *isn't* holding it. Anything else?'

'Plenty. She's got the pistol in her *right* hand. Now take a look at the wound. The pistol was held close to the head just above the left ear – the *left* ear, mark you.'

'H'm,' said Japp. 'That does seem to settle it. She couldn't hold a pistol and fire it in that position with her right hand?'

'Plumb impossible, I should say. You might get your arm round but I doubt if you could fire the shot.'

'That seems pretty obvious then. Someone else shot her and tried to make it look like suicide. What about the locked door and window, though?'

Inspector Jameson answered this.

'Window was closed and bolted, sir, but although the door was locked *we haven't been able to find the key.*'

Japp nodded.

'Yes, that was a bad break. Whoever did it locked the door

63

when he left and hoped the absence of the key wouldn't be noticed.'

Poirot murmured:

'*C'est bête, ça!*'

'Oh, come now, Poirot, old man, you mustn't judge everybody else by the light of your shining intellect! As a matter of fact that's the sort of little detail that's quite apt to be overlooked. Door's locked. People break in. Woman found dead – pistol in her hand – clear case of suicide – she locked herself in to do it. They don't go hunting about for keys. As a matter of fact, Miss Plenderleith's sending for the police was lucky. She might have got one or two of the chauffeurs to come and burst in the door – and then the key question would have been overlooked altogether.'

'Yes, I suppose that is true,' said Hercule Poirot. 'It would have been many people's natural reaction. The police, they are the last resource, are they not?'

He was still staring down at the body.

'Anything strike you?' Japp asked.

The question was careless but his eyes were keen and attentive.

Hercule Poirot shook his head slowly.

'I was looking at her wrist-watch.'

He bent over and just touched it with a finger-tip. It was a dainty jewelled affair on a black moiré strap on the wrist of the hand that held the pistol.

'Rather a swell piece that,' observed Japp. 'Must have cost money!' He cocked his head inquiringly at Poirot. 'Something in that maybe?'

'It is possible – yes.'

Poirot strayed across to the writing-bureau. It was the kind that has a front flap that lets down. This was daintily set out to match the general colour scheme.

There was a somewhat massive silver inkstand in the centre, in front of it a handsome green lacquer blotter. To the left of the blotter was an emerald glass pen-tray containing a silver penholder – a stick of green sealing-wax, a pencil and two stamps. On the right of the blotter was a movable calendar giving the day of the week, date and month. There was also a little glass jar of shot and standing in it a flamboyant green quill pen. Poirot seemed interested in the pen. He took it out and looked at it but the quill was innocent of ink. It was clearly a decoration – nothing more. The silver penholder with the ink-stained nib was the one in use. His eyes strayed to the calendar.

'Tuesday, November fifth,' said Japp. 'Yesterday. That's all correct.'

He turned to Brett.

'How long has she been dead?'

'She was killed at eleven thirty-three yesterday evening,' said Brett promptly.

Then he grinned as he saw Japp's surprised face.

'Sorry, old boy,' he said. 'Had to do the super doctor of fiction! As a matter of fact eleven is about as near as I can put it – with a margin of about an hour either way.'

'Oh, I thought the wrist-watch might have stopped – or something.'

'It's stopped all right, but it's stopped at a quarter past four.'

'And I suppose she couldn't have been killed possibly at a quarter past four.'

'You can put that right out of your mind.'

Poirot had turned back the cover of the blotter.

'Good idea,' said Japp. 'But no luck.'

The blotter showed an innocent white sheet of blotting-paper. Poirot turned over the leaves but they were all the same.

He turned his attention to the waste-paper basket.

It contained two or three torn-up letters and circulars. They were only torn once and were easily reconstructed. An appeal for money from some society for assisting ex-service men, an invitation to a cocktail party on November 3rd, an appointment with a dressmaker. The circulars were an announcement of a furrier's sale and a catalogue from a department store.

'Nothing there,' said Japp.

'No, it is odd ...' said Poirot.

'You mean they usually leave a letter when it's suicide?'

'Exactly.'

'In fact, one more proof that it *isn't* suicide.'

He moved away.

'I'll have my men get to work now. We'd better go down and interview this Miss Plenderleith. Coming, Poirot?'

Poirot still seemed fascinated by the writing-bureau and its appointments.

He left the room, but at the door his eyes went back once more to the flaunting emerald quill pen.

CHAPTER 2

At the foot of the narrow flight of stairs a door gave admission to a large-sized living-room – actually the converted stable. In this room, the walls of which were finished in a roughened plaster effect and on which hung etchings and woodcuts, two people were sitting.

One, in a chair near the fireplace, her hand stretched out to the blaze, was a dark efficient-looking young woman of twenty-seven or eight. The other, an elderly woman of ample proportions who carried a string bag, was panting and talking when the two men entered the room.

' – and as I said, Miss, such a turn it gave me I nearly dropped down where I stood. And to think that this morning of all mornings –'

The other cut her short.

'That will do, Mrs Pierce. These gentlemen are police officers, I think.'

'Miss Plenderleith?' asked Japp, advancing.

The girl nodded.

'That is my name. This is Mrs Pierce who comes in to work for us every day.'

The irrepressible Mrs Pierce broke out again.

'And as I was saying to Miss Plenderleith, to think that this morning of all mornings, my sister's Louisa Maud should have been took with a fit and me the only one handy and as I say flesh and blood is flesh and blood, and I didn't think Mrs Allen would mind, though I never likes to disappoint my ladies –'

Japp broke in with some dexterity.

'Quite so, Mrs Pierce. Now perhaps you would take Inspector Jameson into the kitchen and give him a brief statement.'

Having then got rid of the voluble Mrs Pierce, who departed with Jameson talking thirteen to the dozen, Japp turned his attention once more to the girl.

'I am Chief Inspector Japp. Now, Miss Plenderleith, I should like to know all you can tell me about this business.'

'Certainly. Where shall I begin?'

Her self-possession was admirable. There were no signs of grief or shock save for an almost unnatural rigidity of manner.

'You arrived this morning at what time?'

'I think it was just before half-past ten. Mrs Pierce, the old liar, wasn't here, I found –'

'Is that a frequent occurrence?'

Jane Plenderleith shrugged her shoulders.

'About twice a week she turns up at twelve – or not at all. She's supposed to come at nine. Actually, as I say, twice a week she either "comes over queer," or else some member of her family is overtaken by sickness. All these daily women are like that – fail you now and again. She's not bad as they go.'

'You've had her long?'

'Just over a month. Our last one pinched things.'

'Please go on, Miss Plenderleith.'

'I paid off the taxi, carried in my suitcase, looked round for Mrs P., couldn't see her and went upstairs to my room. I tidied up a bit then I went across to Barbara – Mrs Allen – and found the door locked. I rattled the handle and knocked but could get no reply. I came downstairs and rang up the police station.'

'*Pardon!*' Poirot interposed a quick, deft question. 'It did not occur to you to try and break down the door – with the help of one of the chauffeurs in the mews, say?'

Her eyes turned to him – cool, grey-green eyes. Her glance seemed to sweep over him quickly and appraisingly.

'No, I don't think I thought of that. If anything was wrong, it seemed to me that the police were the people to send for.'

'Then you thought – *pardon, mademoiselle* –that there *was* something wrong?'

'Naturally.'

'Because you could not get a reply to your knocks? But possibly your friend might have taken a sleeping draught or something of that kind –'

'She didn't take sleeping draughts.'

The reply came sharply.

'Or she might have gone away and locked her door before going?'

'Why should she lock it? In any case she would have left a note for me.'

'And she did not – leave a note for you? You are quite sure of that?'

'Of course I am sure of it. I should have seen it at once.'

The sharpness of her tone was accentuated.

Japp said:

'You didn't try and look through the keyhole, Miss Plenderleith?'

'No,' said Jane Plenderleith thoughtfully. 'I never thought of that. But I couldn't have seen anything, could I? Because the key would have been in it?'

Her inquiring gaze, innocent, wide-eyed, met Japp's. Poirot smiled suddenly to himself.

'You did quite right, of course, Miss Plenderleith,' said Japp. 'I suppose you'd no reason to believe that your friend was likely to commit suicide?'

'Oh, no.'

'She hadn't seemed worried – or distressed in any way?'

There was a pause – an appreciable pause before the girl answered.

68

'No.'

'Did you know she had a pistol?'

Jane Plenderleith nodded.

'Yes, she had it out in India. She always kept it in a drawer in her room.'

'H'm. Got a licence for it?'

'I imagine so. I don't know for certain.'

'Now, Miss Plenderleith, will you tell me all you can about Mrs Allen, how long you've known her, where her relations are – everything in fact.'

Jane Plenderleith nodded.

'I've known Barbara about five years. I met her first travelling abroad – in Egypt to be exact. She was on her way home from India. I'd been at the British School in Athens for a bit and was having a few weeks in Egypt before going home. We were on a Nile cruise together. We made friends, decided we liked each other. I was looking at the time for someone to share a flat or a tiny house with me. Barbara was alone in the world. We thought we'd get on well together.'

'And you did get on well together?' asked Poirot.

'Very well. We each had our own friends – Barbara was more social in her likings – my friends were more of the artistic kind. It probably worked better that way.'

Poirot nodded. Japp went on:

'What do you know about Mrs Allen's family and her life before she met you?'

Jane Plenderleith shrugged her shoulders.

'Not very much really. Her maiden name was Armitage, I believe.'

'Her husband?'

'I don't fancy that he was anything to write home about. He drank, I think. I gather he died a year or two after the marriage. There was one child, a little girl, which died when it was three years old. Barbara didn't talk much about her husband. I believe she married him in India when she was about seventeen. Then they went off to Borneo or one of the Godforsaken spots you send ne'er-do-wells to – but as it was obviously a painful subject I didn't refer to it.'

'Do you know if Mrs Allen was in any financial difficulties?'

'No, I'm sure she wasn't.'

'Not in debt – anything of that kind?'

'Oh, no! I'm sure she wasn't in that kind of a jam.'

'Now there's another question I must ask – and I hope you won't be upset about it, Miss Plenderleith. Had Mrs Allen any particular man friend or men friends?'

Jane Plenderleith answered coolly:

'Well, she was engaged to be married if that answers your question.'

'What is the name of the man she was engaged to?'

'Charles Laverton-West. He's M.P. for some place in Hampshire.'

'Had she known him long?'

'A little over a year.'

'And she has been engaged to him – how long?'

'Two – no – nearer three months.'

'As far as you know there has not been any quarrel?'

Miss Plenderleith shook her head.

'No. I should have been surprised if there had been anything of that sort. Barbara wasn't the quarrelling kind.'

'How long is it since you last saw Mrs Allen?'

'Friday last, just before I went away for the weekend.'

'Mrs Allen was remaining in town?'

'Yes. She was going out with her fiancé on the Sunday, I believe.'

'And you yourself, where did you spend the weekend?'

'At Laidells Hall, Laidells, Essex.'

'And the name of the people with whom you were staying?'

'Mr and Mrs Bentinck.'

'You only left them this morning?'

'Yes.'

'You must have left very early?'

'Mr Bentinck motored me up. He starts early because he has to get to the city by ten.'

'I see.'

Japp nodded comprehendingly. Miss Plenderleith's replies had all been crisp and convincing.

Poirot in his turn put a question.

'What is your own opinion of Mr Laverton-West?'

The girl shrugged her shoulders.

'Does that matter?'

'No, it does not matter, perhaps, but I should like to have your opinion.'

'I don't know that I've thought about him one way or the other. He's young – not more than thirty-one or two – ambitious – a good public speaker – means to get on in the world.'

'That is on the credit side – and on the debit?'

'Well,' Miss Plenderleith considered for a moment or two. 'In my opinion he's commonplace – his ideas are not particularly original – and he's slightly pompous.'

'Those are not very serious faults, mademoiselle,' said Poirot, smiling.

'Don't you think so?'

Her tone was slightly ironic.

'They might be to you.'

He was watching her, saw her look a little disconcerted. He pursued his advantage.

'But to Mrs Allen – no, she would not notice them.'

'You're perfectly right. Barbara thought he was wonderful – took him entirely at his own valuation.'

Poirot said gently:

'You were fond of your friend?'

He saw the hand clench on her knee, the tightening of the line of the jaw, yet the answer came in a matter-of-fact voice free from emotion.

'You are quite right. I was.'

Japp said:

'Just one other thing, Miss Plenderleith. You and she didn't have a quarrel? There was no upset between you?'

'None whatever.'

71

'Not over this engagement business?'

'Certainly not. I was glad she was able to be so happy about it.'

There was a momentary pause, then Japp said:

'As far as you know, did Mrs Allen have any enemies?'

This time there was a definite interval before Jane Plenderleith replied. When she did so, her tone had altered very slightly.

'I don't know quite what you mean by enemies?'

'Anyone, for instance, who would profit by her death?'

'Oh, no, that would be ridiculous. She had a very small income anyway.'

'And who inherits that income?'

Jane Plenderleith's voice sounded mildly surprised as she said:

'Do you know, I really don't know. I shouldn't be surprised if I did. That is, if she ever made a will.'

'And no enemies in any other sense?' Japp slid off to another aspect quickly. 'People with a grudge against her?'

'I don't think anyone had a grudge against her. She was a very gentle creature, always anxious to please. She had a really sweet, lovable nature.'

For the first time that hard, matter-of-fact voice broke a little. Poirot nodded gently.

Japp said:

'So it amounts to this – Mrs Allen has been in good spirits lately, she wasn't in any financial difficulty, she was engaged to be married and was happy in her engagement. There was nothing in the world to make her commit suicide. That's right, isn't it?'

There was a momentary silence before Jane said:

'Yes.'

Japp rose.

'Excuse me, I must have a word with Inspector Jameson.' He left the room.

Hercule Poirot remained *tête à tête* with Jane Plenderleith.

CHAPTER 3

For a few minutes there was silence.

Jane Plenderleith shot a swift appraising glance at the little man, but after that she stared in front of her and did not speak. Yet a consciousness of his presence showed itself in a certain nervous tension. Her body was still but not relaxed. When at last Poirot did break the silence the mere sound of his voice seemed to give her a certain relief. In an agreeable everyday voice he asked a question.

'When did you light the fire, mademoiselle?'

'The fire?' Her voice sounded vague and rather absent-minded. 'Oh, as soon as I arrived this morning.'

'Before you went upstairs or afterwards?'

'Before.'

'I see. Yes, naturally ... And it was already laid – or did you have to lay it?'

'It was laid. I only had to put a match to it.'

There was a slight impatience in her voice. Clearly she suspected him of making conversation. Possibly that was what he was doing. At any rate he went on in quiet conversational tones.

'But your friend – in her room I noticed there was a gas fire only?'

Jane Plenderleith answered mechanically.

'This is the only coal fire we have – the others are all gas fires.'

'And you cook with gas, too?'

'I think everyone does nowadays.'

'True. It is much labour saving.'

The little interchange died down. Jane Plenderleith tapped on the ground with her shoe. Then she said abruptly:

'That man – Chief Inspector Japp – is he considered clever?'

'He is very sound. Yes, he is well thought of. He works hard and painstakingly and very little escapes him.'

'I wonder –' muttered the girl.

Poirot watched her. His eyes looked very green in the firelight. He asked quietly:

'It was a great shock to you, your friend's death?'

'Terrible.'

She spoke with abrupt sincerity.

'You did not expect it – no?'

'Of course not.'

'So that it seemed to you at first, perhaps, that it was impossible – that it could not be?'

The quiet sympathy of his tone seemed to break down Jane Plenderleith's defences. She replied eagerly, naturally, without stiffness.

'That's just it. Even if Barbara *did* kill herself, I can't imagine her *killing herself that way*.'

'Yet she had a pistol?'

Jane Plenderleith made an impatient gesture.

'Yes, but that pistol was a – oh! a hang over. She'd been in out-of-the-way places. She kept it out of habit – not with any other idea. I'm sure of that.'

'Ah! and why are you sure of that?'

'Oh, because of the things she said.'

'Such as –?'

His voice was very gentle and friendly. It led her on subtly.

'Well, for instance, we were discussing suicide once and she said much the easiest way would be to turn the gas on and stuff up all the cracks and just go to bed. I said I thought that would be impossible – to lie there waiting. I said I'd far rather shoot myself. And she said no, she could never shoot herself. She'd be too frightened in case it didn't come off and anyway she said she'd hate the bang.'

'I see,' said Poirot. 'As you say, it is odd … Because, as you have just told me, *there was a gas fire in her room.*'

Jane Plenderleith looked at him, slightly startled.

'Yes, there was... I can't understand – no, I can't understand why she didn't do it that way.'

Poirot shook his head.

'Yes, it seems – odd – not natural somehow.'

'The whole thing doesn't seem natural. I still can't believe she killed herself. I suppose it *must* be suicide?'

'Well, there is one other possibility.'

'What do you mean?'

Poirot looked straight at her.

'It might be – murder.'

'Oh, no?' Jane Plenderleith shrank back. 'Oh no! What a horrible suggestion.'

'Horrible, perhaps, but does it strike you as an impossible one?'

'But the door was locked on the inside. So was the window.'

'The door was locked – yes. But there is nothing to show if it were locked from the inside or the outside. You see, *the key was missing*.'

'But then – if it is missing...' She took a minute or two. 'Then it must have been locked from the *outside*. Otherwise it would be somewhere in the room.'

'Ah, but it may be. The room has not been thoroughly searched yet, remember. Or it may have been thrown out of the window and somebody may have picked it up.'

'Murder!' said Jane Plenderleith. She turned over the possibility, her dark clever face eager on the scent. 'I believe you're right.'

'But if it were murder there would have been a motive. Do you know of a motive, mademoiselle?'

Slowly she shook her head. And yet, in spite of the denial, Poirot again got the impression that Jane Plenderleith was deliberately keeping something back. The door opened and Japp came in.

Poirot rose.

'I have been suggesting to Miss Plenderleith,' he said, 'that her friend's death was not suicide.'

Japp looked momentarily put out. He cast a glance of reproach at Poirot.

'It's a bit early to say anything definite,' he remarked. 'We've always got to take all possibilities into account, you understand. That's all there is to it at the moment.'

Jane Plenderleith replied quietly.

'I see.'

Japp came towards her.

'Now then, Miss Plenderleith, have you ever seen this before?'

On the palm of his hand he held out a small oval of dark blue enamel.

Jane Plenderleith shook her head.

'No, never.'

'It's not yours nor Mrs Allen's?'

'No. It's not the kind of thing usually worn by our sex, is it?'

'Oh! so you recognize it.'

'Well, it's pretty obvious, isn't it? That's half of a man's cuff link.'

CHAPTER 4

'That young woman's too cocky by half,' Japp complained.

The two men were once more in Mrs Allen's bedroom. The body had been photographed and removed and the fingerprint man had done his work and departed.

'It would be unadvisable to treat her as a fool,' agreed Poirot. 'She most emphatically is *not* a fool. She is, in fact, a particularly clever and competent young woman.'

'Think she did it?' asked Japp with a momentary ray of hope. 'She might have, you know. We'll have to get her alibi looked into. Some quarrel over this young man – this budding M.P. She's rather *too* scathing about him, I think! Sounds fishy.

Rather as though she were sweet on him herself and he'd turned her down. She's the kind that would bump anyone off if she felt like it, and keep her head while she was doing it, too. Yes, we'll have to look into that alibi. She had it very pat and after all Essex isn't very far away. Plenty of trains. Or a fast car. It's worth while finding out if she went to bed with a headache for instance last night.'

'You are right,' agreed Poirot.

'In any case,' continued Japp, 'she's holding out on us. Eh? Didn't you feel that too? That young woman knows something.'

Poirot nodded thoughtfully.

'Yes, that could be clearly seen.'

'That's always a difficulty in these cases,' Japp complained. 'People *will* hold their tongues – sometimes out of the most honourable motives.'

'For which one can hardly blame them, my friend.'

'No, but it makes it much harder for *us*,' Japp grumbled.

'It merely displays to its full advantage your ingenuity.' Poirot consoled him. 'What about fingerprints, by the way?'

'Well, it's murder all right. No prints whatever on the pistol. Wiped clean before being placed in her hand. Even if she managed to wind her arm round her head in some marvellous acrobatic fashion she could hardly fire off a pistol without hanging on to it and she couldn't wipe it after she was dead.'

'No, no, an outside agency is clearly indicated.'

'Otherwise the prints are disappointing. None on the doorhandle. None on the window. Suggestive, eh? Plenty of Mrs Allen's all over the place.'

'Did Jameson get anything?'

'Out of the daily woman? No. She talked a lot but she didn't really know much. Confirmed the fact that Allen and Plenderleith were on good terms. I've sent Jameson out to make inquiries in the mews. We'll have to have a word with Mr Laverton-West too. Find out where he was and what he was doing last night. In the meantime we'll have a look through her papers.'

He set to without more ado. Occasionally he grunted and tossed something over to Poirot. The search did not take long. There were not many papers in the desk and what there were were neatly arranged and docketed.

Finally Japp leant back and uttered a sigh.

'Not very much, is there?'

'As you say.'

'Most of it quite straightforward – receipted bills, a few bills as yet unpaid – nothing particularly outstanding. Social stuff – invitations. Notes from friends. These –' he laid his hand on a pile of seven or eight letters – 'and her cheque book and passbook. Anything strike you there?'

'Yes, she was overdrawn.'

'Anything else?'

Poirot smiled.

'Is it an examination that you put me through? But yes, I noticed what you are thinking of. Two hundred pounds drawn to self three months ago – and two hundred pounds drawn out yesterday –'

'And nothing on the counterfoil of the cheque book. No other cheques to self except small sums – fifteen pounds the highest. And I'll tell you this – there's no such sum of money in the house. Four pounds ten in a handbag and an odd shilling or two in another bag. That's pretty clear, I think.'

'Meaning that she paid that sum away yesterday.'

'Yes. Now who did she pay it to?'

The door opened and Inspector Jameson entered.

'Well, Jameson, get anything?'

'Yes, sir, several things. To begin with, nobody actually heard the shot. Two or three women say they did because they want to think they did – but that's all there is to it. With all those fireworks going off there isn't a dog's chance.'

Japp grunted.

'Don't suppose there is. Go on.'

'Mrs Allen was at home most of yesterday afternoon and evening. Came in about five o'clock. Then she went out again about six but only to the post box at the end of the mews. At about nine-thirty a car drove up – Standard Swallow saloon – and a man got out. Description about forty-five, well set up military-looking gent, dark blue overcoat, bowler hat, toothbrush moustache. James Hogg, chauffeur from No. 18 says he's seen him calling on Mrs Allen before.'

'Forty-five,' said Japp. 'Can't very well be Laverton-West.'

'This man, whoever he was, stayed here for just under an hour. Left at about ten-twenty. Stopped in the doorway to speak to Mrs. Allen. Small boy, Frederick Hogg, was hanging about quite near and heard what he said.'

'And what did he say?'

'"*Well, think it over and let me know.*" And then she said something and he answered: "*All right. So long.*" After that he got in his car and drove away.'

'That was at ten-twenty,' said Poirot thoughtfully.

Japp rubbed his nose.

'Then at ten-twenty Mrs Allen was still alive,' he said. 'What next?'

'Nothing more, sir, as far as I can learn. The chauffeur at No. 22 got in at half-past ten and he'd promised his kids to let off some fireworks for them. They'd been waiting for him – and all the other kids in the mews too. He let 'em off and everybody around about was busy watching them. After that everyone went to bed.'

'And nobody else was seen to enter No. 14?'

'No – but that's not to say they didn't. Nobody would have noticed.'

'H'm,' said Japp. 'That's true. Well, we'll have to get hold of this "military gentleman with the toothbrush moustache." It's pretty clear that he was the last person to see her alive. I wonder who he was?'

'Miss Plenderleith might tell us,' suggested Poirot.

'She might,' said Japp gloomily. 'On the other hand she might not. I've no doubt she could tell us a good deal if she liked. What about you, Poirot, old boy? You were alone with her for a bit. Didn't you trot out that Father Confessor manner of yours that sometimes makes such a hit?'

Poirot spread out his hands.

'Alas, we talked only of gas fires.'

'Gas fires – gas fires.' Japp sounded disgusted. 'What's the matter with you, old cock? Ever since you've been here the only things you've taken an interest in are quill pens and waste-paper baskets. Oh, yes, I saw you having a quiet look into the one downstairs. Anything in it?'

Poirot sighed.

'A catalogue of bulbs and an old magazine.'

'What's the idea, anyway? If anyone wants to throw away an incriminating document or whatever it is you have in mind they're not likely just to pitch it into a waste-paper basket.'

'That is very true what you say there. Only something quite unimportant would be thrown away like that.'

Poirot spoke meekly. Nevertheless Japp looked at him suspiciously.

'Well,' he said. 'I know what I'm going to do next. What about you?'

'*Eh bien*,' said Poirot. 'I shall complete my search for the unimportant. There is still the dustbin.'

He skipped nimbly out of the room. Japp looked after him with an air of disgust.

'Potty,' he said. 'Absolutely potty.'

Inspector Jameson preserved a respectful silence. His face said with British superiority: 'Foreigners!'

Aloud he said:

'So that's Mr Hercule Poirot! I've heard of him.'

'Old friend of mine,' explained Japp. 'Not half as balmy as he looks, mind you. All the same he's getting on now.'

'Gone a bit gaga as they say, sir,' suggested Inspector Jameson. 'Ah well, age will tell.'

'All the same,' said Japp, 'I wish I knew what he was up to.'

He walked over to the writing-table and stared uneasily at an emerald green quill pen.

CHAPTER 5

Japp was just engaging his third chauffeur's wife in conversation when Poirot, walking noiselessly as a cat, suddenly appeared at his elbow.

'Whew, you made me jump,' said Japp. 'Got anything?'

'Not what I was looking for.'

Japp turned back to Mrs James Hogg.

'And you say you've seen this gentleman before?'

'Oh, yes sir. And my husband too. We knew him at once.'

'Now look here, Mrs Hogg, you're a shrewd woman, I can see. I've no doubt that you know all about everyone in the mews. And you're a woman of judgment – unusually good judgment, I can tell that –' Unblushingly he repeated this remark for the third time. Mrs Hogg bridled slightly and assumed an expression of superhuman intelligence. 'Give me a line on those two young women – Mrs Allen and Miss Plenderleith. What were they like? Gay? Lots of parties? That sort of thing?'

'Oh, no sir, nothing of the kind. They went out a good bit – Mrs Allen especially – but they're *class*, if you know what I mean. Not like some as I could name down the other end. I'm sure the way that Mrs Stevens goes on – if she *is* a Mrs at all which I doubt – well I shouldn't like to tell you what goes on there – I...'

'Quite so,' said Japp, dexterously stopping the flow. 'Now that's very important what you've told me. Mrs Allen and Miss Plenderleith were well liked, then?'

'Oh yes, sir, very nice ladies, both of them – especially Mrs Allen. Always spoke a nice word to the children, she did. Lost her own little girl, I believe, poor dear. Ah well, I've buried three myself. And what I say is...'

'Yes, yes, very sad. And Miss Plenderleith?'

'Well, of course she was a nice lady too, but much more abrupt if you know what I mean. Just go by with a nod, she would, and not stop to pass the time of day. But I've nothing against her – nothing at all.'

'She and Mrs Allen got on well together?'

'Oh, yes sir. No quarrelling – nothing like that. Very happy and contented they were – I'm sure Mrs Pierce will bear me out.'

'Yes, we've talked to her. Do you know Mrs Allen's fiancé by sight?'

'The gentleman she's going to marry? Oh, yes. He's been here quite a bit off and on. Member of Parliament, they do say.'

'It wasn't he who came last night?'

'No, sir, it was *not*.' Mrs Hogg drew herself up. A note of excitement disguised beneath intense primness came into her voice. 'And if you ask me, sir, what you are thinking is all *wrong*. Mrs Allen wasn't *that* kind of lady, I'm sure. It's true there *was* no one in the house, but I do *not* believe anything of the kind – I said so to Hogg only this morning. "No, Hogg," I said, "Mrs Allen was a lady – a real lady – so don't go suggesting things" – knowing what a man's mind is, if you'll excuse my mentioning it. Always coarse in their ideas.'

Passing this insult by, Japp proceeded:

'You saw him arrive and you saw him leave – that's so, isn't it?'

'That's so, sir.'

'And you didn't hear anything else? Any sounds of a quarrel?'

'No, sir, nor likely to. Not, that is to say, that such things couldn't be heard – because the contrary to that is well known – and down the other end the way Mrs Stevens goes for that poor frightened maid of hers is common talk – and one and all we've advised her not to stand it, but there, the wages is good – temper of the devil she may have but pays for it – thirty shillings a week...'

Japp said quickly:

82

'But you didn't hear anything of the kind at No. 14?'

'No, sir. Nor likely to with fireworks popping off here, there and everywhere and my Eddie with his eyebrows singed off as near as nothing.'

'This man left at ten-twenty – that's right, is it?'

'It might be, sir. I couldn't say myself. But Hogg says so and he's a very reliable, steady man.'

'You actually saw him leave. Did you hear what he said?'

'No, sir. I wasn't near enough for that. Just saw him from my windows, standing in the doorway talking to Mrs Allen.'

'See her too?'

'Yes, sir, she was standing just inside the doorway.'

'Notice what she was wearing?'

'Now really, sir, I couldn't say. Not noticing particularly as it were.'

Poirot said:

'You did not even notice if she was wearing day dress or evening dress?'

'No, sir, I can't say I did.'

Poirot looked thoughtfully up at the window above and then across to No. 14. He smiled and for a moment his eye caught Japp's.

'And the gentleman?'

'He was in a dark-blue overcoat and a bowler hat. Very smart and well set up.'

Japp asked a few more questions and then proceeded to his next interview. This was with Master Frederick Hogg, an impish-faced, bright-eyed lad, considerably swollen with self-importance.

'Yes, sir. I heard them talking. "*Think it over and let me know,*" the gent said. Pleasant like, you know. And then she said something and he answered, '*All right. So long.*' And he got into the car – I was holding the door open but he didn't give me nothing,' said Master Hogg with a slight tinge of depression in his tone. 'And he drove away.'

'You didn't hear what Mrs Allen said?'

'No, sir, can't say I did.'

'Can you tell me what she was wearing? What colour, for instance?'

'Couldn't say, sir. You see, I didn't really see her. She must have been round behind the door.'

'Just so,' said Japp. 'Now look here, my boy, I want you to think and answer my next question very carefully. If you don't know and can't remember, say so. Is that clear?'

'Yes, sir.'

Master Hogg looked at him eagerly.

'Which of 'em closed the door, Mrs Allen or the gentleman?'

'The front door?'

'The front door, naturally.'

The child reflected. His eyes screwed themselves up in an effort of remembrance.

'Think the lady probably did – No, she didn't. He did. Pulled it to with a bit of a bang and jumped into the car quick. Looked as though he had a date somewhere.'

'Right. Well, young man, you seem a bright kind of shaver. Here's sixpence for you.'

Dismissing Master Hogg, Japp turned to his friend. Slowly with one accord they nodded.

'Could be!' said Japp.

'There are possibilities,' agreed Poirot.

His eyes shone with a green light. They looked like a cat's.

CHAPTER 6

On re-entering the sitting-room of No. 14, Japp wasted no time in beating about the bush. He came straight to the point.

'Now look here, Miss Plenderleith, don't you think it's better to spill the beans here and now. It's going to come to that in the end.'

Jane Plenderleith raised her eyebrows. She was standing by the mantelpiece, gently warming one foot at the fire.

'I really don't know what you mean.'

'Is that quite true, Miss Plenderleith?'

She shrugged her shoulders.

'I've answered all your questions. I don't see what more I can do.'

'Well, it's my opinion you could do a lot more – if you chose.'

'That's only an opinion, though, isn't it, Chief Inspector?'

Japp grew rather red in the face.

'I think,' said Poirot, 'that mademoiselle would appreciate better the reason for your questions if you told her just how the case stands.'

'That's very simple. Now then, Miss Plenderleith, the facts are as follows. Your friend was found shot through the head with a pistol in her hand and the door and the window fastened. That looked like a plain case of suicide. *But it wasn't suicide.* The medical evidence alone proves that.'

'How?'

All her ironic coolness had disappeared. She leaned forward – intent – watching his face.

'The pistol was in her hand – *but the fingers weren't grasping it.* Moreover there were *no fingerprints at all* on the pistol. And the angle of the wound makes it impossible that the wound should have been self-inflicted. Then again, she left no letter – rather an unusual thing for a suicide. And though the door was locked the key has not been found.'

Jane Plenderleith turned slowly and sat down in a chair facing them.

'So that's it!' she said. 'All along I've felt it was *impossible* that she should have killed herself! I was right! She *didn't* kill herself. Someone else killed her.'

For a moment or two she remained lost in thought. Then she raised her head brusquely.

'Ask me any questions you like,' she said. 'I will answer them to the best of my ability.'

Japp began:

'Last night Mrs Allen had a visitor. He is described as a man of forty-five, military bearing, toothbrush moustache, smartly dressed and driving a Standard Swallow saloon car. Do you know who that is?'

'I can't be sure, of course, but it sounds like Major Eustace.'

'Who is Major Eustace? Tell me all you can about him?'

'He was a man Barbara had known abroad – in India. He turned up about a year ago, and we've seen him on and off since.'

'He was a friend of Mrs Allen's?'

'He behaved like one,' said Jane dryly.

'What was her attitude to him?'

'I don't think she really liked him – in fact, I'm sure she didn't.'

'But she treated him with outward friendliness?'

'Yes.'

'Did she ever seem – think carefully, Miss Plenderleith – afraid of him?'

Jane Plenderleith considered this thoughtfully for a minute or two. Then she said:

'Yes – I think she was. She was always nervous when he was about.'

'Did he and Mr Laverton-West meet at all?'

'Only once, I think. They didn't take to each other much. That is to say, Major Eustace made himself as agreeable as he could to Charles, but Charles wasn't having any. Charles has got a very good nose for anybody who isn't well – quite – quite.'

'And Major Eustace was not – what you call – quite – quite?' asked Poirot.

The girl said dryly:

'No, he wasn't. Bit hairy at the heel. Definitely not out of the top drawer.'

'Alas – I do not know those two expressions. You mean to say he was not the *pukka sahib*?'

A fleeting smile passed across Jane Plenderleith's face, but she replied gravely, 'No.'

'Would it come as a great surprise to you, Miss Plenderleith, if I suggested that this man was blackmailing Mrs Allen?'

Japp sat forward to observe the result of his suggestion.

He was well satisfied. The girl started forward, the colour rose in her cheeks, she brought down her hand sharply on the arm of her chair.

'So that was it! What a fool I was not to have guessed. Of course!'

'You think the suggestion feasible, mademoiselle?' asked Poirot.

'I was a fool not to have thought of it! Barbara's borrowed small sums off me several times during the last six months. And I've seen her sitting poring over her passbook. I knew she was living well within her income, so I didn't bother, but, of course, if she was paying out sums of money –'

'And it would accord with her general demeanour – yes?' asked Poirot.

'Absolutely. She was nervous. Quite jumpy sometimes. Altogether different from what she used to be.'

Poirot said gently:

'Excuse me, but that is not just what you told us before.'

'That was different,' Jane Plenderleith waved an impatient hand. 'She wasn't depressed. I mean she wasn't feeling suicidal or anything like that. But blackmail – yes. I wish she'd told *me*. I'd have sent him to the devil.'

'But he might have gone – not to the devil, but to Mr Charles Laverton-West?' observed Poirot.

'Yes,' said Jane Plenderleith slowly. 'Yes ... that's true...'

'You've no idea of what this man's hold over her may have been?' asked Japp.

The girl shook her head.

'I haven't the faintest idea. I can't believe, knowing Barbara, that it could have been anything really serious. On the other hand –' she paused, then went on. 'What I mean is, Barbara was a bit of a simpleton in some ways. She'd be very easily frightened. In fact, she was the kind of girl who would be a positive gift to a blackmailer! The nasty brute!'

She snapped out the last three words with real venom.

'Unfortunately,' said Poirot, 'the crime seems to have taken place the wrong way round. It is the victim who should kill the blackmailer, not the blackmailer his victim.'

Jane Plenderleith frowned a little.

'No – that is true – but I can imagine circumstances –'

'Such as?'

'Supposing Barbara got desperate. She may have threatened him with that silly little pistol of hers. He tries to wrench it away from her and in the struggle he fires it and kills her. Then he's horrified at what he's done and tries to pretend it was suicide.'

'Might be,' said Japp. 'But there's a difficulty.'

She looked at him inquiringly.

'Major Eustace (if it was him) left here last night at ten-twenty and said goodbye to Mrs Allen on the doorstep.'

'Oh,' the girl's face fell. 'I see.' She paused a minute or two. 'But he might have come back later,' she said slowly.

'Yes, that is possible,' said Poirot.

Japp continued:

'Tell me, Miss Plenderleith, where was Mrs Allen in the habit of receiving guests, here or in the room upstairs?'

'Both. But this room was used for more communal parties or for my own special friends. You see, the arrangement was that Barbara had the big bedroom and used it as a sitting-room as well, and I had the little bedroom and used this room.'

'If Major Eustace came by appointment last night, in which room do you think Mrs Allen would have received him?'

'I think she would probably bring him in here.' The girl sounded a little doubtful. 'It would be less intimate. On the other hand, if she wanted to write a cheque or anything of that kind, she would probably take him upstairs. There are no writing materials down here.'

Japp shook his head.

'There was no question of a cheque. Mrs Allen drew out two hundred pounds in cash yesterday. And so far we've not been able to find any trace of it in the house.'

'And she gave it to that brute? Oh, poor Barbara! Poor, poor Barbara!'

Poirot coughed.

'Unless, as you suggest, it was more or less an accident, it still seems a remarkable fact that he should kill an apparently regular source of income.'

'Accident? It wasn't an accident. He lost his temper and saw red and shot her.'

'That is how you think it happened?'

'Yes.' She added vehemently, 'It was murder – *murder*!'

Poirot said gravely:

'I will not say that you are wrong, mademoiselle.'

Japp said:

'What cigarettes did Mrs Allen smoke?'

'Gaspers. There are some in that box.'

Japp opened the box, took out a cigarette and nodded. He slipped the cigarette into his pocket.

'And you, mademoiselle?' asked Poirot.

'The same.'

'You do not smoke Turkish?'

'Never.'

'Nor Mrs Allen?'

'No. She didn't like them.'

Poirot asked:

'And Mr Laverton-West. What did he smoke?'

She stared hard at him.

'Charles? What does it matter what he smoked? You're not going to pretend that *he* killed her?'

Poirot shrugged his shoulders.

'A man has killed the woman he loved before now, mademoiselle.'

Jane shook her head impatiently.

'Charles wouldn't kill anybody. He's a very careful man.'

'All the same, mademoiselle, it is the careful men who commit the cleverest murders.'

She stared at him.

'But not for the motive you have just advanced, M. Poirot.'

89

He bowed his head.

'No, that is true.'

Japp rose.

'Well, I don't think that there's much more I can do here. I'd like to have one more look round.'

'In case that money should be tucked away somewhere? Certainly. Look anywhere you like. And in my room too – although it isn't likely Barbara would hide it there.'

Japp's search was quick but efficient. The living-room had given up all its secrets in a very few minutes. Then he went upstairs. Jane Plenderleith sat on the arm of a chair, smoking a cigarette and frowning at the fire. Poirot watched her.

After some minutes, he said quietly:

'Do you know if Mr Laverton-West is in London at present?'

'I don't know at all. I rather fancy he's in Hampshire with his people. I suppose I ought to have wired him. How dreadful. I forgot.'

'It is not easy to remember everything, mademoiselle, when a catastrophe occurs. And after all, the bad news, it will keep. One hears it only too soon.'

'Yes, that's true,' the girl said absently.

Japp's footsteps were heard descending the stairs. Jane went out to meet him.

'Well?'

Japp shook his head.

'Nothing helpful, I'm afraid, Miss Plenderleith. I've been over the whole house now. Oh, I suppose I'd better just have a look in this cupboard under the stairs.'

He caught hold of the handle as he spoke, and pulled.

Jane Plenderleith said:

'It's locked.'

Something in her voice made both men look at her sharply.

'Yes,' said Japp pleasantly. 'I can see it's locked. Perhaps you'll get the key.'

The girl was standing as though carved in stone.

'I–I'm not sure where it is.'

90

Japp shot a quick glance at her. His voice continued resolutely pleasant and off-hand.

'Dear me, that's too bad. Don't want to splinter the wood, opening it by force. I'll send Jameson out to get an assortment of keys.'

She moved forward stiffly.

'Oh,' she said. 'One minute. It might be –'

She went back into the living-room and reappeared a moment later holding a fair-sized key in her hand.

'We keep it locked,' she explained, 'because one's umbrellas and things have a habit of getting pinched.'

'Very wise precaution,' said Japp, cheerfully accepting the key.

He turned it in the lock and threw the door open. It was dark inside the cupboard. Japp took out his pocket flashlight and let it play round the inside.

Poirot felt the girl at his side stiffen and stop breathing for a second. His eyes followed the sweep of Japp's torch.

There was not very much in the cupboard. Three umbrellas – one broken, four walking sticks, a set of golf clubs, two tennis racquets, a neatly-folded rug and several sofa cushions in various stages of dilapidation. On the top of these last reposed a small, smart-looking attaché-case.

As Japp stretched out a hand towards it, Jane Plenderleith said quickly:

'That's mine. I – it came back with me this morning. So there can't be anything there.'

'Just as well to make quite sure,' said Japp, his cheery friendliness increasing slightly.

The case was unlocked. Inside it was fitted with shagreen brushes and toilet bottles. There were two magazines in it but nothing else.

Japp examined the whole outfit with meticulous attention. When at last he shut the lid and began a cursory examination of the cushions, the girl gave an audible sigh of relief.

There was nothing else in the cupboard beyond what was plainly to be seen. Japp's examination was soon finished.

He relocked the door and handed the key to Jane Plenderleith.

'Well,' he said, 'that concludes matters. Can you give me Mr Laverton-West's address?'

'Farlescombe Hall, Little Ledbury, Hampshire.'

'Thank you, Miss Plenderleith. That's all for the present. I may be round again later. By the way, mum's the word. Leave it at suicide as far as the general public's concerned.'

'Of course, I quite understand.'

She shook hands with them both.

As they walked away down the mews, Japp exploded:

'What the – the hell was there in that cupboard? There was *something*.'

'Yes, there was something.'

'And I'll bet ten to one it was something to do with the attaché-case! But like the double-dyed mutt I must be, I couldn't find anything. Looked in all the bottles – felt the lining – what the devil could it be?'

Poirot shook his head thoughtfully.

'That girl's in it somehow,' Japp went on. 'Brought that case back this morning? Not on your life, she didn't! Notice that there were two magazines in it?'

'Yes.'

'Well, one of them was for *last July*!'

CHAPTER 7

It was the following day when Japp walked into Poirot's flat, flung his hat on the table in deep disgust and dropped into a chair.

'Well,' he growled. '*She's* out of it!'

'Who is out of it?'

'Plenderleith. Was playing bridge up to midnight. Host,

hostess, naval-commander guest and two servants can all swear to that. No doubt about it, we've got to give up any idea of her being concerned in the business. All the same, I'd like to know *why* she went all hot and bothered about that little attaché-case under the stairs. That's something in *your* line, Poirot. You like solving the kind of triviality that leads nowhere. The Mystery of the Small Attaché-Case. Sounds quite promising!'

'I will give you yet another suggestion for a title. The Mystery of the Smell of Cigarette Smoke.'

'A bit clumsy for a title. Smell – eh? Was *that* why you were sniffing so when we first examined the body? I saw you – *and* heard you! Sniff – sniff – sniff. Thought you had a cold in your head.'

'You were entirely in error.'

Japp sighed.

'I always thought it was the little grey cells of the brain. Don't tell me the cells of your nose are equally superior to anyone else's.'

'No, no, calm yourself.'

'*I* didn't smell any cigarette smoke,' went on Japp suspiciously.

'No more did I, my friend.'

Japp looked at him doubtfully. Then he extracted a cigarette from his pocket.

'That's the kind Mrs Allen smoked – gaspers. Six of those stubs were hers. *The other three were Turkish.*'

'Exactly.'

'Your wonderful nose knew that without looking at them, I suppose!'

'I assure you my nose does not enter into the matter. My nose registered nothing.'

'But the brain cells registered a lot?'

'Well – there were certain indications – do you not think so?'

Japp looked at him sideways.

'Such as?'

'*Eh bien*, there was very definitely something missing from

93

the room. Also something added, I think ... And then, on the writing-bureau...'

'I knew it! We're coming to that damned quill pen!'

'*Du tout.* The quill pen plays a purely negative rôle.'

Japp retreated to safer ground.

'I've got Charles Laverton-West coming to see me at Scotland Yard in half an hour. I thought you might like to be there.'

'I should very much.'

'And you'll be glad to hear we've tracked down Major Eustace. Got a service flat in the Cromwell Road.'

'Excellent.'

'And we've got a little to go on there. Not at all a nice person, Major Eustace. After I've seen Laverton-West, we'll go and see him. That suit you?'

'Perfectly.'

'Well, come along then.'

At half-past eleven, Charles Laverton-West was ushered into Chief Inspector Japp's room. Japp rose and shook hands.

The M.P. was a man of medium height with a very definite personality. He was clean-shaven, with the mobile mouth of an actor, and the slightly prominent eyes that so often go with the gift of oratory. He was good-looking in a quiet, well-bred way.

Though looking pale and somewhat distressed, his manner was perfectly formal and composed.

He took a seat, laid his gloves and hat on the table and looked towards Japp.

'I'd like to say, first of all, Mr Laverton-West, that I fully appreciate how distressing this must be to you.'

Laverton-West waved this aside.

'Do not let us discuss my feelings. Tell me, Chief Inspector, have you any idea what caused my – Mrs Allen to take her own life?'

'You yourself cannot help us in any way?'

'No, indeed.'

'There was no quarrel? No estrangement of any kind between you?'

'Nothing of the kind. It has been the greatest shock to me.'

'Perhaps it will be more understandable, sir, if I tell you that it was not suicide – but murder!'

'Murder?' Charles Laverton-West's eyes popped nearly out of his head. 'You say *murder*?'

'Quite correct. Now, Mr Laverton-West, have you any idea who might be likely to make away with Mrs Allen?'

Laverton-West fairly spluttered out his answer.

'No – no, indeed – nothing of the sort! The mere idea is – is *unimaginable*!'

'She never mentioned any enemies? Anyone who might have a grudge against her?'

'Never.'

'Did you know that she had a pistol?'

'I was not aware of the fact.'

He looked a little startled.

'Miss Plenderleith says that Mrs Allen brought this pistol back from abroad with her some years ago.'

'Really?'

'Of course, we have only Miss Plenderleith's word for that. It is quite possible that Mrs Allen felt herself to be in danger from some source and kept the pistol handy for reasons of her own.'

Charles Laverton-West shook his head doubtfully. He seemed quite bewildered and dazed.

'What is your opinion of Miss Plenderleith, Mr Laverton-West? I mean, does she strike you as a reliable, truthful person?'

The other pondered a minute.

'I think so – yes, I should say so.'

'You don't like her?' suggested Japp, who had been watching him closely.

'I wouldn't say that. She is not the type of young woman I admire. That sarcastic, independent type is not attractive to me, but I should say she was quite truthful.'

95

'H'm,' said Japp. 'Do you know a Major Eustace?'

'Eustace? Eustace? Ah, yes, I remember the name. I met him once at Barbara's – Mrs Allen's. Rather a doubtful customer in my opinion. I said as much to my – to Mrs Allen. He wasn't the type of man I should have encouraged to come to the house after we were married.'

'And what did Mrs Allen say?'

'Oh! she quite agreed. She trusted my judgment implicitly. A man knows other men better than a woman can do. She explained that she couldn't very well be rude to a man whom she had not seen for some time – I think she felt especially a horror of being *snobbish*! Naturally, as my wife, she would find a good many of her old associates well – unsuitable, shall we say?'

'Meaning that in marrying you she was bettering her position?' Japp asked bluntly.

Laverton-West held up a well-manicured hand.

'No, no, not quite that. As a matter of fact, Mrs Allen's mother was a distant relation of my own family. She was fully my equal in birth. But of course, in my position, I have to be especially careful in choosing my friends – and my wife in choosing hers. One is to a certain extent in the limelight.'

'Oh, quite,' said Japp dryly. He went on, 'So you can't help us in any way?'

'No indeed. I am utterly at sea. Barbara! Murdered! It seems incredible.'

'Now, Mr Laverton-West, can you tell me what your own movements were on the night of November fifth?'

'My movements? *My* movements?'

Laverton-West's voice rose in shrill protest.

'Purely a matter of routine,' explained Japp. 'We – er – have to ask everybody.'

Charles Laverton-West looked at him with dignity.

'I should hope that a man in my position might be exempt.'

Japp merely waited.

'I was – now let me see ... Ah, yes. I was at the House. Left at half-past ten. Went for a walk along the Embankment. Watched some of the fireworks.'

'Nice to think there aren't any plots of that kind nowadays,' said Japp cheerily.

Laverton-West gave him a fish-like stare.

'Then I – er – walked home.'

'Reaching home – your London address is Onslow Square, I think – at what time?'

'I hardly know exactly.'

'Eleven? Half-past?'

'Somewhere about then.'

'Perhaps someone let you in.'

'No, I have my key.'

'Meet anybody whilst you were walking?'

'No – er – really, Chief Inspector, I *resent* these questions very much!'

'I assure you, it's just a matter of routine, Mr Laverton-West. They aren't personal, you know.'

The reply seemed to soothe the irate M.P.

'If that is all –'

'That is all for the present, Mr Laverton-West.'

'You will keep me informed –'

'Naturally, sir. By the way, let me introduce M. Hercule Poirot. You may have heard of him.'

Mr Laverton-West's eye fastened itself interestedly on the little Belgian.

'Yes – yes – I have heard the name.'

'Monsieur,' said Poirot, his manner suddenly very foreign. 'Believe me, my heart bleeds for you. Such a loss! Such agony as you must be enduring! Ah, but I will say no more. How magnificently the English hide their emotions.' He whipped out his cigarette case. 'Permit me – Ah, it is empty. Japp?'

Japp slapped his pockets and shook his head.

Laverton-West produced his own cigarette case, murmured, 'Er – have one of mine, M. Poirot.'

'Thank you – thank you,' The little man helped himself.

'As you say, M. Poirot,' resumed the other, 'we English do not parade our emotions. A stiff upper lip – that is our motto.'

He bowed to the two men and went out.

'Bit of a stuffed fish,' said Japp disgustedly. '*And* a boiled owl! The Plenderleith girl was quite right about him. Yet he's a good-looking sort of chap – might go down well with some woman who had no sense of humour. What about that cigarette?'

Poirot handed it over, shaking his head.

'Egyptian. An expensive variety.'

'No, that's no good. A pity, for I've never heard a weaker alibi! In fact, it wasn't an alibi at all... You know, Poirot, it's a pity the boot wasn't on the other leg. If *she'd* been blackmailing him... He's a lovely type for blackmail – would pay out like a lamb! Anything to avoid a scandal.'

'My friend, it is very pretty to reconstruct the case as you would like it to be, but that is not strictly our affair.'

'No, Eustace is our affair. I've got a few lines on him. Definitely a nasty fellow.'

'By the way, did you do as I suggested about Miss Plenderleith?'

'Yes. Wait a sec, I'll ring through and get the latest.'

He picked up the telephone receiver and spoke through it.

After a brief interchange he replaced it and looked up at Poirot.

'Pretty heartless piece of goods. Gone off to play golf. That's a nice thing to do when your friend's been murdered only the day before.'

Poirot uttered an exclamation.

'What's the matter now?' asked Japp.

But Poirot was murmuring to himself.

'Of course ... of course ... but naturally... What an imbecile I am – why, it leapt to the eye!'

Japp said rudely:

'Stop jabbering to yourself and let's go and tackle Eustace.'

He was amazed to see the radiant smile that spread over Poirot's face.

'But – yes – most certainly let us tackle him. For now, see you, I know everything – but everything!'

CHAPTER 8

Major Eustace received the two men with the easy assurance of a man of the world.

His flat was small, a mere *pied à terre*, as he explained. He offered the two men a drink and when that was refused he took out his cigarette case.

Both Japp and Poirot accepted a cigarette. A quick glance passed between them.

'You smoke Turkish, I see,' said Japp as he twirled the cigarette between his fingers.

'Yes. I'm sorry, do you prefer a gasper? I've got one somewhere about.'

'No, no, this will do me very well.' Then he leaned forward – his tone changed. 'Perhaps you can guess, Major Eustace, what it was I came to see you about?'

The other shook his head. His manner was nonchalant. Major Eustace was a tall man, good-looking in a somewhat coarse fashion. There was a puffiness round the eyes – small, crafty eyes that belied the good-humoured geniality of his manner.

He said:

'No – I've no idea what brings such a big gun as a chief inspector to see me. Anything to do with my car?'

'No, it is not your car. I think you knew a Mrs Barbara Allen, Major Eustace?'

The major leant back, puffed out a cloud of smoke, and said in an enlightened voice:

'Oh, so that's it! Of course, I might have guessed. Very sad business.'

'You know about it?'

'Saw it in the paper last night. Too bad.'

'You knew Mrs Allen out in India, I think.'

'Yes, that's some years ago now.'

'Did you also know her husband?'

There was a pause – a mere fraction of a second – but during that fraction the little pig eyes flashed a quick look at the faces of the two men. Then he answered:

'No, as a matter of fact, I never came across Allen.'

'But you know something about him?'

'Heard he was by way of being a bad hat. Of course, that was only rumour.'

'Mrs Allen did not say anything?'

'Never talked about him.'

'You were on intimate terms with her?'

Major Eustace shrugged his shoulders.

'We were old friends, you know, old friends. But we didn't see each other very often.'

'But you did see her that last evening? The evening of November fifth?'

'Yes, as a matter of fact, I did.'

'You called at her house, I think.'

Major Eustace nodded. His voice took on a gentle, regretful note.

'Yes, she asked me to advise her about some investments. Of course, I can see what you're driving at – her state of mind – all that sort of thing. Well, really, it's very difficult to say. Her manner seemed normal enough and yet she *was* a bit jumpy, come to think of it.'

'But she gave you no hint as to what she contemplated doing?'

'Not the least in the world. As a matter of fact, when I said goodbye I said I'd ring her up soon and we'd do a show together.'

'You said you'd ring her up. Those were your last words?'

'Yes.'

100

'Curious. I have information that you said something quite different.'

Eustace changed colour.

'Well, of course, I can't remember the exact words.'

'My information is that what you actually said was, "*Well, think it over and let me know.*"'

'Let me see, yes I believe you're right. Not exactly that. I think I was suggesting she should let me know when she was free.'

'Not quite the same thing, is it?' said Japp.

Major Eustace shrugged his shoulders.

'My dear fellow, you can't expect a man to remember word for word what he said on any given occasion.'

'And what did Mrs Allen reply?'

'She said she'd give me a ring. That is, as near as I can remember.'

'And then you said, "*All right. So long.*"'

'Probably. Something of the kind anyway.'

Japp said quietly:

'You say that Mrs Allen asked you to advise her about her investments. *Did she, by any chance, entrust you with the sum of two hundred pounds in cash to invest for her?*'

Eustace's face flushed a dark purple. He leaned forward and growled out:

'What the devil do you mean by that?'

'Did she or did she not?'

'That's my business, Mr Chief Inspector.'

Japp said quietly:

'Mrs Allen drew out the sum of two hundred pounds in cash from her bank. Some of the money was in five-pound notes. The numbers of these can, of course, be traced.'

'What if she did?'

'*Was* the money for investment – or was it – blackmail, Major Eustace?'

'That's a preposterous idea. What next will you suggest?'

Japp said in his most official manner:

'I think, Major Eustace, that at this point I must ask you if you are willing to come to Scotland Yard and make a statement. There is, of course, no compulsion and you can, if you prefer it, have your solicitor present.'

'Solicitor? What the devil should I want with a solicitor? And what are you cautioning me for?'

'I am inquiring into the circumstances of the death of Mrs Allen.'

'Good God, man, you don't suppose – Why, that's nonsense! Look here, what happened was this. I called round to see Barbara by appointment...'

'That was at what time?'

'At about half-past nine, I should say. We sat and talked...'

'And smoked?'

'Yes, and smoked. Anything damaging in that?' demanded the major belligerently.

'Where did this conversation take place?'

'In the sitting-room. Left of the door as you go in. We talked together quite amicably, as I say. I left a little before half-past ten. I stayed for a minute on the doorstep for a few last words...'

'Last words – precisely,' murmured Poirot.

'Who are *you*, I'd like to know?' Eustace turned and spat the words at him. 'Some kind of damned dago! What are *you* butting in for?'

'I am Hercule Poirot,' said the little man with dignity.

'I don't care if you are the Achilles statue. As I say, Barbara and I parted quite amicably. I drove straight to the Far East Club. Got there at five and twenty to eleven and went straight up to the card-room. Stayed there playing bridge until one-thirty. Now then, put that in your pipe and smoke it.'

'I do not smoke the pipe,' said Poirot. 'It is a pretty *alibi* you have there.'

'It should be a pretty cast iron one anyway! Now then, sir,' he looked at Japp. 'Are you satisfied?'

'You remained in the sitting-room throughout your visit?'

'Yes.'

'You did not go upstairs to Mrs Allen's own boudoir?'

'No, I tell you. We stayed in the one room and didn't leave it.'

Japp looked at him thoughtfully for a minute or two. Then he said:

'How many sets of cuff links have you?'

'Cuff links? Cuff links? What's that got to do with it?'

'You are not bound to answer the question, of course.'

'Answer it? I don't mind answering it. I've got nothing to hide. And I shall demand an apology. There are these ...' he stretched out his arms.

Japp noted the gold and platinum with a nod.

'And I've got these.'

He rose, opened a drawer and taking out a case, he opened it and shoved it rudely almost under Japp's nose.

'Very nice design,' said the chief inspector. 'I see one is broken – bit of enamel chipped off.'

'What of it?'

'You don't remember when that happened, I suppose?'

'A day or two ago, not longer.'

'Would you be surprised to hear that it happened *when you were visiting Mrs Allen*?'

'Why shouldn't it? I've not denied that I was there.' The major spoke haughtily. He continued to bluster, to act the part of the justly indignant man, but his hands were trembling.

Japp leaned forward and said with emphasis:

'Yes, but that bit of cuff link *wasn't found in the sitting-room.* It was found *upstairs* in Mrs Allen's boudoir – there in the room where she was killed, and where a man sat smoking *the same kind of cigarettes as you smoke.*'

The shot told. Eustace fell back into his chair. His eyes went from side to side. The collapse of the bully and the appearance of the craven was not a pretty sight.

'You've got nothing on me.' His voice was almost a whine. 'You're trying to frame me ... But you can't do it. I've got an alibi ... I never came near the house again that night...'

Poirot in his turn, spoke.

'No, you did not come near the house again ... *You did not need to . . .* For perhaps Mrs Allen *was already dead when you left it.*'

'That's impossible – impossible – She was just inside the door – she spoke to me – People must have heard her – seen her...'

Poirot said softly:

'They heard *you* speaking to her ... and pretending to wait for her answer and then speaking again ... It is an old trick that ... People may have *assumed* she was there, but they did not *see* her, because *they could not even say whether she was wearing evening dress or not – not even mention what colour she was wearing...*'

'My God – it isn't true – it isn't true–'

He was shaking now – collapsed...

Japp looked at him with disgust. He spoke crisply.

'I'll have to ask you, sir, to come with me.'

'You're arresting me?'

'Detained for inquiry – we'll put it that way.'

The silence was broken with a long, shuddering sigh. The despairing voice of the erstwhile blustering Major Eustace said:

'I'm sunk...'

Hercule Poirot rubbed his hands together and smiled cheerfully. He seemed to be enjoying himself.

CHAPTER 9

'Pretty the way he went all to pieces,' said Japp with professional appreciation, later that day.

He and Poirot were driving in a car along the Brompton Road.

'He knew the game was up,' said Poirot absently.

'We've got plenty on him,' said Japp. 'Two or three different aliases, a tricky business over a cheque, and a very nice affair when he stayed at the Ritz and called himself Colonel de Bathe. Swindled half a dozen Piccadilly tradesmen. We're holding him on that charge for the moment – until we get this affair finally squared up. What's the idea of this rush to the country, old man?'

'My friend, an affair must be rounded off properly. Everything must be explained. I am on the quest of the mystery you suggested. The Mystery of the Missing Attaché-Case.'

'The Mystery of the Small Attaché-Case – that's what I called it – It isn't missing that I know of.'

'Wait, *mon ami*.'

The car turned into the mews. At the door of No. 14, Jane Plenderleith was just alighting from a small Austin Seven. She was in golfing clothes.

She looked from one to the other of the two men, then produced a key and opened the door.

'Come in, won't you?'

She led the way. Japp followed her into the sitting-room. Poirot remained for a minute or two in the hall, muttering something about:

'*C'est embêtant* – how difficult to get out of these sleeves.'

In a moment or two he also entered the sitting-room minus his overcoat but Japp's lips twitched under his moustache. He had heard the very faint squeak of an opening cupboard door.

Japp threw Poirot an inquiring glance and the other gave a hardly perceptible nod.

'We won't detain you, Miss Plenderleith,' said Japp briskly. 'Only came to ask if you could tell us the name of Mrs Allen's solicitor.'

'Her solicitor?' The girl shook her head. 'I don't even know that she had one.'

'Well, when she rented this house with you, someone must have drawn up the agreement?'

'No, I don't think so. You see, I took the house, the lease is in my name. Barbara paid me half the rent. It was quite informal.'

'I see. Oh! well, I suppose there's nothing doing then.'

'I'm sorry I can't help you,' said Jane politely.

'It doesn't really matter very much.' Japp turned towards the door. 'Been playing golf?'

'Yes.' She flushed. 'I suppose it seems rather heartless to you. But as a matter of fact it got me down rather, being here in this house. I felt I must go out and *do* something – tire myself – or I'd choke!'

She spoke with intensity.

Poirot said quickly:

'I comprehend, mademoiselle. It is most understandable – most natural. To sit in this house and think – no, it would not be pleasant.'

'So long as you understand,' said Jane shortly.

'You belong to a club?'

'Yes, I play at Wentworth.'

'It has been a pleasant day,' said Poirot.

'Alas, there are few leaves left on the trees now! A week ago the woods were magnificent.'

'It was quite lovely today.'

'Good afternoon, Miss Plenderleith,' said Japp formally. 'I'll let you know when there's anything definite. As a matter of fact we have got a man detained on suspicion.'

'What man?'

She looked at them eagerly.

'Major Eustace.'

She nodded and turned away, stooping down to put a match to the fire.

'Well?' said Japp as the car turned the corner of the mews.

Poirot grinned.

'It was quite simple. The key was in the door this time.'

'And –?'

Poirot smiled.

'*Eh, bien*, the golf clubs had gone –'

'Naturally. The girl isn't a fool, whatever else she is. *Anything else gone?*'

Poirot nodded his head.

'Yes, my friend – *the little attaché-case!*'

The accelerator leaped under Japp's foot.

'Damnation!' he said. 'I knew there was *something*. But what the devil is it? I searched that case pretty thoroughly.'

'My poor Japp – but it is – how do you say, "obvious, my dear Watson"?'

Japp threw him an exasperated look.

'Where are we going?' he asked.

Poirot consulted his watch.

'It is not yet four o'clock. We could get to Wentworth, I think, before it is dark.'

'Do you think she really went there?'

'I think so – yes. She would know that we might make inquiries. Oh, yes, I think we will find that she has been there.'

Japp grunted.

'Oh well, come on.' He threaded his way dexterously through the traffic. 'Though what this attaché-case business has to do with the crime I can't imagine. I can't see that it's got anything at all to do with it.'

'Precisely, my friend, I agree with you – it has nothing to do with it.'

'Then why – No, don't tell me! Order and method and everything nicely rounded off! Oh, well, it's a fine day.'

The car was a fast one. They arrived at Wentworth Golf Club a little after half-past four. There was no great congestion there on a week day.

Poirot went straight to the caddie-master and asked for Miss Plenderleith's clubs. She would be playing on a different course tomorrow, he explained.

The caddie-master raised his voice and a boy sorted through some golf clubs standing in a corner. He finally produced a bag bearing the initials, J.P.

'Thank you,' said Poirot. He moved away, then turned

107

carelessly and asked, 'She did not leave with you a small attaché-case also, did she?'

'Not today, sir. May have left it in the clubhouse.'

'She was down here today?'

'Oh, yes, I saw her.'

'Which caddie did she have, do you know? She's mislaid an attaché-case and can't remember where she had it last.'

'She didn't take a caddie. She came in here and bought a couple of balls. Just took out a couple of irons. I rather fancy she had a little case in her hand then.'

Poirot turned away with a word of thanks. The two men walked round the clubhouse. Poirot stood a moment admiring the view.

'It is beautiful, is it not, the dark pine trees – and then the lake. Yes, the lake –'

Japp gave him a quick glance.

'That's the idea, is it?'

Poirot smiled.

'I think it possible that someone may have seen something. I should set the inquiries in motion if I were you.'

CHAPTER 10

Poirot stepped back, his head a little on one side as he surveyed the arrangement of the room. A chair here – another chair there. Yes, that was very nice. And now a ring at the bell – that would be Japp.

The Scotland Yard man came in alertly.

'Quite right, old cock! Straight from the horse's mouth. A young woman was seen to throw something into the lake at Wentworth yesterday. Description of her answers to Jane Plenderleith. We managed to fish it up without much difficulty. A lot of reeds just there.'

'And it was?'

'It was the attaché-case all right! But *why*, in heaven's name? Well, it beats me! Nothing inside it – not even the magazines. Why a presumably sane young woman should want to fling an expensively-fitted dressing-case into a lake – d'you know, I worried all night because I couldn't get the hang of it.'

'*Mon pauvre Japp*! But you need worry no longer. Here is the answer coming. The bell has just rung.'

George, Poirot's immaculate man-servant, opened the door and announced:

'Miss Plenderleith.'

The girl came into the room with her usual air of complete self-assurance. She greeted the two men.

'I asked you to come here –' explained Poirot. 'Sit here, will you not, and you here, Japp – because I have certain news to give you.'

The girl sat down. She looked from one to the other, pushing aside her hat. She took it off and laid it aside impatiently.

'Well,' she said. 'Major Eustace has been arrested.'

'You saw that, I expect, in the morning paper?'

'Yes.'

'He is at the moment charged with a minor offence,' went on Poirot. 'In the meantime we are gathering evidence in connection with the murder.'

'It *was* murder, then?'

The girl asked it eagerly.

Poirot nodded his head.

'Yes,' he said. 'It was murder. The wilful destruction of one human being by another human being.'

She shivered a little.

'Don't,' she murmured. 'It sounds horrible when you say it like that.'

'Yes – but it is horrible!'

He paused – then he said:

'Now, Miss Plenderleith, I am going to tell you just how I arrived at the truth in this matter.'

She looked from Poirot to Japp. The latter was smiling.

'He has his methods, Miss Plenderleith,' he said. 'I humour him, you know. I think we'll listen to what he has to say.'

Poirot began:

'As you know, mademoiselle, I arrived with my friend at the scene of the crime on the morning of November the sixth. We went into the room where the body of Mrs Allen had been found and I was struck at once by several significant details. There were things, you see, in that room that were decidedly odd.'

'Go on,' said the girl.

'To begin with,' said Poirot, 'there was the smell of cigarette smoke.'

'I think you're exaggerating there, Poirot,' said Japp. '*I* didn't smell anything.'

Poirot turned on him in a flash.

'Precisely. *You did not smell any stale smoke. No more did I.* And that was very, very strange – for the door and the window were both closed and on an ashtray there were the stubs of no fewer than ten cigarettes. It was odd, very odd, that the room should smell – as it did, perfectly fresh.'

'So that's what you were getting at!' Japp sighed. 'Always have to get at things in such a tortuous way.'

'Your Sherlock Holmes did the same. He drew attention, remember, to the curious incident of the dog in the night-time – and the answer to that was there was no curious incident. The dog did nothing in the night-time. To proceed:

'The next thing that attracted my attention was a wristwatch worn by the dead woman.'

'What about it?'

'Nothing particular about it, but it was worn on the *right* wrist. Now in my experience it is more usual for a watch to be worn on the left wrist.'

Japp shrugged his shoulders. Before he could speak, Poirot hurried on:

'But as you say, there is nothing very definite about *that*. Some people *prefer* to wear one on the right hand. And now I

110

come to something really interesting – I come, my friends, to the writing-bureau.'

'Yes, I guessed that,' said Japp.

'That was really *very* odd – *very* remarkable! For two reasons. The first reason was that something was missing from that writing-table.'

Jane Plenderleith spoke.

'What was missing?'

Poirot turned to her.

'*A sheet of blotting-paper, mademoiselle.* The blotting-book had on top a clean, untouched piece of blotting-paper.'

Jane shrugged her shoulders.

'Really, M. Poirot. People do occasionally tear off a very much used sheet!'

'Yes, but what do they do with it? Throw it into the waste-paper basket, do they not? *But it was not in the waste-paper basket. I looked.*'

Jane Plenderleith seemed impatient.

'Because it had probably been already thrown away the day before. The sheet was clean because Barbara hadn't written any letters that day.'

'That could hardly be the case, mademoiselle. *For Mrs Allen was seen going to the post-box that evening. Therefore she must have been writing letters.* She could not write downstairs – there were no writing materials. She would be hardly likely to go to *your* room to write. So, then, what had happened to the sheet of paper on which she had blotted her letters? It is true that people sometimes throw things in the fire instead of the waste-paper basket, but there was only a gas fire in the room. *And the fire downstairs had not been alight the previous day, since you told me it was all laid ready when you put a match to it.*'

He paused.

'A curious little problem. I looked everywhere, in the waste-paper baskets, in the dustbin, but I could not find a sheet of used blotting-paper – and that seemed to me very important. It looked as though someone had deliberately taken that sheet of

111

blotting paper away. Why? Because there was writing on it that could easily have been read by holding it up to a mirror.

'But there was a second curious point about the writing-table. Perhaps, Japp, you remember roughly the arrangement of it? Blotter and inkstand in the centre, pen tray to the left, calendar and quill pen to the right. *Eh bien?* You do not see? The quill pen, remember, I examined, it was for show only – it had not been used. Ah! *still* you do not see? I will say it again. Blotter in the centre, pen tray to the left – to the *left*, Japp. But is it not usual to find a pen tray *on the right*, convenient to *the right hand?*

'Ah, now it comes to you, does it not? The pen tray on the *left* – the wrist-watch on the *right* wrist – the blotting-paper removed – and something else brought *into* the room – the ashtray with the cigarette ends!

'That room was fresh and pure smelling, Japp, a room in which the window had been *open*, not closed all night... And I made myself a picture.'

He spun round and faced Jane.

'A picture of you, mademoiselle, driving up in your taxi, paying it off, running up the stairs, calling perhaps, 'Barbara' – and you open the door and you find your friend there lying dead with the pistol clasped in her hand – the left hand, naturally, *since she is left-handed* and therefore, too, the bullet has entered on the *left side of the head*. There is a note there addressed to you. It tells you what it is that has driven her to take her own life. It was, I fancy, a very moving letter ... A young, gentle, unhappy woman driven by blackmail to take her life...

'I think that, almost at once, the idea flashed into your head. This was a certain man's doing. Let him be punished – fully and adequately punished! You take the pistol, wipe it and place it in the *right* hand. You take the note and you tear off the top sheet of the blotting-paper on which the note has been blotted. You go down, light the fire and put them both on the flames. Then you carry up the ashtray – to further the illusion that two people sat there talking – and you also take up a fragment of enamel cuff link that is on the floor. That is a lucky find and you expect it to clinch matters. Then you close the window and lock the door. There must be no suspicion that you have tampered with the room. The police must see it exactly as it is – so you do not seek help in the mews but ring up the police straightaway.

'And so it goes on. You play your chosen rôle with judgment and coolness. You refuse at first to say anything but cleverly you suggest doubts of suicide. Later you are quite ready to set us on the trail of Major Eustace...

'Yes, mademoiselle, it was clever – a very clever murder – for that is what it is. The attempted murder of Major Eustace.'

Jane Plenderleith sprang to her feet.

'It wasn't murder – it was justice. That man *hounded* poor Barbara to her death! She was so sweet and helpless. You see, poor kid, she got involved with a man in India when she first went out. She was only seventeen and he was a married man years older than her. Then she had a baby. She could have put it in a home but she wouldn't hear of that. She went off to some out of the way spot and came back calling herself Mrs Allen. Later the child died. She came back here and she fell in love with Charles – that pompous, stuffed owl; she adored him – and he took her adoration very complacently. If he had been a different kind of man I'd have advised her to tell him everything. But as it was, I urged her to hold her tongue. After all, nobody knew anything about that business except me.

'And then that devil Eustace turned up! You know the rest. He began to bleed her systematically, but it wasn't till that last evening that she realised that she was exposing Charles too, to the risk of scandal. Once married to Charles, Eustace had got her where he wanted her – married to a rich man with a horror of any scandal! When Eustace had gone with the money she had got for him she sat thinking it over. Then she came up and wrote a letter to me. She said she loved Charles and couldn't live without him, but that for his own sake she mustn't marry him. She was taking the best way out, she said.'

Jane flung her head back.

'Do you wonder I did what I did? And you stand there calling it *murder*!'

'Because it is murder,' Poirot's voice was stern. 'Murder can sometimes seem justified, *but it is murder all the same*. You are truthful and clear-minded – face the truth, mademoiselle! Your friend died, in the last resort, *because she had not the courage to live*. We may sympathize with her. We may pity her. But the fact remains – the act was *hers* – not another.'

He paused.

'And you? That man is now in prison, he will serve a long sentence for other matters. Do you really wish, of your own volition, to destroy the life – the *life*, mind – of *any* human being?'

She stared at him. Her eyes darkened. Suddenly she muttered:

'No. You're right. I don't.'

Then, turning on her heel, she went swiftly from the room. The outer door banged...

Japp gave a long – a very prolonged – whistle.

'Well, I'm damned!' he said.

Poirot sat down and smiled at him amiably. It was quite a long time before the silence was broken. Then Japp said:

'Not murder disguised as suicide, but suicide made to look like murder!'

'Yes, and very cleverly done, too. Nothing over-emphasized.'

Japp said suddenly:

'But the attaché-case? Where did that come in?'

'But, my dear, my very dear friend, I have already told you that *it did not come in*.'

'Then why –'

'The golf clubs. The golf clubs, Japp. *They were the golf clubs of a left-handed person*. Jane Plenderleith kept her clubs at Wentworth. Those were Barbara Allen's clubs. No wonder the girl got, as you say, the wind up when we opened that cupboard. Her whole plan might have been ruined. But she is quick, she realized that she had, for one short moment, given herself away. *She* saw that *we* saw. So she does the best thing she can think of on the spur of the moment. She tries to focus our attention on the *wrong object*. She says of the attaché-case "That's mine. I – it came back with me this morning. So there can't be anything there." And, as she hoped, away you go on the false trail. For the same reason, when she sets out the following day to get rid of the golf clubs, she continues to use the attaché-case as a – what is it – kippered herring?'

'Red herring. Do you mean that her real object was –?'

'Consider, my friend. Where is the best place to get rid of a bag of golf clubs? One cannot burn them or put them in a dustbin. If one leaves them somewhere they may be returned to you. Miss Plenderleith took them to a golf course. She leaves them in the clubhouse while she gets a couple of irons from her own bag, and then she goes round without a caddy. Doubtless at judicious intervals she breaks a club in half and throws it into some deep undergrowth, and ends by throwing the empty bag away. If anyone should find a broken golf club here and there it will not create surprise. People have been known to break and throw away *all* their clubs in a mood of intense exasperation over the game! It is, in fact, that kind of game!

'But since she realizes that her actions may still be a matter of interest, she throws that useful red herring – the attaché-case – in a somewhat spectacular manner into the lake – and that, my friend, is the truth of "The Mystery of the Attaché-Case."'

Japp looked at his friend for some moments in silence. Then he rose, clapped him on the shoulder, and burst out laughing.

'Not so bad for an old dog! Upon my word, you take the cake! Come out and have a spot of lunch?'

'With pleasure, my friend, but we will not have the cake. Indeed, an Omelette aux Champignons, Blanquette de Veau, Petits pois à la Francaise, and – to follow – a Baba au Rhum.'

'Lead me to it,' said Japp.

TRIANGLE AT RHODES

CHAPTER 1

Hercule Poirot sat on the white sand and looked out across the sparkling blue water. He was carefully dressed in a dandified fashion in white flannels and a large panama hat protected his head. He belonged to the old-fashioned generation which believed in covering itself carefully from the sun. Miss Pamela Lyall, who sat beside him and talked ceaselessly, represented the modern school of thought in that she was wearing the barest minimum of clothing on her sun-browned person.

Occasionally her flow of conversation stopped whilst she reanointed herself from a bottle of oily fluid which stood beside her.

On the farther side of Miss Pamela Lyall her great friend, Miss Sarah Blake, lay face downwards on a gaudily-striped towel. Miss Blake's tanning was as perfect as possible and her friend cast dissatisfied glances at her more than once.

'I'm so patchy still,' she murmured regretfully. 'M. Poirot – *would* you mind? Just below the right shoulder-blade – I can't reach to rub it in properly.'

M. Poirot obliged and then wiped his oily hand carefully on his handkerchief. Miss Lyall, whose principal interests in life were the observation of people round her and the sound of her own voice, continued to talk.

'I was right about that woman – the one in the *Chanel* model – it *is* Valentine Dacres – Chantry, I mean. I thought it was. I recognized her at once. She's really rather marvellous, isn't she? I mean I can understand how people go quite crazy about her. She just obviously *expects* them to! That's half the battle.

116

Those other people who came last night are called Gold. He's terribly good-looking.'

'Honeymooners?' murmured Sarah in a stifled voice.

Miss Lyall shook her head in an experienced manner.

'Oh, no – her clothes aren't *new* enough. You can always tell brides! Don't you think it's the most fascinating thing in the world to watch people, M. Poirot, and see what you can find out about them by just looking?'

'Not just looking, darling,' said Sarah sweetly. 'You ask a lot of questions, too.'

'I haven't even spoken to the Golds yet,' said Miss Lyall with dignity. 'And anyway I don't see why one shouldn't be interested in one's fellow-creatures? Human nature is simply fascinating. Don't you think so, M. Poirot?'

This time she paused long enough to allow her companion to reply.

Without taking his eyes off the blue water, M. Poirot replied:

'*Ça depend.*'

Pamela was shocked.

'Oh, M. Poirot! I don't think *anything's* so interesting – so *incalculable* as a human being!'

'Incalculable? That, no.'

'Oh, but they *are*. Just as you think you've got them beautifully taped – they do something completely unexpected.'

Hercule Poirot shook his head.

'No, no, that is not true. It is most rare that anyone does an action that is not *dans son caractère*. It is in the end monotonous.'

'I don't agree with you at all!' said Miss Pamela Lyall.

She was silent for quite a minute and a half before returning to the attack.

'As soon as I see people I begin wondering about them – what they're like – what relations they are to each other – what they're thinking and feeling. It's – oh, it's quite thrilling.'

'Hardly that,' said Hercule Poirot. 'Nature repeats herself more than one would imagine. The sea,' he added thoughtfully, 'has infinitely more variety.'

Sarah turned her head sideways and asked:

'You think that human beings tend to reproduce certain patterns? Stereotyped patterns?'

'*Précisément*,' said Poirot, and traced a design in the sand with his finger.

'What's that you're drawing?' asked Pamela curiously.

'A triangle,' said Poirot.

But Pamela's attention had been diverted elsewhere.

'Here are the Chantrys,' she said.

A woman was coming down the beach – a tall woman, very conscious of herself and her body. She gave a half-nod and smile and sat down a little distance away on the beach. The scarlet and gold silk wrap slipped down from her shoulders. She was wearing a white bathing-dress.

Pamela sighed.

'Hasn't she got a lovely figure?'

But Poirot was looking at her face – the face of a woman of thirty-nine who had been famous since sixteen for her beauty.

He knew, as everyone knew, all about Valentine Chantry. She had been famous for many things – for her caprices, for her wealth, for her enormous sapphire-blue eyes, for her matrimonial ventures and adventures. She had had five husbands and innumerable lovers. She had in turn been the wife of an Italian count, of an American steel magnate, of a tennis professional, of a racing motorist. Of these four the American had died, but the others had been shed negligently in the divorce court. Six months ago she had married a fifth time – a commander in the navy.

He it was who came striding down the beach behind her. Silent, dark – with a pugnacious jaw and a sullen manner. A touch of the primeval ape about him.

She said:

'Tony darling – my cigarette case ...'

He had it ready for her – lighted her cigarette – helped her to slip the straps of the white bathing-dress from her shoulders. She lay, arms outstretched in the sun. He sat by her like some wild beast that guards its prey.

118

Pamela said, her voice just lowered sufficiently:

'You know they interest me *frightfully* ... He's such a brute! So silent and – sort of *glowering*. I suppose a woman of her kind likes that. It must be like controlling a tiger! I wonder how long it will last. She gets tired of them very soon, I believe – especially nowadays. All the same, if she tried to get rid of him, I think he might be dangerous.'

Another couple came down the beach – rather shyly. They were the newcomers of the night before. Mr and Mrs Douglas Gold as Miss Lyall knew from her inspection of the hotel visitors' book. She knew, too, for such were the Italian regulations – their Christian names and their ages as set down from their passports.

Mr Douglas Cameron Gold was thirty-one and Mrs Marjorie Emma Gold was thirty-five.

Miss Lyall's hobby in life, as has been said, was the study of human beings. Unlike most English people, she was capable of speaking to strangers on sight instead of allowing four days to a week to elapse before making the first cautious advance as is the customary British habit. She, therefore, noting the slight hesitancy and shyness of Mrs Gold's advance, called out:

'Good morning, isn't it a lovely day?'

Mrs Gold was a small woman – rather like a mouse. She was not bad-looking, indeed her features were regular and her complexion good, but she had a certain air of diffidence and dowdiness that made her liable to be overlooked. Her husband, on the other hand, was extremely good-looking, in an almost theatrical manner. Very fair, crisply curling hair, blue eyes, broad shoulders, narrow hips. He looked more like a young man on the stage than a young man in real life, but the moment he opened his mouth that impression faded. He was quite natural and unaffected, even, perhaps, a little stupid.

Mrs Gold looked gratefully at Pamela and sat down near her.

'What a lovely shade of brown you are. I feel terribly underdone!'

'One has to take a frightful lot of trouble to brown evenly,' sighed Miss Lyall.

119

She paused a minute and then went on:

'You've only just arrived, haven't you?'

'Yes. Last night. We came on the Vapo d'Italia boat.'

'Have you ever been to Rhodes before?'

'No. It is lovely, isn't it?'

Her husband said:

'Pity it's such a long way to come.'

'Yes, if it were only nearer England –'

In a muffled voice Sarah said:

'Yes, but then it would be awful. Rows and rows of people laid out like fish on a slab. Bodies everywhere!'

'That's true, of course,' said Douglas Gold. 'It's a nuisance the Italian exchange is so absolutely ruinous at present.'

'It does make a difference, doesn't it?'

The conversation was running on strictly stereotyped lines. It could hardly have been called brilliant.

A little way along the beach, Valentine Chantry stirred and sat up. With one hand she held her bathing-dress in position across her breast.

She yawned, a wide yet delicate cat-like yawn. She glanced casually down the beach. Her eyes slanted past Marjorie Gold – and stayed thoughtfully on the crisp, golden head of Douglas Gold.

She moved her shoulders sinuously. She spoke and her voice was raised a little higher than it need have been.

'Tony darling – isn't it divine – this sun? I simply *must* have been a sun worshipper once – don't you think so?'

Her husband grunted something in reply that failed to reach the others. Valentine Chantry went on in that high, drawling voice.

'Just pull that towel a little flatter, will you, darling?'

She took infinite pains in the resettling of her beautiful body. Douglas Gold was looking now. His eyes were frankly interested.

Mrs Gold chirped happily in a subdued key to Miss Lyall.

'What a beautiful woman!'

Pamela, as delighted to give as to receive information, replied in a lower voice:

'That's Valentine Chantry – you know, who used to be Valentine Dacres – she *is* rather marvellous, isn't she? He's simply crazy about her – won't let her out of his sight!'

Mrs Gold looked once more along the beach. Then she said:

'The sea really is lovely – so blue. I think we ought to go in now, don't you, Douglas?'

He was still watching Valentine Chantry and took a minute or two to answer. Then he said, rather absently:

'Go in? Oh, yes, rather, in a minute.'

Marjorie Gold got up and strolled down to the water's edge.

Valentine Chantry rolled over a little on one side. Her eyes looked along at Douglas Gold. Her scarlet mouth curved faintly into a smile.

The neck of Mr Douglas Gold became slightly red.

Valentine Chantry said:

'Tony darling – would you mind? I want a little pot of face-cream – it's up on the dressing-table. I meant to bring it down. Do get it for me – there's an angel.'

The commander rose obediently. He stalked off into the hotel.

Marjorie Gold plunged into the sea, calling out:

'It's lovely, Douglas – so warm. Do come.'

Pamela Lyall said to him:

'Aren't you going in?'

He answered vaguely:

'Oh! I like to get well hotted up first.'

Valentine Chantry stirred. Her head was lifted for a moment as though to recall her husband – but he was just passing inside the wall of the hotel garden.

'I like my dip the last thing,' explained Mr Gold.

Mrs Chantry sat up again. She picked up a flask of sun-bathing oil. She had some difficulty with it – the screw top seemed to resist her efforts.

She spoke loudly and petulantly.

'Oh, dear – I *can't* get this thing undone!'

She looked towards the other group –

'I wonder –'

Always gallant, Poirot rose to his feet, but Douglas Gold had the advantage of youth and suppleness. He was by her side in a moment.

'Can I do it for you?'

'Oh, thank you –' It was the sweet, empty drawl again.

'You *are* kind. I'm such a *fool* at undoing things – I always seem to screw them the wrong way. Oh! you've done it! Thank you ever so much –'

Hercule Poirot smiled to himself.

He got up and wandered along the beach in the opposite direction. He did not go very far but his progress was leisurely. As he was on his way back, Mrs Gold came out of the sea and joined him. She had been swimming. Her face, under a singularly unbecoming bathing cap, was radiant.

She said breathlessly, 'I do love the sea. And it's so warm and lovely here.'

She was, he perceived, an enthusiastic bather.

She said, 'Douglas and I are simply mad on bathing. He can stay in for hours.'

And at that Hercule Poirot's eyes slid over her shoulder to the spot on the beach where that enthusiastic bather, Mr Douglas Gold, was sitting talking to Valentine Chantry.

His wife said:

'I can't think why he doesn't come ...'

Her voice held a kind of childish bewilderment.

Poirot's eyes rested thoughtfully on Valentine Chantry. He thought that other women in their time had made that same remark.

Beside him, he heard Mrs Gold draw in her breath sharply.

She said – and her voice was cold:

'She's supposed to be very attractive, I believe. But Douglas doesn't like that type of woman.'

Hercule Poirot did not reply.

Mrs Gold plunged into the sea again.

122

She swam away from the shore with slow, steady strokes. You could see that she loved the water.

Poirot retraced his steps to the group on the beach.

It had been augmented by the arrival of old General Barnes, a veteran who was usually in the company of the young. He was sitting now between Pamela and Sarah, and he and Pamela were engaged in dishing up various scandals with appropriate embellishments.

Commander Chantry had returned from his errand. He and Douglas Gold were sitting on either side of Valentine.

Valentine was sitting up very straight between the two men and talking. She talked easily and lightly in her sweet, drawling voice, turning her head to take first one man and then the other in the conversation.

She was just finishing an anecdote.

'– and what do you think the foolish man said? "It may have been only a minute, but I'd remember you *anywhere*, Mum!" Didn't he, Tony? And you know, I thought it was so *sweet* of him. I do think it's such a kind world – I mean, everybody is so frightfully kind to *me* always – I don't know why – they just are. But I said to Tony – d'you remember, darling – "Tony, if you want to be a teeny-weeny bit jealous, you can be jealous of that commissionaire." Because he really was too adorable…'

There was a pause and Douglas Gold said:

'Good fellows – some of these commissionaires.'

'Oh, yes – but he took such trouble – really an immense amount of trouble – and seemed just pleased to be able to help me.'

Douglas Gold said:

'Nothing odd about that. Anyone would for you, I'm sure.'

She cried delightedly:

'How nice of you! Tony, did you hear that?'

Commander Chantry grunted.

His wife sighed:

'Tony never makes pretty speeches – do you, my lamb?'

Her white hand with its long red nails ruffled up his dark head.

He gave her a sudden sidelong look. She murmured:

'I don't really know how he puts up with me. He's simply frightfully clever – absolutely frantic with brains – and I just go on talking nonsense the whole time, but he doesn't seem to mind. Nobody minds what I do or say – everybody spoils me. I'm sure it's frightfully bad for me.'

Commander Chantry said across her to the other man:

'That your missus in the sea?'

'Yes. Expect it's about time I joined her.'

Valentine murmured:

'But it's so lovely here in the sun. You mustn't go into the sea yet. Tony darling, I don't think I shall actually *bathe* today – not my first day. I might get a chill or something. But why don't you go in now, Tony darling? Mr – Mr Gold will stay and keep me company while you're in.'

Chantry said rather grimly:

'No, thanks. Shan't go in just yet. Your wife seems to be waving to you, Gold.'

Valentine said:

'How well your wife swims. I'm sure she's one of those terribly efficient women who do everything well. They always frighten me so because I feel they despise me. I'm so frightfully bad at everything – an absolute duffer, aren't I, Tony darling?'

But again Commander Chantry only grunted.

His wife murmured affectionately:

'You're too sweet to admit it. Men are so wonderfully loyal – that's what I like about them. I do think men are so much more loyal than women – and they never say nasty things. Women, I always think, are rather *petty*.'

Sarah Blake rolled over on her side towards Poirot.

She murmured between her teeth.

'Examples of pettiness, to suggest that dear Mrs Chantry is in any way not absolute perfection! What a complete idiot the woman is! I really do think Valentine Chantry is very nearly the most idiotic woman I ever met. She can't do anything but say, "Tony, darling," and roll her eyes. I should fancy she'd got cottonwool padding instead of brains.'

Poirot raised his expressive eyebrows.

'*Un peu sévère!*'

'Oh, yes. Put it down as pure "Cat," if you like. She certainly has her methods! Can't she leave *any* man alone? Her husband's looking like thunder.'

Looking out to sea, Poirot remarked:

'Mrs Gold swims well.'

'Yes, she isn't like us who find it a nuisance to get wet. I wonder if Mrs Chantry will ever go into the sea at all while she's out here.'

'Not she,' said General Barnes huskily. 'She won't risk that make-up of hers coming off. Not that she isn't a fine-looking woman although perhaps a bit long in the tooth.'

'She's looking your way, General,' said Sarah wickedly. 'And you're wrong about the make-up. We're all waterproof and kissproof nowadays.'

'Mrs Gold's coming out,' announced Pamela.

'Here we go gathering nuts and may,' hummed Sarah. 'Here comes his wife to fetch him away – fetch him away – fetch him away...'

Mrs Gold came straight up the beach. She had quite a pretty figure but her plain, waterproof cap was rather too serviceable to be attractive.

'Aren't you coming, Douglas?' she demanded impatiently. 'The sea is lovely and warm.'

'Rather.'

Douglas Gold rose hastily to his feet. He paused a moment and as he did so Valentine Chantry looked up at him with a sweet smile.

'Au revoir,' she said.

Gold and his wife went down the beach.

As soon as they were out of earshot, Pamela said critically:

'I don't think, you know, that that was wise. To snatch your husband away from another woman is always bad policy. It makes you seem so possessive. And husbands hate that.'

'You seem to know a lot about husbands, Miss Pamela,' said General Barnes.

125

'Other people's – not my own!'

'Ah! that's where the difference comes in.'

'Yes, but General, I shall have learnt a lot of Do Nots.'

'Well, darling,' said Sarah, 'I shouldn't wear a cap like that for one thing...'

'Seems very sensible to me,' said the General. 'Seems a nice, sensible little woman altogether.'

'You've hit it exactly, General,' said Sarah. 'But you know there's a limit to the sensibleness of sensible women. I have a feeling she won't be so sensible when it's a case of Valentine Chantry.'

She turned her head and exclaimed in a low, excited whisper:

'Look at him now. Just like thunder. That man looks as though he had got the most frightful temper...'

Commander Chantry was indeed scowling after the retreating husband and wife in a singularly unpleasant fashion.

Susan looked up at Poirot.

'Well?' she said. 'What do you make of all this?'

Hercule Poirot did not reply in words, but once again his forefinger traced a design in the sand. The same design – a triangle.

'The eternal triangle,' mused Susan. 'Perhaps you're right. If so, we're in for an exciting time in the next few weeks.'

CHAPTER 2

M. Hercule Poirot was disappointed with Rhodes. He had come to Rhodes for a rest and for a holiday. A holiday, especially, from crime. In late October, so he had been told, Rhodes would be nearly empty. A peaceful, secluded spot.

That, in itself, was true enough. The Chantrys, the Golds, Pamela and Susan, the General and himself and two Italian

126

couples were the only guests. But within that restricted circle the intelligent brain of M. Poirot perceived the inevitable shaping of events to come.

'It is that I am criminal-minded,' he told himself reproachfully. 'I have the indigestion! I imagine things.'

But still he worried.

One morning he came down to find Mrs Gold sitting on the terrace doing needlework.

As he came up to her he had the impression that there was the flicker of a cambric handkerchief swiftly whisked out of sight.

Mrs Gold's eyes were dry, but they were suspiciously bright. Her manner, too, struck him as being a shade too cheerful. The brightness of it was a shade overdone.

She said:

'Good morning, M. Poirot,' with such enthusiasm as to arouse his doubts.

He felt that she could not possibly be quite as pleased to see him as she appeared to be. For she did not, after all, know him very well. And though Hercule Poirot was a conceited little man where his profession was concerned, he was quite modest in his estimate of his personal attractions.

'Good morning, madame,' he responded. 'Another beautiful day.'

'Yes, isn't it fortunate? But Douglas and I are always lucky in our weather.'

'Indeed?'

'Yes. We're really very lucky altogether. You know, M. Poirot, when one sees so much trouble and unhappiness, and so many couples divorcing each other and all that sort of thing, well, one does feel very grateful for one's own happiness.'

'It is pleasant to hear you say so, madame.'

'Yes. Douglas and I are so wonderfully happy together. We've been married five years, you know, and after all, five years is quite a long time nowadays –'

'I have no doubt that in some cases it can seem an eternity, madame,' said Poirot dryly.

127

'– but I really believe that we're happier now than when we were first married. You see, we're so absolutely suited to each other.'

'That, of course, is everything.'

'That's why I feel so sorry for people who aren't happy.'

'You mean –'

'Oh! I was speaking generally, M. Poirot.'

'I see. I see.'

Mrs Gold picked up a strand of silk, held it to the light, approved of it, and went on:

'Mrs Chantry, for instance –'

'Yes, Mrs Chantry?'

'I don't think she's at all a nice woman.'

'No. No, perhaps not.'

'In fact, I'm quite sure she's not a nice woman. But in a way one feels sorry for her. Because in spite of her money and her good looks and all that' – Mrs Gold's fingers were trembling and she was quite unable to thread her needle – 'she's not the sort of woman men really stick to. She's the sort of woman, I think, that men would get tired of very easily. Don't you think so?'

'I myself should certainly get tired of her conversation before any great space of time had passed,' said Poirot cautiously.

'Yes, that's what I mean. She has, of course, a kind of appeal …' Mrs Gold hesitated, her lips trembled, she stabbed uncertainly at her work. A less acute observer than Hercule Poirot could not have failed to notice her distress. She went on inconsequently:

'Men are just like children! They believe *anything* …'

She bent over her work. The tiny wisp of cambric came out again unobtrusively.

Perhaps Hercule Poirot thought it well to change the subject.

He said:

'You do not bathe this morning? And monsieur your husband, is he down on the beach?'

128

Mrs Gold looked up, blinked, resumed her almost defiantly bright manner and replied:

'No, not this morning. We arranged to go round the walls of the old city. But somehow or other we – we missed each other. They started without me.'

The pronoun was revealing, but before Poirot could say anything, General Barnes came up from the beach below and dropped into a chair beside them.

'Good morning, Mrs Gold. Good morning, Poirot. Both deserters this morning? A lot of absentees. You two, and your husband, Mrs Gold – and Mrs Chantry.'

'And Commander Chantry?' inquired Poirot casually.

'Oh, no, he's down there. Miss Pamela's got him in hand.' The General chuckled. 'She's finding him a little bit difficult! One of the strong, silent men you hear about in books.'

Marjorie Gold said with a little shiver:

'He frightens me a little, that man. He – he looks so black sometimes. As though he might do – anything!'

She shivered.

'Just indigestion, I expect,' said the General cheerfully. 'Dyspepsia is responsible for many a reputation for romantic melancholy or ungovernable rages.'

Marjorie Gold smiled a polite little smile.

'And where's your good man?' inquired the General.

Her reply came without hesitation – in a natural, cheerful voice.

'Douglas? Oh, he and Mrs Chantry have gone into the town. I believe they've gone to have a look at the walls of the old city.'

'Ha, yes – very interesting. Time of the knights and all that. You ought to have gone too, little lady.'

Mrs Gold said:

'I'm afraid I came down rather late.'

She got up suddenly with a murmured excuse and went into the hotel.

General Barnes looked after her with a concerned expression, shaking his head gently.

'Nice little woman, that. Worth a dozen painted trollops like someone whose name we won't mention! Ha! Husband's a fool! Doesn't know when he's well off.'

He shook his head again. Then, rising, he went indoors.

Sarah Blake had just come up from the beach and had heard the General's last speech.

Making a face at the departing warrior's back, she remarked as she flung herself into a chair:

'Nice little woman – nice little woman! Men always approve of dowdy women – but when it comes to brass tacks the dress-up trollops win hands down! Sad, but there it is.'

'Mademoiselle,' said Poirot, and his voice was abrupt. 'I do not like all this!'

'Don't you? Nor do I. No, let's be honest, I suppose I *do* like it really. There is a horrid side of one that enjoys accidents and public calamities and unpleasant things that happen to one's friends.'

Poirot asked:

'Where is Commander Chantry?'

'On the beach being dissected by Pamela (*she's* enjoying herself if you like!) and not being improved in temper by the proceeding. He was looking like a thunder cloud when I came up. There are squalls ahead, believe me.'

Poirot murmured:

'There is something I do not understand –'

'It's not easy to *understand*,' said Sarah. 'But what's going to *happen* that's the question.'

Poirot shook his head and murmured:

'As you say, mademoiselle – it is the future that causes one inquietude.'

'What a nice way of putting it,' said Sarah and went into the hotel.

In the doorway she almost collided with Douglas Gold. The young man came out looking rather pleased with himself but at the same time slightly guilty. He said:

'Hallo, M. Poirot,' and added rather self-consciously, 'Been showing Mrs Chantry the Crusaders' walls. Marjorie didn't feel up to going.'

Poirot's eyebrows rose slightly, but even had he wished he would have had no time to make a comment for Valentine Chantry came sweeping out, crying in her high voice:

'Douglas – a pink gin – positively I must have a pink gin.'

Douglas Gold went off to order the drink. Valentine sank into a chair by Poirot. She was looking radiant this morning.

She saw her husband and Pamela coming up towards them and waved a hand, crying out:

'Have a nice bathe, Tony darling? Isn't it a divine morning?'

Commander Chantry did not answer. He swung up the steps, passed her without a word or a look and vanished into the bar.

His hands were clenched by his sides and that faint likeness to a gorilla was accentuated.

Valentine Chantry's perfect but rather foolish mouth fell open.

She said, 'Oh,' rather blankly.

Pamela Lyall's face expressed keen enjoyment of the situation. Masking it as far as was possible to one of her ingenuous disposition she sat down by Valentine Chantry and inquired:

'Have you had a nice morning?'

As Valentine began, 'Simply marvellous. We –' Poirot got up and in his turn strolled gently towards the bar. He found young Gold waiting for the pink gin with a flushed face. He looked disturbed and angry.

He said to Poirot, 'That man's a brute!' And he nodded his head in the direction of the retreating figure of Commander Chantry.

'It is possible,' said Poirot. 'Yes, it is quite possible. But *les femmes*, they like brutes, remember that!'

Douglas muttered:

'I shouldn't be surprised if he ill-treats her!'

'She probably likes that too.'

Douglas Gold looked at him in a puzzled way, took up the pink gin and went out with it.

Hercule Poirot sat on a stool and ordered a *sirop de cassis*.

Whilst he was sipping it with long sighs of enjoyment, Chantry came in and drank several pink gins in rapid succession.

He said suddenly and violently to the world at large rather than to Poirot:

'If Valentine thinks she can get rid of me like she's got rid of a lot of other damned fools, she's mistaken! I've got her and I mean to keep her. No other fellow's going to get her except over my dead body.'

He flung down some money, turned on his heel and went out.

CHAPTER 3

It was three days later that Hercule Poirot went to the Mount of the Prophet. It was a cool, agreeable drive through the golden green fir trees, winding higher and higher, far above the petty wrangling and squabbling of human beings. The car stopped at the restaurant. Poirot got out and wandered into the woods. He came out at last on a spot that seemed truly on top of the world. Far below, deeply and dazzlingly blue, was the sea.

Here at last he was at peace – removed from cares – above the world. Carefully placing his folded overcoat on a tree stump, Hercule Poirot sat down.

'Doubtless *le bon Dieu* knows what he does. But it is odd that he should have permitted himself to fashion certain human beings. *Eh bien*, here for a while at least I am away from these vexing problems.' Thus he mused.

He looked up with a start. A little woman in a brown coat and skirt was hurrying towards him. It was Marjorie Gold and this time she had abandoned all pretence. Her face was wet with tears.

Poirot could not escape. She was upon him.

'M. Poirot. You've got to help me. I'm so miserable I don't know what to do! Oh, what shall I do? What shall I do?'

She looked up at him with a distracted face. Her fingers fastened on his coat sleeve. Then, as something she saw in his face alarmed her, she drew back a little.

'What – what is it?' she faltered.

'You want my advice, madame? It is that you ask?'

She stammered, 'Yes ... Yes ...'

'*Eh bien* – here it is.' He spoke curtly – trenchantly. 'Leave this place at once – *before it is too late.*'

'What?' She stared at him.

'You heard me. Leave this island.'

'Leave the island?'

She stared at him stupefied.

'That is what I say.'

'But why – why?'

'It is my advice to you – *if you value your life.*'

She gave a gasp.

'Oh! what do you mean? You're frightening me – you're frightening me.'

'Yes,' said Poirot gravely, 'that is my intention.'

She sank down, her face in her hands.

'But I can't! He wouldn't come! Douglas wouldn't, I mean. She wouldn't let him. She's got hold of him – body and soul. He won't listen to anything against her ... He's crazy about her ... He believes everything she tells him – that her husband ill-treats her – that she's an injured innocent – that nobody has ever understood her ... He doesn't even think about me any more – I don't count – I'm not real to him. He wants me to give him his freedom – to divorce him. He believes that she'll divorce her husband and marry him. But I'm afraid ... Chantry won't give her up. He's not that kind of man. Last night she showed Douglas bruises on her arm – said her husband had done it. It made Douglas wild. He's so chivalrous ... Oh! I'm *afraid*! What will come of it all? Tell me what to do!'

Hercule Poirot stood looking straight across the water to the blue line of hills on the mainland of Asia. He said:

'I have told you. Leave the island *before it is too late...*'

She shook her head.

'I can't – I can't – unless Douglas...'

Poirot sighed.

He shrugged his shoulders.

CHAPTER 4

Hercule Poirot sat with Pamela Lyall on the beach.

She said with a certain amount of gusto, 'The triangle's going strong! They sat one each side of her last night – glowering at each other! Chantry had had too much to drink. He was positively insulting to Douglas Gold. Gold behaved very well. Kept his temper. The Valentine woman enjoyed it, of course. Purred like the man-eating tiger she is. What do you think will happen?'

Poirot shook his head.

'I am afraid. I am very much afraid...'

'Oh, we all are,' said Miss Lyall hypocritically. She added, 'This business is rather in *your* line. Or it may come to be. Can't you do anything?'

'I have done what I could.'

Miss Lyall leaned forward eagerly.

'What *have* you done?' she asked with pleasurable excitement.

'I advised Mrs Gold to leave the island before it was too late.'

'Oo-er – so you think –' she stopped.

'Yes, mademoiselle?'

'So *that's* what you think is going to happen!' said Pamela slowly. 'But he couldn't – he'd never do a thing like that ...

134

He's so *nice* really. It's all that Chantry woman. He wouldn't –
He wouldn't – do –'

She stopped – then she said softly:

'*Murder*? Is that – is that really the word that's in your
mind?'

'It is in someone's mind, mademoiselle. I will tell you that.'

Pamela gave a sudden shiver.

'I don't believe it,' she declared.

CHAPTER 5

The sequence of events on the night of October the twenty-
ninth was perfectly clear.

To begin with, there was a scene between the two men –
Gold and Chantry. Chantry's voice rose louder and louder and
his last words were overheard by four persons – the cashier at
the desk, the manager, General Barnes and Pamela Lyall.

'You god-damned swine! If you and my wife think you can
put this over on me, you're mistaken! *As long as I'm alive*,
Valentine will remain my wife.'

Then he had flung out of the hotel, his face livid with rage.

That was before dinner. After dinner (how arranged no one
knew) a reconciliation took place. Valentine asked Marjorie
Gold to come out for a moonlight drive. Pamela and Sarah
went with them. Gold and Chantry played billiards together.
Afterwards they joined Hercule Poirot and General Barnes in
the lounge.

For the first time almost, Chantry's face was smiling and
good-tempered.

'Have a good game?' asked the General.

The Commander said:

'This fellow's too good for me! Ran out with a break of forty-
six.'

135

Douglas Gold deprecated this modestly.

'Pure fluke. I assure you it was. What'll you have? I'll go and get hold of a waiter.'

'Pink gin for me, thanks.'

'Right. General?'

'Thanks. I'll have a whisky and soda.'

'Same for me. What about you, M. Poirot?'

'You are most amiable. I should like a *sirop de cassis*.'

'A *sirop* – excuse me?'

'*Sirop de cassis*. The syrup of blackcurrants.'

'Oh, a liqueur! I see. I suppose they have it here? I never heard of it.'

'They have it, yes. But it is not a liqueur.'

Douglas Gold said, laughing:

'Sounds a funny taste to me – but every man his own poison! I'll go and order them.'

Commander Chantry sat down. Though not by nature a talkative or a social man, he was clearly doing his best to be genial.

'Odd how one gets used to doing without any news,' he remarked.

The General grunted.

'Can't say the *Continental Daily Mail* four days old is much use to *me*. Of course I get *The Times* sent to me and *Punch* every week, but they're a devilish long time in coming.'

'Wonder if we'll have a general election over this Palestine business?'

'Whole thing's been badly mismanaged,' declared the General just as Douglas Gold reappeared followed by a waiter with the drinks.

The General had just begun on an anecdote of his military career in India in the year 1905. The two Englishmen were listening politely, if without great interest. Hercule Poirot was sipping his *sirop de cassis*.

The General reached the point of his narrative and there was dutiful laughter all round.

Then the women appeared at the doorway of the lounge.

136

They all four seemed in the best of spirits and were talking and laughing.

'Tony, darling, it was too divine,' cried Valentine as she dropped into a chair by his side. 'The most marvellous idea of Mrs Gold's. You all ought to have come!'

Her husband said:

'What about a drink?'

He looked inquiringly at the others.

'Pink gin for me, darling,' said Valentine.

'Gin and gingerbeer,' said Pamela.

'Sidecar,' said Sarah.

'Right.' Chantry stood up. He pushed his own untouched pink gin over to his wife. 'You have this. I'll order another for myself. What's yours, Mrs Gold?'

Mrs Gold was being helped out of her coat by her husband. She turned smiling:

'Can I have an orangeade, please?'

'Right you are. Orangeade.'

He went towards the door. Mrs Gold smiled up in her husband's face.

'It was so lovely, Douglas. I wish you had come.'

'I wish I had too. We'll go another night, shall we?'

They smiled at each other.

Valentine Chantry picked up the pink gin and drained it.

'Oo! I needed that,' she sighed.

Douglas Gold took Marjorie's coat and laid it on a settee.

As he strolled back to the others he said sharply:

'Hallo, what's the matter?'

Valentine Chantry was leaning back in her chair. Her lips were blue and her hand had gone to her heart.

'I feel – rather queer...'

She gasped, fighting for breath.

Chantry came back into the room. He quickened his step.

'Hallo, Val, what's the matter?'

'I – I don't know ... That drink – it tasted queer...'

'The pink gin?'

137

Chantry swung round his face worked. He caught Douglas Gold by the shoulder.

'That was *my* drink ... Gold, what the hell did you put in it?'

Douglas Gold was staring at the convulsed face of the woman in the chair. He had gone dead white.

'I – I – never –'

Valentine Chantry slipped down in her chair.

General Barnes cried out:

'Get a doctor – quick...'

Five minutes later Valentine Chantry died...

CHAPTER 6

There was no bathing the next morning.

Pamela Lyall, white-faced, clad in a simple dark dress, clutched at Hercule Poirot in the hall and drew him into the little writing-room.

'It's horrible!' she said. 'Horrible! You said so! You foresaw it! Murder!'

He bent his head gravely.

'Oh!' she cried out. She stamped her foot on the floor. 'You should have stopped it! Somehow! It *could* have been stopped!'

'How?' asked Hercule Poirot.

That brought her up short for the moment.

'Couldn't you go to someone – to the police –?'

'And say what? What is there to say – *before the event*? That someone has murder in their heart? I tell you, *mon enfant*, if one human being is determined to kill another human being –'

'You could warn the victim,' insisted Pamela.

'Sometimes,' said Hercule Poirot, 'warnings are useless.'

Pamela said slowly, 'You could warn the murderer – show him that you knew what was intended...'

Poirot nodded appreciatively.

'Yes – a better plan, that. But even then you have to reckon with a criminal's chief vice.'

'What is that?'

'Conceit. A criminal never believes that his crime can fail.'

'But it's absurd – stupid,' cried Pamela. 'The whole crime was childish! Why, the police arrested Douglas Gold at once last night.'

'Yes.' He added thoughtfully, 'Douglas Gold is a very stupid young man.'

'Incredibly stupid! I hear that they found the rest of the poison – whatever it was –?'

'A form of stropanthin. A heart poison.'

'That they actually found the rest of it in his dinner jacket pocket?'

'Quite true.'

'Incredibly stupid!' said Pamela again. 'Perhaps he meant to get rid of it – and the shock of the wrong person being poisoned paralysed him. What a scene it would make on the stage. The lover putting the stropanthin in the husband's glass and then, just when his attention is elsewhere, the wife drinks it instead ... Think of the ghastly moment when Douglas Gold turned round and realized he had killed the woman he loved...'

She gave a little shiver.

'Your triangle. *The Eternal Triangle!* Who would have thought it would end like this?'

'I was afraid of it,' murmured Poirot.

Pamela turned on him.

'You warned *her* – Mrs Gold. Then why didn't you warn him as well?'

'You mean, why didn't I warn Douglas Gold?'

'No. I mean Commander Chantry. You could have told him that he was in danger – after all, *he* was the real obstacle! I've no doubt Douglas Gold relied on being able to bully his wife into giving him a divorce – she's a meek-spirited little woman and terribly fond of him. But Chantry is a mulish sort of devil. He was determined not to give Valentine her freedom.'

Poirot shrugged his shoulders.

'It would have been no good my speaking to Chantry,' he said.

'Perhaps not,' Pamela admitted. 'He'd probably have said he could look after himself and told you to go to the devil. But I do feel there ought to have been *something* one could have done.'

'I did think,' said Poirot slowly, 'of trying to persuade Valentine Chantry to leave the island, but she would not have believed what I had to tell her. She was far too stupid a woman to take in a thing like that. *Pauvre femme*, her stupidity killed her.'

'I don't believe it would have been any good if she *had* left the island,' said Pamela. 'He would simply have followed her.'

'He?'

'Douglas Gold.'

'You think Douglas Gold would have followed her? Oh, no, mademoiselle, you are wrong – you are completely wrong. You have not yet appreciated the truth of this matter. If Valentine Chantry had left the island, her husband would have gone with her.'

Pamela looked puzzled.

'Well, naturally.'

'And then, you see, the crime would simply have taken place somewhere else.'

'I don't understand you?'

'I am saying to you that the same crime would have occurred somewhere else – *that crime being the murder of Valentine Chantry by her husband.*'

Pamela stared.

'Are you trying to say that it was Commander Chantry – Tony Chantry – who murdered Valentine?'

'Yes. You saw him do it! Douglas Gold brought him his drink. He sat with it in front of him. When the women came in we all looked across the room, he had the stropanthin ready, he dropped it into the pink gin and presently, courteously, he passed it along to his wife and she drank it.'

'But the packet of stropanthin was found in Douglas Gold's pocket!'

'A very simple matter to slip it there when we were all crowding round the dying woman.'

It was quite two minutes before Pamela got her breath.

'But I don't understand a word! The triangle – you said yourself –'

Hercule Poirot nodded his head vigorously.

'I said there was a triangle – yes. But you, you imagined *the wrong one*. You were deceived by some very clever acting! You thought, as you were meant to think, that both Tony Chantry and Douglas Gold were in love with Valentine Chantry. You believed, as you were meant to believe, that Douglas Gold, being in love with Valentine Chantry (whose husband refused to divorce her) took the desperate step of administering a powerful heart poison to Chantry and that, by a fatal mistake, Valentine Chantry drank that poison instead. All that is illusion. Chantry has been meaning to do away with his wife for some time. He was bored to death with her, I could see that from the first. He married her for her money. Now he wants to marry another woman – so he planned to get rid of Valentine and keep her money. That entailed murder.'

'Another *woman*?'

Poirot said slowly:

'Yes, yes – *the little Marjorie Gold*. It was the eternal triangle all right! But you saw it the wrong way round. Neither of those two men cared in the least for Valentine Chantry. It was her vanity *and Majorie Gold's very clever stage managing* that made you think they did! A very clever woman, Mrs Gold, and amazingly attractive in her demure Madonna, poor-little-thing-way! I have known four women criminals of the same type. There was Mrs Adams who was acquitted of murdering her husband, but everybody knows she did it. Mary Parker did away with an aunt, a sweetheart and two brothers before she got a little careless and was caught. Then there was Mrs Rowden, she was hanged all right. Mrs Lecray escaped by the skin of her teeth. This woman is exactly the same type. I recognized it as soon as I saw her! That type takes to crime like a duck to water! And a very pretty bit of well-planned work it was. Tell me, what *evidence* did you ever have that Douglas Gold was in love with Valentine Chantry? When you come to think it out, you will realize that there was only Mrs Gold's confidences and Chantry's jealous bluster. Yes? You see?'

'It's horrible,' cried Pamela.

'They were a clever pair,' said Poirot with professional detachment. 'They planned to "meet" here and stage their crime. That Marjorie Gold, she is a cold-blooded devil! She would have sent her poor, innocent fool of a husband to the scaffold without the least remorse.'

Pamela cried out:

'But he was arrested and taken away by the police last night.'

'Ah,' said Hercule Poirot, 'but after that, me, I had a few little words with the police. It is true that I did not see Chantry put the stropanthin in the glass. I, like everyone else, looked up when the ladies came in. But the moment I realized that Valentine Chantry had been poisoned, I watched her husband without taking my eyes off him. And so, you see, I actually saw him slip the packet of stropanthin in Douglas Gold's coat pocket...'

He added with a grim expression on his face:

'I am a good witness. My name is well known. The moment the police heard my story they realized that it put an entirely different complexion on the matter.'

'And then?' demanded Pamela, fascinated.

'*Eh bien*, then they asked Commander Chantry a few questions. He tried to bluster it out, but he is not really clever, he soon broke down.'

'So Douglas Gold was set at liberty?'

'Yes.'

'And – Marjorie Gold?'

Poirot's face grew stern.

'I warned her,' he said. 'Yes, I warned her ... Up on the Mount of the Prophet ... It was the only chance of averting the crime. I as good as told her that I suspected her. She understood. But she believed herself too clever ... I told her to leave the island *if* she valued her life. She chose – to remain...'

142

THE DREAM

Hercule Poirot gave the house a steady appraising glance. His eyes wandered a moment to its surroundings, the shops, the big factory building on the right, the blocks of cheap mansion flats opposite.

Then once more his eyes returned to Northway House, relic of an earlier age – an age of space and leisure, when green fields had surrounded its well-bred arrogance. Now it was an anachronism, submerged and forgotten in the hectic sea of modern London, and not one man in fifty could have told you where it stood.

Furthermore, very few people could have told you to whom it belonged, though its owner's name would have been recognized as one of the world's richest men. But money can quench publicity as well as flaunt it. Benedict Farley, that eccentric millionaire, chose not to advertise his choice of residence. He himself was rarely seen, seldom making a public appearance. From time to time, he appeared at board meetings, his lean figure, beaked nose, and rasping voice easily dominating the assembled directors. Apart from that, he was just a well-known figure of legend. There were his strange meannesses, his incredible generosities, as well as more personal details – his famous patchwork dressing-gown, now reputed to be twenty-eight years old, his invariable diet of cabbage soup and caviare, his hatred of cats. All these things the public knew.

Hercule Poirot knew them also. It was all he did know of the man he was about to visit. The letter which was in his coat pocket told him little more.

After surveying this melancholy landmark of a past age for a minute or two in silence, he walked up the steps to the front door and pressed the bell, glancing as he did so at the neat wrist-watch which had at last replaced an old favourite – the large turnip-faced watch of earlier days. Yes, it was exactly nine-thirty. As ever, Hercule Poirot was exact to the minute.

The door opened after just the right interval. A perfect specimen of the genus butler stood outlined against the lighted hall.

'Mr Benedict Farley?' asked Hercule Poirot.

The impersonal glance surveyed him from head to foot, inoffensively but effectively.

En gros et en détail, thought Hercule Poirot to himself with appreciation.

'You have an appointment, sir?' asked the suave voice.

'Yes.'

'Your name, sir?'

'Monsieur Hercule Poirot.'

The butler bowed and drew back. Hercule Poirot entered the house. The butler closed the door behind him.

But there was yet one more formality before the deft hands took hat and stick from the visitor.

'You will excuse me, sir. I was to ask for a letter.'

With deliberation Poirot took from his pocket the folded letter and handed it to the butler. The latter gave it a mere glance, then returned it with a bow. Hercule Poirot returned it to his pocket. Its contents were simple.

Northway House, W.8

M. Hercule Poirot
Dear Sir,

Mr Benedict Farley would like to have the benefit of your advice. If convenient to yourself he would be glad if you would call upon him at the above address at 9.30 tomorrow (Thursday) evening.

Yours truly,

Hugo Cornworthy
(Secretary)

P.S. Please bring this letter with you.

144

Deftly the butler relieved Poirot of hat, stick and overcoat. He said:

'Will you please come up to Mr Cornworthy's room?'

He led the way up the broad staircase. Poirot followed him, looking with appreciation at such *objets d'art* as were of an opulent and florid nature! His taste in art was always somewhat bourgeois.

On the first floor the butler knocked on a door.

Hercule Poirot's eyebrows rose very slightly. It was the first jarring note. For the best butlers do not knock at doors – and yet indubitably this was a first-class butler!

It was, so to speak, the first intimation of contact with the eccentricity of a millionaire.

A voice from within called out something. The butler threw open the door. He announced (and again Poirot sensed the deliberate departure from orthodoxy):

'The gentleman you are expecting, sir.'

Poirot passed into the room. It was a fair-sized room, very plainly furnished in a workmanlike fashion. Filing cabinets, books of reference, a couple of easy-chairs, and a large and imposing desk covered with neatly docketed papers. The corners of the room were dim, for the only light came from a big green-shaded reading lamp which stood on a small table by the arm of one of the easy-chairs. It was placed so as to cast its full light on anyone approaching from the door. Hercule Poirot blinked a little, realizing that the lamp bulb was at least 150 watts. In the arm-chair sat a thin figure in a patchwork dressing-gown – Benedict Farley. His head was stuck forward in a characteristic attitude, his beaked nose projecting like that of a bird. A crest of white hair like that of a cockatoo rose above his forehead. His eyes glittered behind thick lenses as he peered suspiciously at his visitor.

'Hey,' he said at last – and his voice was shrill and harsh, with a rasping note in it. 'So you're Hercule Poirot, hey?'

'At your service,' said Poirot politely and bowed, one hand on the back of the chair.

'Sit down – sit down,' said the old man testily.

Hercule Poirot sat down – in the full glare of the lamp. From behind it the old man seemed to be studying him attentively.

'How do I know you're Hercule Poirot – hey?' he demanded fretfully. 'Tell me that – hey?'

Once more Poirot drew the letter from his pocket and handed it to Farley.

'Yes,' admitted the millionaire grudgingly. 'That's it. That's what I got Cornworthy to write.' He folded it up and tossed it back. 'So you're the fellow, are you?'

With a little wave of his hand Poirot said:

'I assure you there is no deception!'

Benedict Farley chuckled suddenly.

'That's what the conjurer says before he takes the goldfish out of the hat! Saying that is part of the trick, you know!'

Poirot did not reply. Farley said suddenly:

'Think I'm a suspicious old man, hey? So I am. Don't trust anybody! That's my motto. Can't trust anybody when you're rich. No, no, it doesn't do.'

'You wished,' Poirot hinted gently, 'to consult me?'

The old man nodded.

'Go to the expert and don't count the cost. You'll notice, M. Poirot, I haven't asked you your fee. I'm not going to! Send me in the bill later – *I* shan't cut up rough over it. Damned fools at the dairy thought they could charge me two and nine for eggs when two and seven's the market price – lot of swindlers! I won't be swindled. But the man at the top's different. He's worth the money. I'm at the top myself – I know.'

Hercule Poirot made no reply. He listened attentively, his head poised a little on one side.

Behind his impassive exterior he was conscious of a feeling of disappointment. He could not exactly put his finger on it. So far Benedict Farley had run true to type – that is, he had conformed to the popular idea of himself; and yet – Poirot was disappointed.

'The man,' he said disgustedly to himself, 'is a mountebank – nothing but a mountebank!'

He had known other millionaires, eccentric men too, but in nearly every case he had been conscious of a certain force, an inner energy that had commanded his respect. If they had worn a patchwork dressing-gown, it would have been because they liked wearing such a dressing-gown. But the dressing-gown of Benedict Farley, or so it seemed to Poirot, was essentially a stage property. And the man himself was essentially stagy. Every word he spoke was uttered, so Poirot felt assured, sheerly for effect.

He repeated again unemotionally, 'You wished to consult me, Mr Farley?'

Abruptly the millionaire's manner changed.

He leaned forward. His voice dropped to a croak.

'Yes. Yes . . . I want to hear what you've got to say – what you think. . . . Go to the top! That's my way! The best doctor – the best detective – it's between the two of them.'

'As yet, Monsieur, I do not understand.'

'Naturally,' snapped Farley. 'I haven't begun to tell you.'

He leaned forward once more and shot out an abrupt question.

'What do you know, M. Poirot, about dreams?'

The little man's eyebrows rose. Whatever he had expected, it was not this.

'For that, M. Farley, I should recommend Napoleon's *Book of Dreams* – or the latest practising psychologist from Harley Street.'

Benedict Farley said soberly, 'I've tried both. . . .'

There was a pause, then the millionaire spoke, at first almost in a whisper, then with a voice growing higher and higher.

'It's the same dream – night after night. And I'm afraid, I

147

tell you – I'm afraid. . . . It's always the same. I'm sitting in my room next door to this. Sitting at my desk, writing. There's a clock there and I glance at it and see the time – exactly twenty-eight minutes past three. Always the same time, you understand.

'*And when I see the time, M. Poirot, I know I've got to do it. I don't want to do it – I loathe doing it – but I've got to. . . .*'

His voice had risen shrilly.

Unperturbed, Poirot said, 'And what is it that you have to do?'

'At twenty-eight minutes past three,' Benedict Farley said hoarsely, 'I open the second drawer down on the right of my desk, take out the revolver that I keep there, load it and walk over to the window. And then – and then –'

'Yes?'

Benedict Farley said in a whisper:

'*Then I shoot myself. . . .*'

There was silence.

Then Poirot said, 'That is your dream?'

'Yes.'

'The same every night?'

'Yes.'

'What happens after you shoot yourself?'

'I wake up.'

Poirot nodded his head slowly and thoughtfully. 'As a matter of interest, do you keep a revolver in that particular drawer?'

'Yes.'

'Why?'

'I have always done so. It is as well to be prepared.'

'Prepared for what?'

Farley said irritably, 'A man in my position has to be on his guard. All rich men have enemies.'

Poirot did not pursue the subject. He remained silent for a moment or two, then he said:

148

'Why exactly did you send for me?'

'I will tell you. First of all I consulted a doctor – three doctors to be exact.'

'Yes?'

'The first told me it was all a question of diet. He was an elderly man. The second was a young man of the modern school. He assured me that it all hinged on a certain event that took place in infancy at that particular time of day – three twenty-eight. I am so determined, he says, not to remember the event, that I symbolize it by destroying myself. That is his explanation.'

'And the third doctor?' asked Poirot.

Benedict Farley's voice rose in shrill anger.

'He's a young man too. He has a preposterous theory! He asserts that I, myself, am tired of life, that my life is so unbearable to me that I deliberately want to end it! But since to acknowledge that fact would be to acknowledge that essentially I am a failure, I refuse in my waking moments to face the truth. But when I am asleep, all inhibitions are removed, and I proceed to do that *which I really wish to do*. I put an end to myself.'

'His view is that you really wish, unknown to yourself, to commit suicide?' said Poirot.

Benedict Farley cried shrilly:

'And that's impossible – impossible! I'm perfectly happy! I've got everything I want – everything money can buy! It's fantastic – unbelievable even to suggest a thing like that!'

Poirot looked at him with interest. Perhaps something in the shaking hands, the trembling shrillness of the voice, warned him that the denial was *too* vehement, that its very insistence was in itself suspect. He contented himself with saying:

'And where do I come in, Monsieur?'

Benedict Farley calmed down suddenly. He tapped with an emphatic finger on the table beside him.

'There's another possibility. And if it's right, you're the man to know about it! You're famous, you've had hundreds of cases – fantastic, improbable cases! You'd know if anyone does.'

'Know what?'

Farley's voice dropped to a whisper.

'Supposing someone wants to kill me. . . . Could they do it this way? Could they make me dream that dream night after night?'

'Hypnotism, you mean?'

'Yes.'

Hercule Poirot considered the question.

'It would be possible, I suppose,' he said at last. 'It is more a question for a doctor.'

'You don't know of such a case in your experience?'

'Not precisely on those lines, no.'

'You see what I'm driving at? I'm made to dream the same dream, night after night, night after night – and then – one day the suggestion is too much for me – *and I act upon it*. I do what I've dreamed of so often – kill myself!'

Slowly Hercule Poirot shook his head.

'You don't think that is possible?' asked Farley.

'*Possible?*' Poirot shook his head. 'That is not a word I care to meddle with.'

'But you think it improbable?'

'Most improbable.'

Benedict Farley murmured. 'The doctor said so too. . . .' Then his voice rising shrilly again, he cried out, 'But why do I have this dream? Why? Why?'

Hercule Poirot shook his head. Benedict Farley said abruptly, 'You're sure you've never come across anything like this in your experience?'

'Never.'

'That's what I wanted to know.'

Delicately, Poirot cleared his throat.

'You permit,' he said, 'a question?'

'What is it? What is it? Say what you like.'

'Who is it you suspect of wanting to kill you?'

Farley snapped out, 'Nobody. Nobody at all.'

'But the idea presented itself to your mind?' Poirot persisted.

'I wanted to know – if it was a possibility.'

'Speaking from my own experience, I should say No. Have you ever been hypnotized, by the way?'

'Of course not. D'you think I'd lend myself to such tomfoolery?'

'Then I think one can say that your theory is definitely improbable.'

'But the dream, you fool, the dream.'

'The dream is certainly remarkable,' said Poirot thoughtfully. He paused and then went on. 'I should like to see the scene of this drama – the table, the clock, and the revolver.'

'Of course, I'll take you next door.'

Wrapping the folds of his dressing-gown round him, the old man half-rose from his chair. Then suddenly, as though a thought had struck him, he resumed his seat.

'No,' he said. 'There's nothing to see there. I've told you all there is to tell.'

'But I should like to see for myself –'

'There's no need,' Farley snapped. 'You've given me your opinion. That's the end.'

Poirot shrugged his shoulders. 'As you please.' He rose to his feet. 'I am sorry, Mr Farley, that I have not been able to be of assistance to you.'

Benedict Farley was staring straight ahead of him.

'Don't want a lot of hanky-pankying around,' he growled out. 'I've told you the facts – you can't make anything of them. That closes the matter. You can send me a bill for the consultation fee.'

'I shall not fail to do so,' said the detective drily. He walked towards the door.

'Stop a minute.' The millionaire called him back. 'That letter – I want it.'

'The letter from your secretary?'

'Yes.'

Poirot's eyebrows rose. He put his hand into his pocket, drew out a folded sheet, and handed it to the old man. The latter scrutinized it, then put it down on the table beside him with a nod.

Once more Hercule Poirot walked to the door. He was puzzled. His busy mind was going over and over the story he had been told. Yet in the midst of his mental preoccupation, a nagging sense of something wrong obtruded itself. And that something had to do with himself – not with Benedict Farley.

With his hand on the door knob, his mind cleared. He, Hercule Poirot, had been guilty of an error! He turned back into the room once more.

'A thousand pardons! In the interest of your problem I have committed a folly! That letter I handed to you – by mischance I put my hand into my right-hand pocket instead of the left –'

'What's all this? What's all this?'

'The letter that I handed you just now – an apology from my laundress concerning the treatment of my collars.' Poirot was smiling, apologetic. He dipped into his left-hand pocket. 'This is *your* letter.'

Benedict Farley snatched at it – grunted: 'Why the devil can't you mind what you're doing?'

Poirot retrieved his laundress's communication, apologized gracefully once more, and left the room.

He paused for a moment outside on the landing. It was a spacious one. Directly facing him was a big old oak settle with a refectory table in front of it. On the table were magazines. There were also two arm-chairs and a table with flowers. It reminded him a little of a dentist's waiting-room.

152

The butler was in the hall below waiting to let him out.

'Can I get you a taxi, sir?'

'No, I thank you. The night is fine. I will walk.'

Hercule Poirot paused a moment on the pavement waiting for a lull in the traffic before crossing the busy street.

A frown creased his forehead.

'No,' he said to himself. 'I do not understand at all. Nothing makes sense. Regrettable to have to admit it, but I, Hercule Poirot, am completely baffled.'

That was what might be termed the first act of the drama. The second act followed a week later. It opened with a telephone call from one John Stillingfleet, MD.

He said with a remarkable lack of medical decorum:

'That you, Poirot, old horse? Stillingfleet here.'

'Yes, my friend. What is it?'

'I'm speaking from Northway House – Benedict Farley's.'

'Ah, yes?' Poirot's voice quickened with interest. 'What of – Mr Farley?'

'Farley's dead. Shot himself this afternoon.'

There was a pause, then Poirot said:

'Yes . . .'

'I notice you're not overcome with surprise. Know something about it, old horse?'

'Why should you think that?'

'Well, it isn't brilliant deduction or telepathy or anything like that. We found a note from Farley to you making an appointment about a week ago.'

'I see.'

'We've got a tame police inspector here – got to be careful, you know, when one of these millionaire blokes bumps himself off. Wondered whether you could throw any light on the case. If so, perhaps you'd come round?'

'I will come immediately.'

'Good for you, old boy. Some dirty work at the crossroads – eh?'

Poirot merely repeated that he would set forth immediately.

'Don't want to spill the beans over the telephone? Quite right. So long.'

A quarter of an hour later Poirot was sitting in the library, a low long room at the back of Northway House on the ground floor. There were five other persons in the room. Inspector Barnett, Dr Stillingfleet, Mrs Farley, the widow of the millionaire, Joanna Farley, his only daughter, and Hugo Cornworthy, his private secretary.

Of these, Inspector Barnett was a discreet soldierly-looking man. Dr Stillingfleet, whose professional manner was entirely different from his telephonic style, was a tall, long-faced young man of thirty. Mrs Farley was obviously very much younger than her husband. She was a handsome dark-haired woman. Her mouth was hard and her black eyes gave absolutely no clue to her emotions. She appeared perfectly self-possessed. Joanna Farley had fair hair and a freckled face. The prominence of her nose and chin was clearly inherited from her father. Her eyes were intelligent and shrewd. Hugo Cornworthy was a good-looking young fellow, very correctly dressed. He seemed intelligent and efficient.

After greetings and introductions, Poirot narrated simply and clearly the circumstances of his visit and the story told him by Benedict Farley. He could not complain of any lack of interest.

'Most extraordinary story I've ever heard!' said the inspector. 'A dream, eh? Did you know anything about this, Mrs Farley?'

She bowed her head.

'My husband mentioned it to me. It upset him very much. I – I told him it was indigestion – his diet, you know, was very peculiar – and suggested his calling in Dr Stillingfleet.'

The young man shook his head.

'He didn't consult me. From M. Poirot's story, I gather he went to Harley Street.'

'I would like your advice on that point, Doctor,' said Poirot. 'Mr Farley told me that he consulted three specialists. What do you think of the theories they advanced?'

Stillingfleet frowned.

'It's difficult to say. You've got to take into account that what he passed on to you wasn't exactly what had been said to him. It was a layman's interpretation.'

'You mean he had got the phraseology wrong?'

'Not exactly. I mean they would put a thing to him in professional terms, he'd get the meaning a little distorted, and then recast it in his own language.'

'So that what he told me was not really what the doctors said.'

'That's what it amounts to. He's just got it all a little wrong, if you know what I mean.'

Poirot nodded thoughtfully. 'Is it known whom he consulted?' he asked.

Mrs Farley shook her head, and Joanna Farley remarked:

'None of us had any idea he had consulted anyone.'

'Did he speak to *you* about his dream?' asked Poirot.

The girl shook her head.

'And you, Mr Cornworthy?'

'No, he said nothing at all. I took down a letter to you at his dictation, but I had no idea why he wished to consult you. I thought it might possibly have something to do with some business irregularity.'

Poirot asked: 'And now as to the actual facts of Mr Farley's death?'

Inspector Barnett looked interrogatively at Mrs Farley and at Dr Stillingfleet, and then took upon himself the role of spokesman.

'Mr Farley was in the habit of working in his own room on the first floor every afternoon. I understand that there was a big amalgamation of business in prospect –'

He looked at Hugo Cornworthy who said, 'Consolidated Coachlines.'

'In connection with that,' continued Inspector Barnett, 'Mr Farley had agreed to give an interview to two members of the Press. He very seldom did anything of the kind – only about once in five years, I understand. Accordingly two reporters, one from the Associated Newsgroups, and one from Amalgamated Press-sheets, arrived at a quarter past three by appointment. They waited on the first floor outside Mr Farley's door – which was the customary place for people to wait who had an appointment with Mr Farley. At twenty past three a messenger arrived from the office of Consolidated Coachlines with some urgent papers. He was shown into Mr Farley's room where he handed over the documents. Mr Farley accompanied him to the door, and from there spoke to the two members of the Press. He said:

'"I'm sorry, gentlemen, to have to keep you waiting, but I have some urgent business to attend to. I will be as quick as I can."

'The two gentlemen, Mr Adams and Mr Stoddart, assured Mr Farley that they would await his convenience. He went back into his room, shut the door – and was never seen alive again!'

'Continue,' said Poirot.

'At a little after four o'clock,' went on the inspector, 'Mr Cornworthy here came out of his room which is next door to Mr Farley's and was surprised to see the two reporters still waiting. He wanted Mr Farley's signature to some letters and thought he had also better remind him that these two gentlemen were waiting. He accordingly went into Mr Farley's room. To his surprise he could not at first see Mr Farley and thought the room was empty. Then he caught sight of a boot sticking out behind the desk (which is placed in front of the window). He went quickly across and discovered Mr Farley lying there dead, with a revolver beside him.

'Mr Cornworthy hurried out of the room and directed the butler to ring up Dr Stillingfleet. By the latter's advice, Mr Cornworthy also informed the police.'

'Was the shot heard?' asked Poirot.

'No. The traffic is very noisy here, the landing window was open. What with lorries and motor horns it would be most unlikely if it had been noticed.'

Poirot nodded thoughtfully. 'What time is it supposed he died?' he asked.

Stillingfleet said:

'I examined the body as soon as I got here – that is, at thirty-two minutes past four. Mr Farley had been dead at least an hour.'

Poirot's face was very grave.

'So then, it seems possible that his death could have occurred at the time he mentioned to me – that is, at twenty-eight minutes past three.'

'Exactly,' said Stillingfleet.

'Any fingermarks on the revolver?'

'Yes, his own.'

'And the revolver itself?'

The inspector took up the tale.

'Was one which he kept in the second right-hand drawer of his desk, just as he told you. Mrs Farley has identified it positively. Moreover, you understand, there is only one entrance to the room, the door giving on to the landing. The two reporters were sitting exactly opposite that door and they swear that no one entered the room from the time Mr Farley spoke to them, until Mr Cornworthy entered it at a little after four o'clock.'

'So that there is every reason to suppose that Mr Farley committed suicide.'

Inspector Barnett smiled a little.

'There would have been no doubt at all but for one point.'

'And that?'

'The letter written to you.'

Poirot smiled too.

'I see! Where Hercule Poirot is concerned – immediately the suspicion of murder arises!'

'Precisely,' said the inspector dryly. 'However, after your clearing up of the situation –'

Poirot interrupted him. 'One little minute.' He turned to Mrs Farley. 'Had your husband ever been hypnotized?'

'Never.'

'Had he studied the question of hypnotism? Was he interested in the subject?'

She shook her head. 'I don't think so.'

Suddenly her self-control seemed to break down. 'That horrible dream! It's uncanny! That he should have dreamed that – night after night – and then – it's as though he were – *hounded* to death!'

Poirot remembered Benedict Farley saying— '*I proceed to do that which I really wish to do. I put an end to myself.*'

He said, 'Had it ever occurred to you that your husband might be tempted to do away with himself?'

'No – at least – sometimes he was very queer. . . .'

Joanna Farley's voice broke in clear and scornful. 'Father would never have killed himself. He was far too careful of himself.'

Dr Stillingfleet said, 'It isn't the people who threaten to commit suicide who usually do it, you know, Miss Farley. That's why suicides sometimes seem unaccountable.'

Poirot rose to his feet. 'Is it permitted,' he asked, 'that I see the room where the tragedy occurred?'

'Certainly. Dr Stillingfleet –'

The doctor accompanied Poirot upstairs.

Benedict Farley's room was a much larger one than the secretary's next door. It was luxuriously furnished with deep leather-covered arm-chairs, a thick pile carpet, and a superb outsize writing-desk.

Poirot passed behind the latter to where a dark stain on the carpet showed just before the window. He remembered the millionaire saying, '*At twenty-eight minutes past three I open the second drawer on the right of my desk, take out the revolver that I keep there, load it, and walk over to the window. And then – and then I shoot myself.'*

He nodded slowly. Then he said:

'The window was open like this?'

'Yes. But nobody could have got in that way.'

Poirot put his head out. There was no sill or parapet and no pipes near. Not even a cat could have gained access that way. Opposite rose the blank wall of the factory, a dead wall with no windows in it.

Stillingfleet said, 'Funny room for a rich man to choose as his own sanctum, with that outlook. It's like looking out on to a prison wall.'

'Yes,' said Poirot. He drew his head in and stared at the expanse of solid brick. 'I think,' he said, 'that that wall is important.'

Stillingfleet looked at him curiously. 'You mean – psychologically?'

Poirot had moved to the desk. Idly, or so it seemed, he picked up a pair of what are usually called lazy-tongs. He pressed the handles; the tongs shot out to their full length. Delicately, Poirot picked up a burnt match stump with them from beside a chair some feet away and conveyed it carefully to the wastepaper basket.

'When you've finished playing with those things. . . .' said Stillingfleet irritably.

Hercule Poirot murmured, 'An ingenious invention,' and replaced the tongs neatly on the writing-table. Then he asked:

'Where were Mrs Farley and Miss Farley at the time of the – death?'

'Mrs Farley was resting in her room on the floor above this. Miss Farley was painting in her studio at the top of the house.'

Hercule Poirot drummed idly with his fingers on the table for a minute or two. Then he said:

'I should like to see Miss Farley. Do you think you could ask her to come here for a minute or two?'

159

'If you like.'

Stillingfleet glanced at him curiously, then left the room. In another minute or two the door opened and Joanna Farley came in.

'You do not mind, Mademoiselle, if I ask you a few questions?'

She returned his glance coolly. 'Please ask anything you choose.'

'Did you know that your father kept a revolver in his desk?'

'No.'

'Where were you and your mother – that is to say your stepmother – that is right?'

'Yes, Louise is my father's second wife. She is only eight years older than I am. You were about to say –?'

'Where were you and she on Thursday of last week? That is to say, on Thursday night.'

She reflected for a minute or two.

'Thursday? Let me see. Oh, yes, we had gone to the theatre. To see *Little Dog Laughed*.'

'Your father did not suggest accompanying you?'

'He never went out to theatres.'

'What did he usually do in the evenings?'

'He sat in here and read.'

'He was not a very sociable man?'

The girl looked at him directly. 'My father,' she said, 'had a singularly unpleasant personality. No one who lived in close association with him could possibly be fond of him.'

'That, Mademoiselle, is a very candid statement.'

'I am saving you time, M. Poirot. I realize quite well what you are getting at. My stepmother married my father for his money. I live here because I have no money to live elsewhere. There is a man I wish to marry – a poor man; my father saw to it that he lost his job. He wanted me, you see, to marry well – an easy matter since I was to be his heiress!'

'Your father's fortune passes to you?'

'Yes. That is, he left Louise, my stepmother, a quarter of a

160

million free of tax, and there are other legacies, but the residue goes to me.' She smiled suddenly. 'So you see, M. Poirot, I had every reason to desire my father's death!'

'I see, Mademoiselle, that you have inherited your father's intelligence.'

She said thoughtfully, 'Father was clever. . . . One felt that with him – that he had force – driving power – but it had all turned sour – bitter – there was no humanity left. . . .'

Hercule Poirot said softly, '*Grand Dieu*, but what an imbecile I am. . . .'

Joanna Farley turned towards the door. 'Is there anything more?'

'Two little questions. These tongs here,' he picked up the lazy-tongs, 'were they always on the table?'

'Yes. Father used them for picking up things. He didn't like stooping.'

'One other question. Was your father's eyesight good?'

She stared at him.

'Oh, no – he couldn't see at all – I mean he couldn't see without his glasses. His sight had always been bad from a boy.'

'But with his glasses?'

'Oh, he could see all right then, of course.'

'He could read newspapers and fine print?'

'Oh, yes.'

'That is all, Mademoiselle.'

She went out of the room.

Poirot murmured, 'I was stupid. It was there, all the time, under my nose. And because it was so near I could not see it.'

He leaned out of the window once more. Down below, in the narrow way between the house and the factory, he saw a small dark object.

Hercule Poirot nodded, satisfied, and went downstairs again.

The others were still in the library. Poirot addressed himself to the secretary:

'I want you, Mr Cornworthy, to recount to me in detail the

exact circumstances of Mr Farley's summons to me. When, for instance, did Mr Farley dictate that letter?'

'On Wednesday afternoon – at five-thirty, as far as I can remember.'

'Were there any special directions about posting it?'

'He told me to post it myself.'

'And you did so?'

'Yes.'

'Did he give any special instructions to the butler about admitting me?'

'Yes. He told me to tell Holmes (Holmes is the butler) that a gentleman would be calling at nine-thirty. He was to ask the gentleman's name. He was also to ask to see the letter.'

'Rather peculiar precaution to take, don't you think?'

Cornworthy shrugged his shoulders.

'Mr Farley,' he said carefully, 'was rather a peculiar man.'

'Any other instructions?'

'Yes. He told me to take the evening off.'

'Did you do so?'

'Yes, immediately after dinner I went to the cinema.'

'When did you return?'

'I let myself in about a quarter past eleven.'

'Did you see Mr Farley again that evening?'

'No.'

'And he did not mention the matter the next morning?'

'No.'

Poirot paused a moment, then resumed, 'When I arrived I was not shown into Mr Farley's own room.'

'No. He told me that I was to tell Holmes to show you into my room.'

'Why was that? Do you know?'

Cornworthy shook his head. 'I never questioned any of Mr Farley's orders,' he said dryly. 'He would have resented it if I had.'

'Did he usually receive visitors in his own room?'

'Usually, but not always. Sometimes he saw them in my room.'

'Was there any reason for that?'

Hugo Cornworthy considered.

'No – I hardly think so – I've never really thought about it.'

Turning to Mrs Farley, Poirot asked:

'You permit that I ring for your butler?'

'Certainly, M. Poirot.'

Very correct, very urbane, Holmes answered the bell.

'You rang, madam?'

Mrs Farley indicated Poirot with a gesture. Holmes turned politely. 'Yes, sir?'

'What were your instructions, Holmes, on the Thursday night when I came here?'

Holmes cleared his throat, then said:

'After dinner Mr Cornworthy told me that Mr Farley expected a Mr Hercule Poirot at nine-thirty. I was to ascertain the gentleman's name, and I was to verify the information by glancing at a letter. Then I was to show him up to Mr Cornworthy's room.'

'Were you also told to knock on the door?'

An expression of distaste crossed the butler's countenance.

'That was one of Mr Farley's orders. I was always to knock when introducing visitors – business visitors, that is,' he added.

'Ah, that puzzled me! Were you given any other instructions concerning me?'

'No, sir. When Mr Cornworthy had told me what I have just repeated to you he went out.'

'What time was that?'

'Ten minutes to nine, sir.'

'Did you see Mr Farley after that?'

'Yes, sir, I took him up a glass of hot water as usual at nine o'clock.'

'Was he then in his own room or in Mr Cornworthy's?'

'He was in his own room, sir.'

'You noticed nothing unusual about that room?'

163

'Unusual? No, sir.'

'Where were Mrs Farley and Miss Farley?'

'They had gone to the theatre, sir.'

'Thank you, Holmes, that will do.'

Holmes bowed and left the room. Poirot turned to the millionaire's widow.

'One more question, Mrs Farley. Had your husband good sight?'

'No. Not without his glasses.'

'He was very short-sighted?'

'Oh, yes, he was quite helpless without his spectacles.'

'He had several pairs of glasses?'

'Yes.'

'Ah,' said Poirot. He leaned back. 'I think that that concludes the case. . . .'

There was silence in the room. They were all looking at the little man who sat there complacently stroking his moustache. On the inspector's face was perplexity, Dr Stillingfleet was frowning, Cornworthy merely stared uncomprehendingly, Mrs Farley gazed in blank astonishment, Joanna Farley looked eager.

Mrs Farley broke the silence.

'I don't understand, M. Poirot.' Her voice was fretful. 'The dream –'

'Yes,' said Poirot. 'That dream was very important.'

Mrs Farley shivered. She said:

'I've never believed in anything supernatural before – but now – to dream it night after night beforehand –'

'It's extraordinary,' said Stillingfleet. 'Extraordinary! If we hadn't got your word for it, Poirot, and if you hadn't had it straight from the horse's mouth –' he coughed in embarrassment, and readopting his professional manner, 'I beg your pardon, Mrs Farley. If Mr Farley himself had not told that story –'

'Exactly,' said Poirot. His eyes, which had been half-closed, opened suddenly. They were very green. *'If Benedict Farley hadn't told me –'*

He paused a minute, looking round at a circle of blank faces.

'There are certain things, you comprehend, that happened that evening which I was quite at a loss to explain. First, why make such a point of my bringing that letter with me?'

'Identification,' suggested Cornworthy.

'No, no, my dear young man. Really that idea is too ridiculous. There must be some much more valid reason. For not only did Mr Farley require to see that letter produced, but he definitely demanded that I should leave it behind me. And moreover even then he did not destroy it! It was found among his papers this afternoon. *Why did he keep it?'*

Joanna Farley's voice broke in. 'He wanted, in case anything happened to him, that the facts of his strange dream should be made known.'

Poirot nodded approvingly.

'You are astute, Mademoiselle. That must be – that can only be – the point of the keeping of the letter. When Mr Farley was dead, the story of that strange dream was to be told! That dream was very important. That dream, Mademoiselle, was *vital*!

'I will come now,' he went on, 'to the second point. After hearing his story I ask Mr Farley to show me the desk and the revolver. He seems about to get up to do so, then suddenly refuses. Why did he refuse?'

This time no one advanced an answer.

'I will put that question differently. *What was there in that next room that Mr Farley did not want me to see?'*

There was still silence.

'Yes,' said Poirot, 'it is difficult, that. And yet there was some reason – some *urgent* reason why Mr Farley received me in his secretary's room and refused point blank to take me into his own room. *There was something in that room he could not afford to have me see*.

'And now I come to the third inexplicable thing that

165

happened on that evening. Mr Farley, just as I was leaving, requested me to hand him the letter I had received. By inadvertence I handed him a communication from my laundress. He glanced at it and laid it down beside him. Just before I left the room I discovered my error – and rectified it! After that I left the house and – I admit it – I was completely at sea! The whole affair and especially that last incident seemed to me quite inexplicable.'

He looked round from one to the other.

'You do not see?'

Stillingfleet said, 'I don't really see how your laundress comes into it, Poirot.'

'My laundress,' said Poirot, 'was very important. That miserable woman who ruins my collars, was, for the first time in her life, useful to somebody. Surely you see – it is so obvious. Mr Farley glanced at that communication – *one glance* would have told him that it was the wrong letter – and yet he knew nothing. Why? *Because he could not see it properly!*'

Inspector Barnett said sharply, 'Didn't he have his glasses on?'

Hercule Poirot smiled. 'Yes,' he said. 'He had his glasses on. That is what makes it so very interesting.'

He leaned forward.

'Mr Farley's dream was very important. He dreamed, you see, that he committed suicide. And a little later on, he did commit suicide. That is to say he was alone in a room and was found there with a revolver by him, and no one entered or left the room at the time that he was shot. What does that mean? It means, does it not, that it *must* be suicide!'

'Yes,' said Stillingfleet.

Hercule Poirot shook his head.

'On the contrary,' he said. 'It was murder. An unusual and a very cleverly planned murder.'

Again he leaned forward, tapping the table, his eyes green and shining.

'Why did Mr Farley not allow me to go into his own room that evening? What was there in there that I must not be allowed to see? I think, my friends, that there was – Benedict Farley himself!'

He smiled at the blank faces.

'Yes, yes, it is not nonsense what I say. Why could the Mr Farley to whom I had been talking not realize the difference between two totally dissimilar letters? Because, *mes amis*, he was a man of *normal sight* wearing a pair of very powerful glasses. Those glasses would render a man of normal eyesight practically blind. Isn't that so, Doctor?'

Stillingfleet murmured, 'That's so – of course.'

'Why did I feel that in talking to Mr Farley I was talking to a *mountebank*, to an actor playing a part! Consider the setting. The dim room, the green-shaded light turned blindingly away from the figure in the chair. What did I see – the famous patchwork dressing-gown, the beaked nose (faked with that useful substance, nose putty) the white crest of hair, the powerful lenses concealing the eyes. What evidence is there that Mr Farley ever had a dream? Only the story I was told and the evidence of *Mrs Farley*. What evidence is there that Benedict Farley kept a revolver in his desk? Again only the story told me and the word of Mrs Farley. Two people carried this fraud through – Mrs Farley and Hugo Cornworthy. Cornworthy wrote the letter to me, gave instructions to the butler, went out ostensibly to the cinema, but let himself in again immediately with a key, went to his room, made himself up, and played the part of Benedict Farley.

'And so we come to this afternoon. The opportunity for which Mr Cornworthy has been waiting arrives. There are two witnesses on the landing to swear that no one goes in or out of Benedict Farley's room. Cornworthy waits until a particularly heavy batch of traffic is about to pass. Then he leans out of his window, and with the lazy-tongs which he has purloined from the desk next door he holds an object against the window of that room. Benedict Farley comes to the window. Cornworthy snatches back the tongs and as Farley leans out, and the lorries are passing outside, Cornworthy shoots him with the revolver that he has ready. There is a blank wall opposite, remember. There can be no witness of the crime. Cornworthy waits for over half-an hour, then gathers up some papers, conceals the lazy-tongs and the revolver between them and goes out on to the landing and into the next room. He replaces the tongs on the desk, lays down the revolver after pressing the dead man's fingers on it, and hurries out with the news of Mr Farley's "suicide."

'He arranges that the letter to me shall be found and that I shall arrive with my story – the story I heard *from Mr Farley's own lips* – of his extraordinary "dream" – the strange compulsion he felt to kill himself! A few credulous people will discuss the hypnotism theory – but the main result will be to confirm without a doubt that the actual hand that held the revolver was Benedict Farley's own.'

Hercule Poirot's eyes went to the widow's face – he noted with satisfaction the dismay – the ashy pallor – the blind fear. . . .

'And in due course,' he finished gently, 'the happy ending would have been achieved. A quarter of a million and two hearts that beat as one. . . .'

John Stillingfleet, MD, and Hercule Poirot walked along the side of Northway House. On their right was the towering wall of the factory. Above them, on their left, were the windows of Benedict Farley's and Hugo Cornworthy's rooms. Hercule Poirot stopped and picked up a small object – a black stuffed cat.

'*Voilà*,' he said. 'That is what Cornworthy held in the lazy-tongs against Farley's window. You remember, he hated cats? Naturally he rushed to the window.'

'Why on earth didn't Cornworthy come out and pick it up after he'd dropped it?'

'How could he? To do so would have been definitely suspicious. After all, if this object were found what would anyone think – that some child had wandered round here and dropped it.'

'Yes,' said Stillingfleet with a sigh. 'That's probably what the ordinary person *would* have thought. But not good old Hercule! D'you know, old horse, up to the very last minute I thought you were leading up to some subtle theory of high-falutin' psychological "suggested" murder? I bet those two thought so too! Nasty bit of goods, the Farley. Goodness, how she cracked! Cornworthy might have got away with it if she hadn't had hysterics and tried to spoil your beauty by going for you with her nails. I only got her off you just in time.'

He paused a minute and then said:

'I rather like the girl. Grit, you know, and brains. I suppose I'd be thought to be a fortune hunter if I had a shot at her . . . ?'

'You are too late, my friend. There is already someone *sur le tapis*. Her father's death has opened the way to happiness.'

'Take it all round, *she* had a pretty good motive for bumping off the unpleasant parent.'

'Motive and opportunity are not enough,' said Poirot. 'There must also be the criminal temperament!'

'I wonder if you'll ever commit a crime, Poirot?' said Stillingfleet. 'I bet you could get away with it all right. As a matter of fact, it would be *too* easy for you – I mean the thing would be off as definitely too unsporting.'

'That,' said Poirot, 'is a typical English idea.'

FOUR AND TWENTY BLACKBIRDS

Hercule Poirot was dining with his friend, Henry Bonnington at the Gallant Endeavour in the King's Road, Chelsea.

Mr Bonnington was fond of the Gallant Endeavour. He liked the leisurely atmosphere, he liked the food which was 'plain' and 'English' and 'not a lot of made up messes.' He liked to tell people who dined with him there just exactly where Augustus John had been wont to sit and draw their attention to the famous artists' names in the visitors' book. Mr Bonnington was himself the least artistic of men – but he took a certain pride in the artistic activities of others.

Molly, the sympathetic waitress, greeted Mr Bonnington as an old friend. She prided herself on remembering her customers' likes and dislikes in the way of food.

'Good evening, sir,' she said, as the two men took their seats at a corner table. 'You're in luck today – turkey stuffed with chestnuts – that's your favourite, isn't it? And ever such a nice Stilton we've got! Will you have soup first or fish?'

Mr Bonnington deliberated the point. He said to Poirot warningly as the latter studied the menu:

'None of your French kickshaws now. Good well-cooked English food.'

'My friend,' Hercule Poirot waved his hand, 'I ask no better! I put myself in your hands unreservedly.'

'Ah – hruup – er – hm,' replied Mr Bonnington and gave careful attention to the matter.

These weighty matters, and the question of wine, settled, Mr Bonnington leaned back with a sigh and unfolded his napkin as Molly sped away.

'Good girl, that,' he said approvingly. 'Was quite a beauty once – artists used to paint her. She knows about food, too – and that's a great deal more important. Women are very unsound on food as a rule. There's many a woman if she goes out with a fellow she fancies – won't even notice what she eats. She'll just order the first thing she sees.'

Hercule Poirot shook his head.

'*C'est terrible.*'

'Men aren't like that, thank God!' said Mr Bonnington complacently.

'Never?' There was a twinkle in Hercule Poirot's eye.

'Well, perhaps when they're very young,' conceded Mr Bonnington. 'Young puppies! Young fellows nowadays are all the same – no guts – no stamina. I've no use for the young – and they,' he added with strict impartiality, 'have no use for me. Perhaps they're right! But to hear some of these young fellows talk you'd think no man had a right to be *alive* after sixty! From the way they go on, you'd wonder more of them didn't help their elderly relations out of the world.'

'It is possible,' said Hercule Poirot, 'that they do.'

'Nice mind you've got, Poirot, I must say. All this police work saps your ideals.'

Hercule Poirot smiled.

'*Tout de même,*' he said. 'It would be interesting to make a table of accidental deaths over the age of sixty. I assure you it would raise some curious speculations in your mind.'

'The trouble with you is that you've started going to look for crime – instead of waiting for crime to come to you.'

'I apologize,' said Poirot. 'I talk what you call "the shop." Tell me, my friend, of your own affairs. How does the world go with you?'

'Mess!' said Mr Bonnington. 'That's what's the matter with the world nowadays. Too much mess. And too much fine language. The fine language helps to conceal the mess. Like a highly-flavoured sauce concealing the fact that the fish

171

underneath it is none of the best! Give me an honest fillet of sole and no messy sauce over it.'

It was given him at that moment by Molly and he grunted approval.

'You know just what I like, my girl,' he said.

'Well, you come here pretty regular, don't you, sir? I ought to know what you like.'

Hercule Poirot said:

'Do people then always like the same things? Do not they like a change sometimes?'

'Not gentlemen, sir. Ladies like variety – gentlemen always like the same thing.'

'What did I tell you?' grunted Bonnington. 'Women are fundamentally unsound where food is concerned!'

He looked round the restaurant.

'The world's a funny place. See that odd-looking old fellow with a beard in the corner? Molly'll tell you he's always here Tuesdays and Thursday nights. He has come here for close on ten years now – he's a kind of landmark in the place. Yet nobody here knows his name or where he lives or what his business is. It's odd when you come to think of it.'

When the waitress brought the portions of turkey he said:

'I see you've still got Old Father Time over there?'

'That's right, sir. Tuesdays and Thursdays, his days are. Not but what he came in here on a *Monday* last week! It quite upset me! I felt I'd got my dates wrong and that it must be Tuesday without my knowing it! But he came in the next night as well – so the Monday was just a kind of extra, so to speak.'

'An interesting deviation from habit,' murmured Poirot. 'I wonder what the reason was?'

'Well, sir, if you ask me, I think he'd had some kind of upset or worry.'

'Why did you think that? His manner?'

'No, sir – not his manner exactly. He was very quiet as he

always is. Never says much except good evening when he comes and goes. No, it was his *order*.'

'His order?'

'I dare say you gentlemen will laugh at me,' Molly flushed up, 'but when a gentleman has been here for ten years, you get to know his likes and dislikes. He never could bear suet pudding or blackberries and I've never known him take thick soup – but on that Monday night he ordered thick tomato soup, beefsteak and kidney pudding and blackberry tart! Seemed as though he just didn't notice *what* he ordered!'

'Do you know,' said Hercule Poirot, 'I find that extraordinarily interesting.'

Molly looked gratified and departed.

'Well, Poirot,' said Henry Bonnington with a chuckle. 'Let's have a few deductions from you. All in your best manner.'

'I would prefer to hear yours first.'

'Want me to be Watson, eh? Well, old fellow went to a doctor and the doctor changed his diet.'

'To thick tomato soup, steak and kidney pudding and blackberry tart? I cannot imagine any doctor doing that.'

'Don't believe it, old boy. Doctors will put you on to anything.'

'That is the only solution that occurs to you?'

Henry Bonnington said:

'Well, seriously, I suppose there's only one explanation possible. Our unknown friend was in the grip of some powerful mental emotion. He was so perturbed by it that he literally did not notice what he was ordering or eating.'

He paused a minute and then said:

'You'll be telling me next that you know just *what* was on his mind. You'll say perhaps that he was making up his mind to commit a murder.'

He laughed at his own suggestion.

Hercule Poirot did not laugh.

He has admitted that at that moment he was seriously worried. He claims that he ought then to have had some inkling of what was likely to occur.

His friends assure him that such an idea is quite fantastic.

It was some three weeks later that Hercule Poirot and Bonnington met again – this time their meeting was in the Tube.

They nodded to each other, swaying about, hanging on to adjacent straps. Then at Piccadilly Circus there was a general exodus and they found seats right at the forward end of the car – a peaceful spot since nobody passed in or out that way.

'That's better,' said Mr Bonnington. 'Selfish lot, the human race, they won't pass up the car however much you ask 'em to!'

Hercule Poirot shrugged his shoulders.

'What will you?' he said. 'Life is too uncertain.'

'That's it. Here today, gone tomorrow,' said Mr Bonnington with a kind of gloomy relish. 'And talking of that, d'you remember that old boy we noticed at the Gallant Endeavour? I shouldn't wonder if *he'd* hopped it to a better world. He's not been there for a whole week. Molly's quite upset about it.'

Hercule Poirot sat up. His green eyes flashed.

'Indeed?' he said. 'Indeed?'

Bonnington said:

'D'you remember I suggested he'd been to a doctor and been put on a diet? Diet's nonsense of course – but I shouldn't wonder if he had consulted a doctor about his health and what the doctor said gave him a bit of a jolt. That would account for him ordering things off the menu without noticing what he was doing. Quite likely the jolt he got hurried him out of the world sooner than he would have gone otherwise. Doctors ought to be careful what they tell a chap.'

'They usually are,' said Hercule Poirot.

'This is my station,' said Mr Bonnington. 'Bye, bye. Don't suppose we shall ever know now who the old boy was – not even his name. Funny world!'

He hurried out of the carriage.

Hercule Poirot, sitting frowning, looked as though he did not think it was such a funny world.

He went home and gave certain instructions to his faithful valet, George.

Hercule Poirot ran his finger down a list of names. It was a record of deaths within a certain area.

Poirot's finger stopped.

'Henry Gascoigne. Sixty-nine. I might try him first.'

Later in the day, Hercule Poirot was sitting in Dr MacAndrew's surgery just off the King's Road. MacAndrew was a tall red-haired Scotsman with an intelligent face.

'Gascoigne?' he said. 'Yes, that's right. Eccentric old bird. Lived alone in one of those derelict old houses that are being cleared away in order to build a block of modern flats. I hadn't attended him before, but I'd seen him about and I knew who he was. It was the dairy people got the wind up first. The milk bottles began to pile up outside. In the end the people next door sent word to the police and they broke the door in and found him. He'd pitched down the stairs and broken his neck. Had on an old dressing-gown with a ragged cord – might easily have tripped himself up with it.'

'I see,' said Hercule Poirot. 'It was quite simple – an accident.'

'That's right.'

'Had he any relations?'

'There's a nephew. Used to come along and see his uncle about once a month. Lorrimer, his name is, George Lorrimer. He's a medico himself. Lives at Wimbledon.'

'Was he upset at the old man's death?'

'I don't know that I'd say he was upset. I mean, he had an affection for the old man, but he didn't really know him very well.'

'How long had Mr Gascoigne been dead when you saw him?'

'Ah!' said Dr MacAndrew. 'This is where we get official. Not less than forty-eight hours and not more than seventy-two hours. He was found on the morning of the sixth. Actually, we got closer than that. He'd got a letter in the pocket of his dressing-gown – written on the third – posted in Wimbledon that afternoon – would have been delivered somewhere around nine-twenty p.m. That puts the time of death at after nine-twenty on the evening of the third. That agrees with the contents of the stomach and the processes of digestion. He had had a meal about two hours before death. I examined him on the morning of the sixth and his condition was quite consistent with death having occurred about sixty hours previously – round about ten p.m. on the third.'

'It all seems very consistent. Tell me, when was he last seen alive?'

'He was seen in the King's Road about seven o'clock that same evening, Thursday the third, and he dined at the Gallant Endeavour restaurant at seven-thirty. It seems he always dined there on Thursdays. He was by way of being an artist, you know. An extremely bad one.'

'He had no other relations? Only this nephew?'

'There was a twin brother. The whole story is rather curious. They hadn't seen each other for years. It seems the other brother, Anthony Gascoigne, married a very rich woman and gave up art – and the brothers quarrelled over it. Hadn't seen each other since, I believe. But oddly enough, *they died on the same day*. The elder twin passed away at three o'clock on the afternoon of the third. Once before I've known a case of twins dying on the same day – in different parts of the world! Probably just a coincidence – but there it is.'

'Is the other brother's wife alive?'

'No, she died some years ago.'

'Where did Anthony Gascoigne live?'

'He had a house on Kingston Hill. He was, I believe, from what Dr Lorrimer tells me, very much of a recluse.'

Hercule Poirot nodded thoughtfully.

The Scotsman looked at him keenly.

'What exactly have you got in your mind, M. Poirot?' he asked bluntly. 'I've answered your questions – as was my duty seeing the credentials you brought. But I'm in the dark as to what it's all about.'

Poirot said slowly:

'A simple case of accidental death, that's what you said. What I have in mind is equally simple – a simple push.'

Dr MacAndrew looked startled.

'In other words, murder! Have you any grounds for that belief?'

'No,' said Poirot. 'It is a mere supposition.'

'There must be something –' persisted the other.

Poirot did not speak. MacAndrew said:

'If it's the nephew, Lorrimer, you suspect, I don't mind telling you here and now that you are barking up the wrong tree. Lorrimer was playing bridge in Wimbledon from eight-thirty till midnight. That came out at the inquest.'

Poirot murmured:

'And presumably it was verified. The police are careful.'

The doctor said:

'Perhaps you know something against him?'

'I didn't know that there was such a person until you mentioned him.'

'Then you suspect somebody else?'

'No, no. It is not that at all. It's a case of the routine habits of the human animal. That is very important. And the dead M. Gascoigne does not fit in. It is all wrong, you see.'

'I really don't understand.'

Hercule Poirot murmured:

'The trouble is, there is too much sauce over the bad fish.'

'My dear sir?'

Hercule Poirot smiled.

'You will be having me locked up as a lunatic soon, *Monsieur le Docteur*. But I am not really a mental case – just a man who has a liking for order and method and who is worried when he comes across a fact *that does not fit in*. I must ask you to forgive me for having given you so much trouble.'

He rose and the doctor rose also.

'You know,' said MacAndrew, 'honestly I can't see anything the least bit suspicious about the death of Henry Gascoigne. I say he fell – you say somebody pushed him. It's all – well – in the air.'

Hercule Poirot sighed.

'Yes,' he said. 'It is workmanlike. Somebody has made the good job of it!'

'You still think –'

The little man spread out his hands.

'I'm an obstinate man – a man with a little idea – and nothing to support it! By the way, did Henry Gascoigne have false teeth?'

'No, his own teeth were in excellent preservation. Very creditable indeed at his age.'

'He looked after them well – they were white and well brushed?'

'Yes, I noticed them particularly. Teeth tend to grow a little yellow as one grows older, but they were in good condition.'

'Not discoloured in any way?'

'No. I don't think he was a smoker if that is what you mean.'

'I did not mean that precisely – it was just a long shot – which probably will not come off! Goodbye, Dr MacAndrew, and thank you for your kindness.'

He shook the doctor's hand and departed.

'And now,' he said, 'for the long shot.'

At the Gallant Endeavour, he sat down at the same table which he had shared with Bonnington. The girl who served him was not Molly. Molly, the girl told him, was away on a holiday.

178

It was only just seven and Hercule Poirot found no difficulty in entering into conversation with the girl on the subject of old Mr Gascoigne.

'Yes,' she said. 'He'd been here for years and years. But none of us girls ever knew his name. We saw about the inquest in the paper, and there was a picture of him. "There," I said to Molly. "If that isn't our 'Old Father Time'" as we used to call him.'

'He dined here on the evening of his death, did he not?'

'That's right, Thursday, the third. He was always here on a Thursday. Tuesdays and Thursdays – punctual as a clock.'

'You don't remember, I suppose, what he had for dinner?'

'Now let me see, it was mulligatawny soup, that's right, and beefsteak pudding or was it the mutton? – no pudding, that's right, and blackberry and apple pie and cheese. And then to think of him going home and falling down those stairs that very same evening. A frayed dressing-gown cord they said it was as caused it. Of course, his clothes were always something awful – old-fashioned and put on anyhow, and all tattered, and yet he *had* a kind of air, all the same, as though he was *somebody*! Oh, we get all sorts of interesting customers here.'

She moved off.

Hercule Poirot ate his filleted sole. His eyes showed a green light.

'It is odd,' he said to himself, 'how the cleverest people slip over details. Bonnington will be interested.'

But the time had not yet come for leisurely discussion with Bonnington.

Armed with introductions from a certain influential quarter, Hercule Poirot found no difficulty at all in dealing with the coroner for the district.

'A curious figure, the deceased man Gascoigne,' he observed. 'A lonely, eccentric old fellow. But his decease seems to arouse an unusual amount of attention?'

He looked with some curiosity at his visitor as he spoke.

179

Hercule Poirot chose his words carefully.

'There are circumstances connected with it, Monsieur, which make investigation desirable.'

'Well, how can I help you?'

'It is, I believe, within your province to order documents produced in your court to be destroyed, or to be impounded – as you think fit. A certain letter was found in the pocket of Henry Gascoigne's dressing-gown, was it not?'

'That is so.'

'A letter from his nephew, Dr George Lorrimer?'

'Quite correct. The letter was produced at the inquest as helping to fix the time of death.'

'Which was corroborated by the medical evidence?'

'Exactly.'

'Is that letter still available?'

Hercule Poirot waited rather anxiously for the reply.

When he heard that the letter was still available for examination he drew a sigh of relief.

When it was finally produced he studied it with some care. It was written in a slightly cramped handwriting with a stylographic pen.

It ran as follows:

Dear Uncle Henry,

I am sorry to tell you that I have had no success as regards Uncle Anthony. He showed no enthusiasm for a visit from you and would give me no reply to your request that he would let bygones be bygones. He is, of course, extremely ill, and his mind is inclined to wander. I should fancy that the end is very near. He seemed hardly to remember who you were.

I am sorry to have failed you, but I can assure you that I did my best.

Your affectionate nephew,

George Lorrimer

The letter itself was dated 3rd November. Poirot glanced at the envelope's postmark – 4.30 p.m. 3 Nov.

He murmured:

'It is beautifully in order, is it not?'

Kingston Hill was his next objective. After a little trouble, with the exercise of good-humoured pertinacity, he obtained an interview with Amelia Hill, cook-housekeeper to the late Anthony Gascoigne.

Mrs Hill was inclined to be stiff and suspicious at first, but the charming geniality of this strange-looking foreigner would have had its effect on a stone. Mrs Amelia Hill began to unbend.

She found herself, as had so many other women before her, pouring out her troubles to a really sympathetic listener.

For fourteen years she had had charge of Mr Gascoigne's household – *not* an easy job! No, indeed! Many a woman would have quailed under the burdens *she* had had to bear! Eccentric the poor gentleman was and no denying it. Remarkably close with his money – a kind of mania with him it was – and he as rich a gentleman as might be! But Mrs Hill had served him faithfully, and put up with his ways, and naturally she'd expected at any rate a *remembrance*. But no – nothing at all! Just an old will that left all his money to his wife and if she predeceased him then everything to his brother, Henry. A will made years ago. It didn't seem fair!

Gradually Hercule Poirot detached her from her main theme of unsatisfied cupidity. It was indeed a heartless injustice! Mrs Hill could not be blamed for feeling hurt and surprised. It was well known that Mr Gascoigne was tight-fisted about money. It had even been said that the dead man had refused his only brother assistance. Mrs Hill probably knew all about that.

'Was it that that Dr Lorrimer came to see him about?' asked Mrs Hill. 'I knew it was something about his brother, but I thought it was just that his brother wanted to be reconciled. They'd quarrelled years ago.'

'I understand,' said Poirot, 'that Mr Gascoigne refused absolutely?'

'That's right enough,' said Mrs Hill with a nod. '"*Henry?*" he says, rather weak like. "*What's this about Henry? Haven't seen him for years and don't want to. Quarrelsome fellow, Henry.*" Just that.'

The conversation then reverted to Mrs Hill's own special grievances, and the unfeeling attitude of the late Mr Gascoigne's solicitor.

With some difficulty Hercule Poirot took his leave without breaking off the conversation too abruptly.

And so, just after the dinner hour, he came to Elmcrest, Dorset Road, Wimbledon, the residence of Dr George Lorrimer.

The doctor was in. Hercule Poirot was shown into the surgery and there presently Dr George Lorrimer came to him, obviously just risen from the dinner table.

'I'm not a patient, Doctor,' said Hercule Poirot. 'And my coming here is, perhaps, somewhat of an impertinence – but I'm an old man and I believe in plain and direct dealing. I do not care for lawyers and their long-winded roundabout methods.'

He had certainly aroused Lorrimer's interest. The doctor was a clean-shaven man of middle height. His hair was brown but his eyelashes were almost white which gave his eyes a pale, boiled appearance. His manner was brisk and not without humour.

'Lawyers?' he said, raising his eyebrows. 'Hate the fellows! You rouse my curiosity, my dear sir. Pray sit down.'

Poirot did so and then produced one of his professional cards which he handed to the doctor.

George Lorrimer's white eyelashes blinked.

Poirot leaned forward confidentially. 'A good many of my clients are women,' he said.

'Naturally,' said Dr George Lorrimer, with a slight twinkle.

'As you say, naturally,' agreed Poirot. 'Women distrust the

official police. They prefer private investigations. They do not want to have their troubles made public. An elderly woman came to consult me a few days ago. She was unhappy about a husband she'd quarrelled with many years before. This husband of hers was your uncle, the late Mr Gascoigne.'

George Lorrimer's face went purple.

'My uncle? Nonsense! His wife died many years ago.'

'Not your uncle, Mr *Anthony* Gascoigne. Your uncle, Mr *Henry* Gascoigne.'

'Uncle Henry? But *he* wasn't married!'

'Oh yes, he was,' said Hercule Poirot, lying unblushingly. 'Not a doubt of it. The lady even brought along her marriage certificate.'

'It's a lie!' cried George Lorrimer. His face was now as purple as a plum. 'I don't believe it. You're an impudent liar.'

'It is too bad, is it not?' said Poirot. 'You have committed murder for nothing.'

'Murder?' Lorrimer's voice quavered. His pale eyes bulged with terror.

'By the way,' said Poirot, 'I see you have been eating blackberry tart again. An unwise habit. Blackberries are said to be full of vitamins, but they may be deadly in other ways. On this occasion I rather fancy they have helped to put a rope round a man's neck – your neck, Dr Lorrimer.'

'You see, *mon ami*, where you went wrong was over your fundamental assumption.' Hercule Poirot, beaming placidly across the table at his friend, waved an expository hand. 'A man under severe mental stress doesn't choose that time to do something that he's never done before. His reflexes just follow the track of least resistance. A man who is upset about something *might* conceivably come down to dinner dressed in his pyjamas – but they will be his *own* pyjamas – not somebody else's.

'A man who dislikes thick soup, suet pudding and blackberries suddenly orders all three one evening. *You* say, because he is thinking of something else. But *I* say *that a man who has got something on his mind will order automatically the dish he has ordered most often before.*

'*Eh bien*, then, what other explanation could there be? I simply could not think of a reasonable explanation. And I was worried! The incident was all wrong. It did not fit! I have an orderly mind and I like things to fit. Mr Gascoigne's dinner order worried me.

'Then you told me that the man had disappeared. He had missed a Tuesday and a Thursday the first time for years. I liked that even less. A queer hypothesis sprang up in my mind. If I were right about it *the man was dead*. I made inquiries. The man *was* dead. And he was very neatly and tidily dead. In other words the bad fish was covered up with the sauce!

'He had been seen in the King's Road at seven o'clock. He had had dinner here at seven-thirty – two hours before he died. It all fitted in – the evidence of the stomach contents, the evidence of the letter. Much too much sauce! You couldn't see the fish at all!

'Devoted nephew wrote the letter, devoted nephew had beautiful alibi for time of death. Death very simple – a fall down the stairs. Simple accident? Simple murder? Everyone says the former.

'Devoted nephew only surviving relative. Devoted nephew will inherit – but is there anything *to* inherit? Uncle notoriously poor.

'But there is a brother. And brother in his time had married a rich wife. And brother lives in a big rich house on Kingston Hill, so it would seem that rich wife must have left him all her money. You see the sequence – rich wife leaves money to Anthony, Anthony leaves money to Henry, Henry's money goes to George – a complete chain.'

'All very pretty in theory,' said Bonnington. 'But what did you do?'

'Once you *know* – you can usually get hold of what you want. Henry had died two hours after a *meal* – that is all the inquest really bothered about. But supposing the meal was not dinner, but *lunch*. Put yourself in George's place. George wants money – badly. Anthony Gascoigne is dying – but his death is no good to George. His money goes to Henry, and Henry Gascoigne may live for years. So Henry must die too – and the sooner the better – but his death must take place *after* Anthony's, and at the same time George must have an alibi. Henry's habit of dining regularly at a restaurant on two evenings of the week suggest an alibi to George. Being a cautious fellow, he tries his plan out first. *He impersonates his uncle on Monday evening at the restaurant in question.* It goes without a hitch. Everyone there accepts him as his uncle. He is satisfied. He has only to wait till Uncle Anthony shows definite signs of pegging out. The time comes. He writes a letter to his uncle on the afternoon of the second November but dates it the third. He comes up to town on the afternoon of the third, calls on his uncle, and carries his scheme into action. A sharp shove and down the stairs goes Uncle Henry. George hunts about for the letter he has written, and shoves it in the pocket of his uncle's dressing-gown. At seven-thirty he is at the Gallant Endeavour, beard, bushy eyebrows all complete. Undoubtedly Mr Henry Gascoigne is alive at seven-thirty. Then a rapid metamorphosis in a lavatory and back full speed in his car to Wimbledon and an evening of bridge. The perfect alibi.'

Mr Bonnington looked at him.

'But the postmark on the letter?'

'Oh, that was very simple. The postmark was smudgy. Why? It had been altered with lamp black from second November to third November. You would not notice it *unless you were looking for it*. And finally there were the blackbirds.'

'Blackbirds?'

'Four-and-twenty blackbirds baked in a pie! Or blackberries if you prefer to be literal! George, you comprehend, was after all not quite a good enough actor. Do you remember the fellow who blacked himself all over to play Othello? That is the kind of actor you have got to be in crime. George *looked* like his uncle and *walked* like his uncle and *spoke* like his uncle and had his uncles' beard and eyebrows, but he forgot to *eat* like his uncle. He ordered the dishes that he himself liked. Blackberries discolour the teeth – the corpse's teeth were not discoloured, and yet Henry Gascoigne ate blackberries at the Gallant Endeavour that night. But there were no blackberries in the stomach. I asked this morning. And George had been fool enough to keep the beard and the rest of the make-up. Oh! plenty of evidence once you look for it. I called on George and rattled him. That finished it! He had been eating blackberries again, by the way. A greedy fellow – cared a lot about his food. *Eh bien*, greed will hang him all right unless I am very much mistaken.'

A waitress brought them two portions of blackberry and apple tart.

'Take it away,' said Mr Bonnington. 'One can't be too careful. Bring me a small helping of sago pudding.'

'Colonel Clapperton!' said General Forbes.

He said it with an effect midway between a snort and a sniff.

Miss Ellie Henderson leaned forward, a strand of her soft grey hair blowing across her face. Her eyes, dark and snapping, gleamed with a wicked pleasure.

'Such a *soldierly*-looking man!' she said with malicious intent, and smoothed back the lock of hair to await the result.

'Soldierly!' exploded General Forbes. He tugged at his military moustache and his face became bright red.

'In the Guards, wasn't he?' murmured Miss Henderson, completing her work.

'Guards? Guards? Pack of nonsense. Fellow was on the music hall stage! Fact! Joined up and was out in France counting tins of plum and apple. Huns dropped a stray bomb and he went home with a flesh wound in the arm. Somehow or other got into Lady Carrington's hospital.'

'So that's how they met.'

'Fact! Fellow played the wounded hero. Lady Carrington had no sense and oceans of money. Old Carrington had been in munitions. She'd been a widow only six months. This fellow snaps her up in no time. She wangled him a job at the War Office. *Colonel* Clapperton! Pah!' he snorted.

'And before the war he was on the music hall stage,' mused Miss Henderson, trying to reconcile the distinguished grey-haired Colonel Clapperton with a red-nosed comedian singing mirth-provoking songs.

'Fact!' said General Forbes. 'Heard it from old Bassington-ffrench. And he heard it from old Badger Cotterill who'd got it from Snooks Parker.'

Miss Henderson nodded brightly. 'That does seem to settle it!' she said.

A fleeting smile showed for a minute on the face of a small

187

man sitting near them. Miss Henderson noticed the smile. She was observant. It had shown appreciation of the irony underlying her last remark – irony which the General never for a moment suspected.

The General himself did not notice the smile. He glanced at his watch, rose and remarked: 'Exercise. Got to keep oneself fit on a boat,' and passed out through the open door on to the deck.

Miss Henderson glanced at the man who had smiled. It was a well-bred glance indicating that she was ready to enter into conversation with a fellow traveller.

'He is energetic – yes?' said the little man.

'He goes round the deck forty-eight times exactly,' said Miss Henderson. 'What an old gossip! And they say *we* are the scandal-loving sex.'

'What an impoliteness!'

'Frenchmen are always polite,' said Miss Henderson – there was the nuance of a question in her voice.

The little man responded promptly. 'Belgian, mademoiselle.'

'Oh! Belgian.'

'Hercule Poirot. At your service.'

The name aroused some memory. Surely she had heard it before –? 'Are you enjoying this trip, M. Poirot?'

'Frankly, no. It was an imbecility to allow myself to be persuaded to come. I detest *la mer*. Never does it remain tranquil – no, not for a little minute.'

'Well, you admit it's quite calm now.'

M. Poirot admitted this grudgingly. '*A ce moment*, yes. That is why I revive. I once more interest myself in what passes around me – your very adept handling of the General Forbes, for instance.'

'You mean – ' Miss Henderson paused.

Hercule Poirot bowed. 'Your methods of extracting the scandalous matter. Admirable!'

Miss Henderson laughed in an unashamed manner. 'That touch about the Guards? I knew that would bring the old boy

188

up spluttering and gasping.' She leaned forward confidentially. 'I admit I *like* scandal – the more ill-natured, the better!'

Poirot looked thoughtfully at her – her slim well-preserved figure, her keen dark eyes, her grey hair; a woman of forty-five who was content to look her age.

Ellie said abruptly: 'I have it! Aren't you the great detective?'

Poirot bowed. 'You are too amiable, mademoiselle.' But he made no disclaimer.

'How thrilling,' said Miss Henderson. 'Are you "hot on the trail" as they say in books? Have we a criminal secretly in our midst? Or am I being indiscreet?'

'Not at all. Not at all. It pains me to disappoint your expectations, but I am simply here, like everyone else, to amuse myself.'

He said it in such a gloomy voice that Miss Henderson laughed.

'Oh! Well, you will be able to get ashore tomorrow at Alexandria. You have been to Egypt before?'

'Never, mademoiselle.'

Miss Henderson rose somewhat abruptly.

'I think I shall join the General on his constitutional,' she announced.

Poirot sprang politely to his feet.

She gave him a little nod and passed on to the deck.

A faint puzzled look showed for a moment in Poirot's eyes, then, a little smile creasing his lips, he rose, put his head through the door and glanced down the deck. Miss Henderson was leaning against the rail talking to a tall, soldierly-looking man.

Poirot's smile deepened. He drew himself back into the smoking-room with the same exaggerated care with which a tortoise withdraws itself into its shell. For the moment he had the smoking-room to himself, though he rightly conjectured that that would not last long.

It did not. Mrs Clapperton, her carefully waved platinum head protected with a net, her massaged and dieted form dressed in a smart sports suit, came through the door from the bar with the purposeful air of a woman who has always been able to pay top price for anything she needed.

She said: 'John – ? Oh! Good morning, M. Poirot – have you seen John?'

'He's on the starboard deck, madame. Shall I – ?'

She arrested him with a gesture. 'I'll sit here a minute.' She sat down in a regal fashion in the chair opposite him. From the distance she had looked a possible twenty-eight. Now, in spite of her exquisitely made-up face, her delicately plucked eyebrows, she looked not her actual forty-nine years, but a possible fifty-five. Her eyes were a hard pale blue with tiny pupils.

'I was sorry not to have seen you at dinner last night,' she said. 'It was just a shade choppy, of course – '

'*Précisément*,' said Poirot with feeling.

'Luckily, I am an excellent sailor,' said Mrs Clapperton. 'I say luckily, because, with my weak heart, seasickness would probably be the death of me.'

'You have the weak heart, madame?'

'Yes, I have to be *most* careful. I must *not* overtire myself! *All* the specialists say so!' Mrs Clapperton had embarked on the – to her – ever-fascinating topic of her health. 'John, poor darling, wears himself out trying to prevent me from doing too much. I live so intensely, if you know what I mean, M. Poirot?'

'Yes, yes.'

'He always says to me: "Try to be more of a vegetable, Adeline." But I can't. Life was meant to be *lived*, I feel. As a matter of fact I wore myself out as a girl in the war. My hospital – you've heard of my hospital? Of course I had nurses and matrons and all that – but *I* actually ran it.' She sighed.

'Your vitality is marvellous, dear lady,' said Poirot, with the slightly mechanical air of one responding to his cue.

Mrs Clapperton gave a girlish laugh.

'Everyone tells me how young I am! It's absurd. I never try to pretend I'm a day less than forty-three,' she continued with slightly mendacious candour, 'but a lot of people find it hard to believe. "You're so *alive*, Adeline," they say to me. But really, M. Poirot, what would one *be* if one wasn't alive?'

'Dead,' said Poirot.

Mrs Clapperton frowned. The reply was not to her liking. The man, she decided, was trying to be funny. She got up and said coldly: 'I must find John.'

As she stepped through the door she dropped her handbag. It opened and the contents flew far and wide. Poirot rushed gallantly to the rescue. It was some few minutes before the lipsticks, vanity boxes, cigarette case and lighter and other odds and ends were collected. Mrs Clapperton thanked him politely, then she swept down the deck and said, 'John – '

Colonel Clapperton was still deep in conversation with Miss Henderson. He swung round and came quickly to meet his wife. He bent over her protectively. Her deck chair – was it in the right place? Wouldn't it be better – ? His manner was courteous – full of gentle consideration. Clearly an adored wife spoilt by an adoring husband.

Miss Ellie Henderson looked out at the horizon as though something about it rather disgusted her.

Standing in the smoking-room door, Poirot looked on.

A hoarse quavering voice behind him said: 'I'd take a hatchet to that woman if I were her husband.' The old gentleman known disrespectfully among the younger set on board as the Grandfather of All the Tea Planters, had just shuffled in. 'Boy!' he called. 'Get me a whisky peg.'

Poirot stooped to retrieve a torn scrap of notepaper, an overlooked item from the contents of Mrs Clapperton's bag. Part of a prescription, he noted, containing digitalin. He put it in his pocket, meaning to restore it to Mrs Clapperton later.

'Yes,' went on the aged passenger. 'Poisonous woman. I remember a woman like that in Poona. In '87 that was.'

'Did anyone take a hatchet to her?' inquired Poirot.

The old gentleman shook his head sadly.

'Worried her husband into his grave within the year. Clapperton ought to assert himself. Gives his wife her head too much.'

'She holds the purse strings,' said Poirot gravely.

'Ha, ha!' chuckled the old gentleman. 'You've put the matter in a nutshell. Holds the purse strings. Ha, ha!'

Two girls burst into the smoking-room. One had a round face with freckles and dark hair streaming out in a windswept confusion, the other had freckles and curly chestnut hair.

'A rescue – a rescue!' cried Kitty Mooney. 'Pam and I are going to rescue Colonel Clapperton.'

'From his wife,' gasped Pamela Cregan.

'We think he's a *pet* ...'

'And she's just awful – she won't let him do *anything*,' the two girls exclaimed.

'And if he isn't with her, he's usually grabbed by the Henderson woman ...'

'Who's quite nice. But terribly *old* ...'

They ran out, gasping in between giggles. 'A rescue – a rescue ...'

That the rescue of Colonel Clapperton was no isolated sally, but a fixed project, was made clear that same evening when the eighteen-year-old Pam Cregan came up to Hercule Poirot, and murmured: 'Watch us, M. Poirot. He's going to be cut out from under her nose and taken to walk in the moonlight on the boat deck.'

It was just at that moment that Colonel Clapperton was saying: 'I grant you the price of a Rolls-Royce. But it's practically good for a lifetime. Now my car – '

'*My* car, I think, John.' Mrs Clapperton's voice was shrill and penetrating.

He showed no annoyance at her ungraciousness. Either he was used to it by this time, or else –

'Or else?' thought Poirot and let himself speculate.

'Certainly, my dear, *your* car,' Clapperton bowed to his wife and finished what he had been saying, perfectly unruffled.

'*Voilà ce qu'on appelle le pukka sahib*,' thought Poirot. 'But the General Forbes says that Clapperton is no gentleman at all. I wonder now.'

There was a suggestion of bridge. Mrs Clapperton, General Forbes and a hawk-eyed couple sat down to it. Miss Henderson had excused herself and gone out on deck.

'What about your husband?' asked General Forbes, hesitating.

'John won't play,' said Mrs Clapperton. 'Most tiresome of him.'

The four bridge players began shuffling the cards.

Pam and Kitty advanced on Colonel Clapperton. Each one took an arm.

'You're coming with us!' said Pam. 'To the boat deck. There's a moon.'

'Don't be foolish, John,' said Mrs Clapperton. 'You'll catch a chill.'

'Not with us, he won't,' said Kitty. 'We're hot stuff!'

He went with them, laughing.

Poirot noticed that Mrs Clapperton said No Bid to her initial bid of Two Clubs.

He strolled out on to the promenade deck. Miss Henderson was standing by the rail. She looked round expectantly as he came to stand beside her and he saw the drop in her expression.

They chatted for a while. Then presently as he fell silent she asked: 'What are you thinking about?'

Poirot replied: 'I am wondering about my knowledge of English. Mrs Clapperton said: "John won't play bridge." Is not "can't play" the usual term?'

'She takes it as a personal insult that he doesn't, I suppose,' said Ellie drily. 'The man was a fool ever to have married her.'

In the darkness Poirot smiled. 'You don't think it's just possible that the marriage may be a success?' he asked diffidently.

'With a woman like that?'

Poirot shrugged his shoulders. 'Many odious women have devoted husbands. An enigma of nature. You will admit that nothing she says or does appears to gall him.' Miss Henderson was considering her reply when Mrs Clapperton's voice floated out through the smoking-room window.

'No – I don't think I will play another rubber. So stuffy. I think I'll go up and get some air on the boat deck.'

'Good night,' said Miss Henderson. 'I'm going to bed.' She disappeared abruptly.

Poirot strolled forward to the lounge – deserted save for Colonel Clapperton and the two girls. He was doing card tricks for them and noting the dexterity of his shuffling and handling of the cards, Poirot remembered the General's story of a career on the music hall stage.

'I see you enjoy the cards even though you do not play bridge,' he remarked.

'I've my reasons for not playing bridge,' said Clapperton, his charming smile breaking out. 'I'll show you. We'll play one hand.'

He dealt the cards rapidly. 'Pick up your hands. Well, what about it?' He laughed at the bewildered expression on Kitty's face. He laid down his hand and the others followed suit. Kitty held the entire club suit, M. Poirot the hearts, Pam the diamonds and Colonel Clapperton the spades.

'You see?' he said. 'A man who can deal his partner and his adversaries any hand he pleases had better stand aloof from a friendly game! If the luck goes too much his way, ill-natured things might be said.'

'Oh!' gasped Kitty. 'How *could* you do that? It all looked perfect ordinary.'

'The quickness of the hand deceives the eye,' said Poirot sententiously – and caught the sudden change in the Colonel's expression.

It was as though he realized that he had been off his guard for a moment or two.

Poirot smiled. The conjuror had shown himself through the mask of the pukka sahib.

The ship reached Alexandria at dawn the following morning.

As Poirot came up from breakfast he found the two girls all ready to go on shore. They were talking to Colonel Clapperton.

'We ought to get off now,' urged Kitty. 'The passport people will be going off the ship presently. You'll come with us won't you? You wouldn't let us go ashore all by ourselves? Awful things might happen to us.'

'I certainly don't think you ought to go by yourselves,' said Clapperton, smiling. 'But I'm not sure my wife feels up to it.'

'That's too bad,' said Pam. 'But she can have a nice long rest.'

Colonel Clapperton looked a little irresolute. Evidently the desire to play truant was strong upon him. He noticed Poirot.

'Hullo, M. Poirot – you going ashore?'

'No, I think not,' M. Poirot replied.

'I'll – I'll – just have a word with Adeline,' decided Colonel Clapperton.

'We'll come with you,' said Pam. She flashed a wink at Poirot. 'Perhaps we can persuade her to come too,' she added gravely.

Colonel Clapperton seemed to welcome this suggestion. He looked decidedly relieved.

'Come along then, the pair of you,' he said lightly. They all three went along the passage of B deck together.

Poirot, whose cabin was just opposite the Clappertons', followed them out of curiosity.

Colonel Clapperton rapped a little nervously at the cabin door.

'Adeline, my dear, are you up?'

The sleepy voice of Mrs Clapperton from within replied: 'Oh, bother – what is it?'

'It's John. What about going ashore?'

'Certainly not.' The voice was shrill and decisive. 'I've had a very bad night. I shall stay in bed most of the day.'

Pam nipped in quickly. 'Oh, Mrs Clapperton, I'm so sorry. We did so want you to come with us. Are you sure you're not up to it?'

'I'm quite certain.' Mrs Clapperton's voice sounded even shriller.

The Colonel was turning the door-handle without result.

'What is it, John? The door's locked. I don't want to be disturbed by the stewards.'

'Sorry, my dear, sorry. Just wanted my Baedeker.'

'Well, you can't have it,' snapped Mrs Clapperton. 'I'm not going to get out of bed. Do go away, John, and let me have a little peace.'

'Certainly, certainly, my dear.' The Colonel backed away from the door. Pam and Kitty closed in on him.

'Let's start at once. Thank goodness your hat's on your head. Oh, gracious – your passport isn't in the cabin, is it?'

'As a matter of fact it's in my pocket – ' began the Colonel.

Kitty squeezed his arm. 'Glory be!' she exclaimed. 'Now, come on.'

Leaning over the rail, Poirot watched the three of them leave the ship. He heard a faint intake of breath beside him and turned to see Miss Henderson. Her eyes were fastened on the three retreating figures.

'So they've gone ashore,' she said flatly.

'Yes. Are you going?'

She had a shade hat, he noticed, and a smart bag and shoes. There was a shore-going appearance about her. Nevertheless, after the most infinitesimal of pauses, she shook her head.

'No,' she said. 'I think I'll stay on board. I have a lot of letters to write.'

She turned and left him.

Puffing after his morning tour of forty-eight rounds of the deck, General Forbes took her place. 'Aha!' he exclaimed as his eyes noted the retreating figures of the Colonel and the two girls. 'So *that's* the game! Where's the Madam?'

Poirot explained that Mrs Clapperton was having a quiet day in bed.

'Don't you believe it!' the old warrior closed one knowing eye. 'She'll be up for tiffin – and if the poor devil's found to be absent without leave, there'll be ructions.'

But the General's prognostications were not fulfilled. Mrs Clapperton did not appear at lunch and by the time the Colonel and his attendant damsels returned to the ship at four o'clock, she had not shown herself.

Poirot was in his cabin and heard the husband's slightly guilty knock on his cabin door. Heard the knock repeated, the cabin door tried, and finally heard the Colonel's call to a steward.

'Look here, I can't get an answer. Have you a key?'

Poirot rose quickly from his bunk and came out into the passage.

The news went like wildfire round the ship. With horrified incredulity people heard that Mrs Clapperton had been found dead in her bunk – a native dagger driven through her heart. A string of amber beads was found on the floor of her cabin.

Rumour succeeded rumour. All bead sellers who had been allowed on board that day were being rounded up and questioned! A large sum in cash had disappeared from a drawer in the cabin! The notes had been traced! They had not been traced! Jewellery worth a fortune had been taken! No jewellery had been taken at all! A steward had been arrested and had confessed to the murder!

'What is the truth of it all?' demanded Miss Ellie Henderson waylaying Poirot. Her face was pale and troubled.

'My dear lady, how should I know?'

'Of course you know,' said Miss Henderson.

It was late in the evening. Most people had retired to their cabins. Miss Henderson led Poirot to a couple of deck chairs on the sheltered side of the ship. 'Now tell me,' she commanded.

Poirot surveyed her thoughtfully. 'It's an interesting case,' he said.

'Is it true that she had some very valuable jewellery stolen?'

Poirot shook his head. 'No. No jewellery was taken. A small amount of loose cash that was in a drawer has disappeared, though.'

'I'll never feel safe on a ship again,' said Miss Henderson with a shiver. 'Any clue as to which of those coffee-coloured brutes did it?'

'No,' said Hercule Poirot. 'The whole thing is rather – strange.'

'What do you mean?' asked Ellie sharply.

Poirot spread out his hands. '*Eh bien* – take the facts. Mrs Clapperton had been dead at least five hours when she was found. Some money had disappeared. A string of beads was on the floor by her bed. The door was locked and the key was missing. The window – *window*, not port-hole – gives on the deck and was open.'

'Well?' asked the woman impatiently.

'Do you not think it is curious for a murder to be committed under those particular circumstances? Remember that the postcard sellers, money changers and bead sellers who are allowed on board are all well known to the police.'

'The stewards usually lock your cabin, all the same,' Ellie pointed out.

'Yes, to prevent any chance of petty pilfering. But this – was murder.'

'What exactly are you thinking of, M. Poirot?' Her voice sounded a little breathless.

'I am thinking of the *locked door*.'

Miss Henderson considered this. 'I don't see anything in that. The man left by the door, locked it and took the key with him so as to avoid having the murder discovered too soon. Quite intelligent of him, for it wasn't discovered until four o'clock in the afternoon.'

'No, no, mademoiselle, you don't appreciate the point I'm trying to make. I'm not worried as to how he got *out*, but as to how he got *in*.'

'The window of course.'

'*C'est possible*. But it would be a very narrow fit – and there were people passing up and down the deck all the time, remember.'

'Then through the door,' said Miss Henderson impatiently.

'But you forget, mademoiselle. *Mrs Clapperton had locked the door on the inside*. She had done so before Colonel Clapperton left the boat this morning. He actually tried it – so we *know* that is so.'

'Nonsense. It probably stuck – or he didn't turn the handle properly.'

'But it does not rest on his word. We actually heard *Mrs Clapperton herself say so*.'

'We?'

'Miss Mooney, Miss Cregan, Colonel Clapperton and myself.'

Ellie Henderson tapped a neatly shod foot. She did not speak for a moment or two. Then she said in a slightly irritable tone: 'Well – what exactly do you deduce from that? If Mrs Clapperton could lock the door she could unlock it too, I suppose.'

'Precisely, precisely.' Poirot turned a beaming face upon her. 'And you see where that leaves us. *Mrs Clapperton unlocked the door and let the murderer in.* Now would she be likely to do that for a bead seller?'

Ellie objected: 'She might not have known who it was. He may have knocked – she got up and opened the door – and he forced his way in and killed her.'

Poirot shook his head. '*Au contraire.* She was lying peacefully in bed when she was stabbed.'

Miss Henderson stared at him. 'What's your idea?' she asked abruptly.

Poirot smiled. 'Well, it looks, does it not, as though she *knew* the person she admitted ...'

'You mean,' said Miss Henderson and her voice sounded a little harsh, '*that the murderer is a passenger on the ship*?'

Poirot nodded. 'It seems indicated.'

'And the string of beads left on the floor was a blind?'

'Precisely.'

'The theft of the money also?'

'Exactly.'

There was a pause, then Miss Henderson said slowly: 'I thought Mrs Clapperton a very unpleasant woman and I don't think anyone on board really liked her – but there wasn't anyone who had any reason to kill her.'

'Except her husband, perhaps,' said Poirot.

'You don't really think – ' She stopped.

'It is the opinion of every person on this ship that Colonel Clapperton would have been quite justified in "taking a hatchet to her". That was, I think, the expression used.'

Ellie Henderson looked at him – waiting.

'But I am bound to say,' went on Poirot, 'that I myself have not noted any signs of exasperation on the good Colonel's part. Also what is more important, he had an alibi. He was with those

199

two girls all day and did not return to the ship till four o'clock. By then, Mrs Clapperton had been dead many hours.'

There was another minute of silence. Ellie Henderson said softly: 'But you still think – a passenger on the ship?'

Poirot bowed his head.

Ellie Henderson laughed suddenly – a reckless defiant laugh. 'Your theory may be difficult to prove, M. Poirot. There are a good many passengers on this ship.'

Poirot bowed to her. 'I will use a phrase from one of your detective stories. "I have my methods, Watson." '

The following evening, at dinner, every passenger found a typewritten slip by his plate requesting him to be in the main lounge at 8.30. When the company were assembled, the Captain stepped on to the raised platform where the orchestra usually played and addressed them.

'Ladies and gentlemen, you all know of the tragedy which took place yesterday. I am sure you all wish to co-operate in bringing the perpetrator of that foul crime to justice.' He paused and cleared his throat. 'We have on board with us M. Hercule Poirot who is probably known to you all as a man who has had wide experience in – er – such matters. I hope you will listen carefully to what he has to say.'

It was at this moment that Colonel Clapperton, who had not been at dinner, came in and sat down next to General Forbes. He looked like a man bewildered by sorrow – not at all like a man conscious of great relief. Either he was a very good actor or else he had been genuinely fond of his disagreeable wife.

'M. Hercule Poirot,' said the Captain and stepped down. Poirot took his place. He looked comically self-important as he beamed on his audience.

'*Messieurs, mesdames*,' he began. 'It is most kind of you to be so indulgent as to listen to me. *M. le Capitaine* has told you that I have had a certain experience in these matters. I have, it is true, a little idea of my own about how to get to the bottom of this particular case.' He made a sign and a steward pushed forward and passed on to him a bulky, shapeless object wrapped in a sheet.

'What I am about to do may surprise you a little,' Poirot warned them. 'It may occur to you that I am eccentric, perhaps mad. Nevertheless I assure you that behind my madness there is – as you English say – a method.'

His eyes met those of Miss Henderson for just a minute. He began unwrapping the bulky object.

'I have here, *messieurs* and *mesdames*, an important witness to the truth of who killed Mrs Clapperton.' With a deft hand he whisked away the last enveloping cloth, and the object it concealed was revealed – an almost life-sized wooden doll, dressed in a velvet suit and lace collar.

'Now, Arthur,' said Poirot and his voice changed subtly – it was no longer foreign – it had instead a confident English, a slightly Cockney inflection. 'Can you tell me – I repeat – can you tell me – anything at all about the death of Mrs Clapperton?'

The doll's neck oscillated a little, its wooden lower jaw dropped and wavered and a shrill high-pitched woman's voice spoke:

'*What is it, John? The door's locked. I don't want to be disturbed by the stewards . . .*'

There was a cry – an overturned chair – a man stood swaying, his hand to his throat – trying to speak – trying . . . Then suddenly, his figure seemed to crumple up. He pitched headlong.

It was Colonel Clapperton.

Poirot and the ship's doctor rose from their knees by the prostrate figure.

'All over, I'm afraid. Heart,' said the doctor briefly.

Poirot nodded. 'The shock of having his trick seen through,' he said.

He turned to General Forbes. 'It was you, General, who gave me a valuable hint with your mention of the music hall stage. I puzzle – I think – and then it comes to me. Supposing that before the war Clapperton was a *ventriloquist*. In that case, it would be perfectly possible for three people to hear Mrs Clapperton speak from inside her cabin *when she was already dead* ...'

Ellie Henderson was beside him. Her eyes were dark and full of pain. 'Did you know his heart was weak?' she asked.

'I guessed it ... Mrs Clapperton talked of her own heart being affected, but she struck me as the type of woman who likes to be thought ill. Then I picked up a torn prescription with a very strong dose of digitalin in it. Digitalin is a heart medicine but it couldn't be Mrs Clapperton's because digitalin dilates the pupils of the eyes. I have never noticed such a phenomenon with her – but when I looked at his eyes I saw the signs at once.'

Ellie murmured: 'So you thought – it might end – this way?'

'The best way, don't you think, mademoiselle?' he said gently.

He saw the tears rise in her eyes. She said: 'You've known. You've known all along ... That I cared ... But he didn't do it for *me* ... It was those girls – youth – it made him feel his slavery. He wanted to be free before it was too late ... Yes, I'm sure that's how it was ... When did you guess – that it was he?'

'His self-control was too perfect,' said Poirot simply. 'No matter how galling his wife's conduct, it never seemed to touch him. That meant either that he was so used to it that it no longer stung him, or else – *eh bien* – I decided on the latter alternative ... And I was right ...

'And then there was his insistence on his conjuring ability – the evening before the crime he pretended to give himself away. But a man like Clapperton doesn't give himself away. There must be a reason. So long as people thought he had been a *conjuror* they weren't likely to think of his having been a *ventriloquist*.'

'And the voice we heard – Mrs Clapperton's voice?'

'One of the stewardesses had a voice not unlike hers. I induced her to hide behind the stage and taught her the words to say.'

'It was a trick – a cruel trick,' cried out Ellie.

'I do not approve of murder,' said Hercule Poirot.

THE THIRD-FLOOR FLAT

'Bother!' said Pat.

With a deepening frown she rummaged wildly in the silken trifle she called an evening bag. Two young men and another girl watched her anxiously. They were all standing outside the closed door of Patricia Garnett's flat.

'It's no good,' said Pat. 'It's not there. And now what shall we do?'

'What is life without a latchkey?' murmured Jimmy Faulkener.

He was a short, broad-shouldered young man, with good-tempered blue eyes.

Pat turned on him angrily. 'Don't make jokes, Jimmy. This is serious.'

'Look again, Pat,' said Donovan Bailey. 'It must be there somewhere.'

He had a lazy, pleasant voice that matched his lean, dark figure.

'If you ever brought it out,' said the other girl, Mildred Hope.

'Of course I brought it out,' said Pat. 'I believe I gave it to one of you two.' She turned on the men accusingly. 'I told Donovan to take it for me.'

But she was not to find a scapegoat so easily. Donovan put in a firm disclaimer, and Jimmy backed him up.

'I saw you put it in your bag, myself,' said Jimmy.

'Well, then, one of you dropped it out when you picked up my bag. I've dropped it once or twice.'

'Once or twice!' said Donovan. 'You've dropped it a dozen times at least, besides leaving it behind on every possible occasion.'

'I can't see why everything on earth doesn't drop out of it the whole time,' said Jimmy.

'The point is – how are we going to get in?' said Mildred.

She was a sensible girl, who kept to the point, but she was not nearly so attractive as the impulsive and troublesome Pat.

All four of them regarded the closed door blankly.

'Couldn't the porter help?' suggested Jimmy. 'Hasn't he got a master key or something of that kind?'

Pat shook her head. There were only two keys. One was inside the flat hung up in the kitchen and the other was – or should be – in the maligned bag.

'If only the flat were on the ground floor,' wailed Pat. 'We could have broken open a window or something. Donovan, you wouldn't like to be a cat burglar, would you?'

Donovan declined firmly but politely to be a cat burglar.

'A flat on the fourth floor is a bit of an undertaking,' said Jimmy.

'How about a fire-escape?' suggested Donovan.

'There isn't one.'

'There should be,' said Jimmy. 'A building five storeys high ought to have a fire escape.'

'I dare say,' said Pat. 'But what should be doesn't help us. How am I ever to get into my flat?'

'Isn't there a sort of thingummybob?' said Donovan. 'A thing the tradesmen send up chops and brussels sprouts in?'

'The service lift,' said Pat. 'Oh yes, but it's only a sort of wire-basket thing. Oh wait – I know. What about the coal lift?'

'Now that,' said Donovan, 'is an idea.'

Mildred made a discouraging suggestion. 'It'll be bolted,' she said. 'In Pat's kitchen, I mean, on the inside.'

But the idea was instantly negatived.

'Don't you believe it,' said Donovan.

'Not in *Pat's* kitchen,' said Jimmy. 'Pat never locks and bolts things.'

'I don't think it's bolted,' said Pat. 'I took the dustbin off this morning, and I'm sure I never bolted it afterwards, and I don't think I've been near it since.'

'Well,' said Donovan, 'that fact's going to be very useful to us tonight, but, all the same, young Pat, let me point out to you

204

that these slack habits are leaving you at the mercy of burglars
– non-feline – every night.'

Pat disregarded these admonitions.

'Come on,' she cried, and began racing down the four flights
of stairs. The others followed her. Pat led them through a dark
recess, apparently full to overflowing of perambulators, and
through another door into the well of the flats, and guided them
to the right lift. There was, at the moment, a dustbin on it.
Donovan lifted it off and stepped gingerly on to the platform in
its place. He wrinkled up his nose.

'A little noisome,' he remarked. 'But what of that? Do I go
alone on this venture or is anyone coming with me?'

'I'll come, too,' said Jimmy.

He stepped on by Donovan's side.

'I suppose the lift will bear me,' he added doubtfully.

'You can't weigh much more than a ton of coal,' said Pat,
who had never been particularly strong on her weights-and-
measures table.

'And, anyway, we shall soon find out,' said Donovan
cheerfully, as he hauled on the rope.

With a grinding noise they disappeared from sight.

'This thing makes an awful noise,' remarked Jimmy, as they
passed up through blackness. 'What will the people in the other
flats think?'

'Ghosts or burglars, I expect,' said Donovan. 'Hauling this
rope is quite heavy work. The porter of Friars Mansions does
more work than I ever suspected. I say, Jimmy, old son, are you
counting the floors?'

'Oh, Lord! No. I forgot about it.'

'Well, I have, which is just as well. That's the third we're
passing now. The next is ours.'

'And now, I suppose,' grumbled Jimmy, 'we shall find that
Pat did bolt the door after all.'

But these fears were unfounded. The wooden door swung
back at a touch, and Donovan and Jimmy stepped out into the
inky blacknesss of Pat's kitchen.

'We ought to have a torch for this wild night work,'
exclaimed Donovan. 'If I know Pat, everything's on the floor,

and we shall smash endless crockery before I can get to the light switch. Don't move about, Jimmy, till I get the light on.'

He felt his way cautiously over the floor, uttering one fervent 'Damn!' as a corner of the kitchen table took him unawares in the ribs. He reached the switch, and in another moment another 'Damn!' floated out of the darkness.

'What's the matter?' asked Jimmy.

'Light won't come on. Dud bulb, I suppose. Wait a minute. I'll turn the sitting-room light on.'

The sitting-room was the door immediately across the passage. Jimmy heard Donovan go out of the door, and presently fresh muffled curses reached him. He himself edged his way cautiously across the kitchen.

'What's the matter?'

'I don't know. Rooms get bewitched at night, I believe. Everything seems to be in a different place. Chairs and tables where you least expected them. Oh, hell! Here's another!'

But at this moment Jimmy fortunately connected with the electric-light switch and pressed it down. In another minute two young men were looking at each other in silent horror.

This room was not Pat's sitting-room. They were in the wrong flat.

To begin with, the room was about ten times more crowded than Pat's, which explained Donovan's pathetic bewilderment at repeatedly cannoning into chairs and tables. There was a large round table in the centre of the room covered with a baize cloth, and there was an aspidistra in the window. It was, in fact, the kind of room whose owner, the young men felt sure, would be difficult to explain to. With silent horror they gazed down at the table, on which lay a little pile of letters.

'Mrs Ernestine Grant,' breathed Donovan, picking them up and reading the name. 'Oh, help! Do you think she's heard us?'

'It's a miracle she hasn't heard you,' said Jimmy. 'What with your language and the way you've been crashing into the furniture. Come on, for the Lord's sake, let's get out of here quickly.'

They hastily switched off the light and retraced their steps on tiptoe to the lift. Jimmy breathed a sigh of relief as they regained the fastness of its depths without further incident.

'I do like a woman to be a good, sound sleeper,' he said approvingly. 'Mrs Ernestine Grant has her points.'

'I see it now,' said Donovan; 'why we made the mistake in the floor, I mean. Out in that well we started up from the basement.'

He heaved on the rope, and the lift shot up. 'We're right this time.'

'I devoutly trust we are,' said Jimmy as he stepped out into another inky void. 'My nerves won't stand many more shocks of this kind.'

But no further nerve strain was imposed. The first click of the light showed them Pat's kitchen, and in another minute they were opening the front door and admitting the two girls who were waiting outside.

'You have been a long time,' grumbled Pat. 'Mildred and I have been waiting here ages.'

'We've had an adventure,' said Donovan. 'We might have been hauled off to the police-station as dangerous malefactors.'

Pat had passed on into the sitting-room, where she switched on the light and dropped her wrap on the sofa. She listened with lively interest to Donovan's account of his adventures.

'I'm glad she didn't catch you,' she commented. 'I'm sure she's an old curmudgeon. I got a note from her this morning – wanted to see me some time – something she had to complain about – my piano, I suppose. People who don't like pianos over their heads shouldn't come and live in flats. I say, Donovan, you've hurt your hand. It's all over blood. Go and wash it under the tap.'

Donovan looked down at his hand in surprise. He went out of the room obediently and presently his voice called to Jimmy.

'Hullo,' said the other, 'what's up? You haven't hurt yourself badly, have you?'

'I haven't hurt myself at all.'

There was something so queer in Donovan's voice that Jimmy stared at him in surprise. Donovan held out his washed hand and Jimmy saw that there was no mark or cut of any kind on it.

'That's odd,' he said, frowning. 'There was quite a lot of blood. Where did it come from?' And then suddenly he realized what his quicker-witted friend had already seen. 'By Jove,' he said. 'It must have come from that flat.' He stopped, thinking over the possibilities his word implied. 'You're sure it was – er – blood?' he said. 'Not paint?'

Donovan shook his head. 'It was blood, all right,' he said, and shivered.

They looked at each other. The same thought was clearly in each of their minds. It was Jimmy who voiced it first.

'I say,' he said awkwardly. 'Do you think we ought to – well – go down again – and have – a – look around? See it's all right, you know?'

'What about the girls?'

'We won't say anything to them. Pat's going to put on an apron and make us an omelette. We'll be back by the time they wonder where we are.'

'Oh, well, come on,' said Donovan. 'I suppose we've got to go through with it. I dare say there isn't anything really wrong.'

But his tone lacked conviction. They got into the lift and descended to the floor below. They found their way across the kitchen without much difficulty and once more switched on the sitting-room light.

'It must have been in here,' said Donovan, 'that – that I got the stuff on me. I never touched anything in the kitchen.'

He looked round him. Jimmy did the same, and they both frowned. Everything looked neat and commonplace and miles removed from any suggestion of violence or gore.

Suddenly Jimmy started violently and caught his companion's arm.

'Look!'

Donovan followed the pointing finger, and in his turn uttered an exclamation. From beneath the heavy rep curtains there protruded a foot – a woman's foot in a gaping patent leather shoe.

Jimmy went to the curtains and drew them sharply apart. In

the recess of the window a woman's huddled body lay on the floor, a sticky dark pool beside it. She was dead, there was no doubt of that. Jimmy was attempting to raise her up when Donovan stopped him.

'You'd better not do that. She oughtn't to be touched till the police come.'

'The police. Oh, of course. I say, Donovan, what a ghastly business. Who do you think she is? Mrs Ernestine Grant?'

'Looks like it. At any rate, if there's anyone else in the flat they're keeping jolly quiet.'

'What do we do next?' asked Jimmy. 'Run out and get a policeman or ring up from Pat's flat?'

'I should think ringing up would be best. Come on, we might as well go out the front door. We can't spend the whole night going up and down in that evil-smelling lift.'

Jimmy agreed. Just as they were passing through the door he hesitated. 'Look here; do you think one of us ought to stay – just to keep an eye on things – till the police come?'

'Yes, I think you're right. If you'll stay I'll run up and telephone.'

He ran quickly up the stairs and rang the bell of the flat above. Pat came to open it, a very pretty Pat with a flushed face and a cooking apron on. Her eyes widened in surprise.

'You? But how – Donovan, what is it? Is anything the matter?'

He took both her hands in his. 'It's all right, Pat – only we've made a rather unpleasant discovery in the flat below. A woman – dead.'

'Oh!' She gave a little gasp. 'How horrible. Has she had a fit or something?'

'No. It looks – well – it looks rather as though she had been murdered.'

'Oh, Donovan!'

'I know. It's pretty beastly.'

Her hands were still in his. She had left them there – was even clinging to him. Darling Pat – how he loved her. Did she care at all for him? Sometimes he thought she did. Sometimes

209

he was afraid that Jimmy Faulkener – remembrances of Jimmy waiting patiently below made him start guiltily.

'Pat, dear, we must telephone to the police.'

'Monsieur is right,' said a voice behind him. 'And in the meantime, while we are waiting their arrival, perhaps I can be of some slight assistance.'

They had been standing in the doorway of the flat, and now they peered out on the landing. A figure was standing on the stairs a little way above them. It moved down and into their range of vision.

They stood staring at the little man with a very fierce moustache and an egg-shaped head. He wore a resplendent dressing-gown and embroidered slippers. He bowed gallantly to Patricia.

'Mademoiselle!' he said. 'I am, as perhaps you know, the tenant of the flat above. I like to be up high – in the air – the view over London. I take the flat in the name of Mr O'Connor. But I am not an Irishman. I have another name. That is why I venture to put myself at your service. Permit me.' With a flourish he pulled out a card and handed it to Pat. She read it.

'M. Hercule Poirot. Oh!' She caught her breath. '*The* M. Poirot! The great detective? And you will really help?'

'That is my intention, mademoiselle. I nearly offered my help earlier in the evening.'

Pat looked puzzled.

'I heard you discussing how to gain admission to your flat. Me, I am very clever at picking locks. I could, without doubt, have opened your door for you, but I hesitated to suggest it. You would have had the grave suspicions of me.'

Pat laughed.

'Now, monsieur,' said Poirot to Donovan. 'Go in, I pray of you, and telephone to the police. I will descend to the flat below.'

Pat came down the stairs with him. They found Jimmy on guard, and Pat explained Poirot's presence. Jimmy, in his turn, explained to Poirot his and Donovan's adventures. The detective listened attentively.

210

'The lift door was unbolted, you say? You emerged into the kitchen, but the light it would not turn on.'

He directed his footsteps to the kitchen as he spoke. His fingers pressed the switch.

'*Tiens! Voilà ce qui est curieux!*' he said as the light flashed on. 'It functions perfectly now. I wonder – ' He held up a finger to ensure silence and listened. A faint sound broke the stillness – the sound of an unmistakable snore. 'Ah!' said Poirot. '*La chambre de domestique.*'

He tiptoed across the kitchen into a little pantry, out of which led a door. He opened the door and switched on the light. The room was the kind of dog kennel designed by the builders of flats to accommodate a human being. The floor space was almost entirely occupied by the bed. In the bed was a rosy-cheeked girl lying on her back with her mouth wide open, snoring placidly.

Poirot switched off the light and beat a retreat.

'She will not wake,' he said. 'We will let her sleep till the police come.'

He went back to the sitting-room. Donovan had joined them.

'The police will be here almost immediately, they say,' he said breathlessly. 'We are to touch nothing.'

Poirot nodded. 'We will not touch,' he said. 'We will look, that is all.'

He moved into the room. Mildred had come down with Donovan, and all four young people stood in the doorway and watched him with breathless interest.

'What I can't understand, sir, is this,' said Donovan. 'I never went near the window – how did the blood come on my hand?'

'My young friend, the answer to that stares you in the face. Of what colour is the tablecloth? Red, is it not? and doubtless you did put your hand on the table.'

'Yes, I did. Is that – ? He stopped.

Poirot nodded. He was bending over the table. He indicated with his hand a dark patch on the red.

'It was here that the crime was committed,' he said solemnly. 'The body was moved afterwards.'

Then he stood upright and looked slowly round the room. He did not move, he handled nothing, but nevertheless the four watching felt as though every object in that rather frowsty place gave up its secret to his observant eye.

Hercule Poirot nodded his head as though satisfied. A little sigh escaped him. 'I see,' he said.

'You see what?' asked Donovan curiously.

'I see,' said Poirot, 'what you doubtless felt – that the room is overfull of furniture.'

Donovan smiled ruefully. 'I did go barging about a bit,' he confessed. 'Of course, everything was in a different place to Pat's room, and I couldn't make it out.'

'Not everything,' said Poirot.

Donovan looked at him inquiringly.

'I mean,' said Poirot apologetically, 'that certain things are always fixed. In a block of flats the door, the window, the fireplace – they are in the same place in the rooms which are below each other.'

'Isn't that rather splitting hairs?' asked Mildred. She was looking at Poirot with faint disapproval.

'One should always speak with absolute accuracy. That is a little – how do you say? – fad of mine.'

There was the noise of footsteps on the stairs, and three men came in. They were a police inspector, a constable, and the divisional surgeon. The inspector recognized Poirot and greeted him in an almost reverential manner. Then he turned to the others.

'I shall want statements from everyone,' he began, 'but in the first place – '

Poirot interrupted. 'A little suggestion. We will go back to the flat upstairs and mademoiselle here shall do what she was planning to do – make us an omelette. Me, I have a passion for the omelettes. Then, *M. l'Inspecteur*, when you have finished here, you will mount to us and ask questions at your leisure.'

It was arranged accordingly, and Poirot went up with them.

'M. Poirot,' said Pat, 'I think you're a perfect dear. And you shall have a lovely omelette. I really make omelettes frightfully well.'

'That is good. Once, mademoiselle, I loved a beautiful young English girl, who resembled you greatly – but alas! – she could not cook. So perhaps everything was for the best.'

There was a faint sadness in his voice, and Jimmy Faulkener looked at him curiously.

Once in the flat, however, he exerted himself to please and amuse. The grim tragedy below was almost forgotten.

The omelette had been consumed and duly praised by the time that Inspector Rice's footsteps were heard. He came in accompanied by the doctor, having left the constable below.

'Well, Monsieur Poirot,' he said. 'It all seems clear and above-board – not much in your line, though we may find it hard to catch the man. I'd just like to hear how the discovery came to be made.'

Donovan and Jimmy between them recounted the happenings of the evening. The inspector turned reproachfully to Pat.

'You shouldn't leave your lift door unbolted, miss. You really shouldn't.'

'I shan't again,' said Pat, with a shiver. 'Somebody might come in and murder me like that poor woman below.'

'Ah, but they didn't come in that way, though,' said the inspector.

'You will recount to us what you have discovered, yes?' said Poirot.

'I don't know as I ought to – but seeing it's you, M. Poirot –'

'*Précisément*,' said Poirot. 'And these young people – they will be discreet.'

'The newspapers will get hold of it, anyway, soon enough,' said the inspector. 'There's no real secret about the matter. Well, the dead woman's Mrs Grant, all right. I had the porter up to identify her. Woman of about thirty-five. She was sitting at the table, and she was shot with an automatic pistol of small calibre, probably by someone sitting opposite her at table. She fell forward, and that's how the bloodstain came on the table.'

'But wouldn't someone have heard the shot?' asked Mildred.

'The pistol was fitted with a silencer. No, you wouldn't hear anything. By the way, did you hear the screech the maid let out when we told her her mistress was dead? No. Well, that just shows how unlikely it was that anyone would hear the other.'

'Has the maid no story to tell?' asked Poirot.

'It was her evening out. She's got her own key. She came in about ten o'clock. Everything was quiet. She thought her mistress had gone to bed.'

'She did not look in the sitting-room, then?'

'Yes, she took the letters in there which had come by the evening post, but she saw nothing unusual – any more than Mr Faulkener and Mr Bailey did. You see, the murderer had concealed the body rather neatly behind the curtains.'

'But it was a curious thing to do, don't you think?'

Poirot's voice was very gentle, yet it held something that made the inspector look up quickly.

'Didn't want the crime discovered till he'd had time to make his getaway.'

'Perhaps, perhaps – but continue with what you were saying.'

'The maid went out at five o'clock. The doctor here puts the time of death as – roughly – about four to five hours ago. That's right, isn't it?'

The doctor, who was a man of few words, contented himself with jerking his head affirmatively.

'It's a quarter to twelve now. The actual time can, I think, be narrowed down to a fairly definite hour.'

He took out a crumpled sheet of paper.

'We found this in the pocket of the dead woman's dress. You needn't be afraid of handling it. There are no fingerprints on it.'

Poirot smoothed out the sheet. Across it some words were printed in small, prim capitals.

I WILL COME TO SEE YOU THIS EVENING AT HALF PAST SEVEN.

J.F.

'A compromising document to leave behind,' commented Poirot, as he handed it back.

'Well, he didn't know she'd got it in her pocket,' said the inspector. 'He probably thought she'd destroyed it. We've evidence that he was a careful man, though. The pistol she was shot with we found under the body – and there again no fingerprints. They'd been wiped off very carefully with a silk handkerchief.'

'How do you know,' said Poirot, 'that it was a silk handkerchief?'

'Because we found it,' said the inspector triumphantly. 'At the last, as he was drawing the curtains, he must have let it fall unnoticed.'

He handed across a big white silk handkerchief – a good-quality handkerchief. It did not need the inspector's finger to draw Poirot's attention to the mark on it in the centre. It was neatly marked and quite legible. Poirot read the name out.

'John Fraser.'

'That's it,' said the inspector. 'John Fraser – J.F. in the note. We know the name of the man we have to look for, and I dare say when we find out a little about the dead woman, and her relations come forward, we shall soon get a line on him.'

'I wonder,' said Poirot. 'No, *mon cher*, somehow I do not think he will be easy to find, your John Fraser. He is a strange man – careful, since he marks his handkerchiefs and wipes the pistol with which he has committed the crime – yet careless since he loses his handkerchief and does not search for a letter that might incriminate him.'

'Flurried, that's what he was,' said the inspector.

'It is possible,' said Poirot. 'Yes, it is possible. And he was not seen entering the building?'

'There are all sorts of people going in and out all the time. These are big blocks. I suppose none of you – ' he addressed the four collectively – 'saw anyone coming out of the flat?'

Pat shook her head. 'We went out earlier – about seven o'clock.'

'I see.' The inspector rose. Poirot accompanied him to the door.

'As a little favour, may I examine the flat below?'

'Why, certainly, M. Poirot. I know what they think of you at

215

headquarters. I'll leave you a key. I've got two. It will be empty. The maid cleared out to some relatives, too scared to stay there alone.'

'I thank you,' said M. Poirot. He went back into the flat, thoughtful.

'You're not satisfied, M. Poirot?' said Jimmy.

'No,' said Poirot. 'I am not satisfied.'

Donovan looked at him curiously. 'What is it that – well, worries you?'

Poirot did not answer. He remained silent for a minute or two, frowning, as though in thought, then he made a sudden impatient movement of the shoulders.

'I will say good night to you, mademoiselle. You must be tired. You have had much cooking to do – eh?'

Pat laughed. 'Only the omelette. I didn't do dinner. Donovan and Jimmy came and called for us, and we went out to a little place in Soho.'

'And then without doubt, you went to a theatre?'

'Yes. *The Brown Eyes of Caroline*.'

'Ah!' said Poirot. 'It should have been blue eyes – the blue eyes of mademoiselle.'

He made a sentimental gesture, and then once more wished Pat good night, also Mildred, who was staying the night by special request, as Pat admitted frankly that she would get the horrors if left alone on this particular night.

The two young men accompanied Poirot. When the door was shut, and they were preparing to say goodbye to him on the landing, Poirot forestalled them.

'My young friends, you heard me say I was not satisfied? *Eh bien*, it is true – I am not. I go now to make some little investigations of my own. You would like to accompany me – yes?'

An eager assent greeted this proposal. Poirot led the way to the flat below and inserted the key the inspector had given him in the lock. On entering, he did not, as the others had expected, enter the sitting-room. Instead he went straight to the kitchen. In a little recess which served as a scullery a big iron bin was standing. Poirot uncovered this and, doubling himself up, began to rootle in it with the energy of a ferocious terrier.

Both Jimmy and Donovan stared at him in amazement.

Suddenly with a cry of triumph he emerged. In his hand he held aloft a small stoppered bottle.

'*Voilà*!' he said. 'I find what I seek.' He sniffed at it delicately. 'Alas! I am *enrhumé* – I have the cold in the head.'

Donovan took the bottle from him and sniffed in his turn, but could smell nothing. He took out the stopper and held the bottle to his nose before Poirot's warning cry could stop him.

Immediately he fell like a log. Poirot, by springing forward, partly broke his fall.

'Imbecile!' he cried. 'The idea. To remove the stopper in that foolhardy manner! Did he not observe how delicately I handled it? Monsieur – Faulkener – is it not? Will you be so good as to get me a little brandy? I observed a decanter in the sitting-room.'

Jimmy hurried off, but by the time he returned, Donovan was sitting up and declaring himself quite all right again. He had to listen to a short lecture from Poirot on the necessity of caution in sniffing at possibly poisonous substances.

'I think I'll be off home,' said Donovan, rising shakily to his feet. 'That is, if I can't be any more use here. I feel a bit wonky still.'

'Assuredly,' said Poirot. 'That is the best thing you can do. M. Faulkener, attend me here a little minute. I will return on the instant.'

He accompanied Donovan to the door and beyond. They remained outside on the landing talking for some minutes. When Poirot at last re-entered the flat he found Jimmy standing in the sitting-room gazing round him with puzzled eyes.

'Well, M. Poirot,' he said, 'what next?'

'There is nothing next. The case is finished.'

'What?'

'I know everything – now.'

Jimmy stared at him. 'That little bottle you found?'

'Exactly. That little bottle.'

Jimmy shook his head. 'I can't make head or tail of it. For some reason or other I can see you are dissatisfied with the evidence against this John Fraser, whoever he may be.'

'Whoever he may be,' repeated Poirot softly. 'If he is anyone at all – well, I shall be surprised.'

'I don't understand.'

'He is a name – that is all – a name carefully marked on a handkerchief!'

'And the letter?'

'Did you notice that it was printed? Now, why? I will tell you. Handwriting might be recognized, and a typewritten letter is more easily traced than you would imagine – but if a real John Fraser wrote that letter those two points would not have appealed to him! No, it was written on purpose, and put in the dead woman's pocket for us to find. There is no such person as John Fraser.'

Jimmy looked at him inquiringly.

'And so,' went on Poirot, 'I went back to the point that first struck me. You heard me say that certain things in a room were always in the same place under given circumstances. I gave three instances. I might have mentioned a fourth – the electric-light switch, my friend.'

Jimmy still stared uncomprehendingly. Poirot went on.

'Your friend Donovan did not go near the window – it was by resting his hand on this table that he got it covered in blood! But I asked myself at once – why did he rest it there? What was he doing groping about this room in darkness? For remember, my friend, the electric-light switch is always in the same place – by the door. Why, when he came to this room, did he not at once feel for the light and turn it on? That was the natural, the normal thing to do. According to him, he tried to turn on the light in the kitchen, but failed. Yet when I tried the switch it was in perfect working order. Did he, then, not wish the light to go on just then? If it had gone on you would both have seen at once that you were in the wrong flat. There would have been no reason to come into this room.'

'What are you driving at, M. Poirot? I don't understand. What do you mean?'

'I mean – this.'

Poirot held up a Yale door key.

'The key of this flat?'

'No, *mon ami*, the key of the flat above. Mademoiselle Patricia's key, which M. Donovan Bailey abstracted from her bag some time during the evening.'

'But why – why?'

'*Parbleu*! So that he could do what he wanted to do – gain admission to this flat in a perfectly unsuspicious manner. He made sure that the lift door was unbolted earlier in the evening.'

'Where did you get the key?'

Poirot's smile broadened. 'I found it just now – where I looked for it – in M. Donovan's pocket. See you, that little bottle I pretended to find was a ruse. M. Donovan is taken in. He does what I knew he would do – unstoppers it and sniffs. And in that little bottle is ethyl chloride, a very powerful instant anaesthetic. It gives me just the moment or two of unconsciousness I need. I take from his pocket the two things that I knew would be there. This key was one of them – the other – '

He stopped and then went on.

'I questioned at the time the reason the inspector gave for the body being concealed behind the curtain. To gain time? No, there was more than that. And so I thought of just one thing – the post, my friend. The evening post that comes at half past nine or thereabouts. Say the murderer does not find something he expects to find, but that something may be delivered by post later. Clearly, then, he must come back. But the crime must not be discovered by the maid when she comes in, or the police would take possession of the flat, so he hides the body behind the curtain. And the maid suspects nothing and lays the letters on the table as usual.'

'The letters?'

'Yes, the letters.' Poirot drew something from his pocket. 'This is the second article I took from M. Donovan when he was unconscious.' He showed the superscription – a typewritten envelope addressed to Mrs Ernestine Grant. 'But I will ask you one thing first. M. Faulkener, before we look at the

219

contents of this letter. Are you or are you not in love with Mademoiselle Patricia?'

'I care for Pat damnably – but I've never thought I had a chance.'

'You thought that she cared for M. Donovan? It may be that she had begun to care for him – but it was only a beginning, my friend. It is for you to make her forget – to stand by her in her trouble.'

'Trouble?' said Jimmy sharply.

'Yes, trouble. We will do all we can to keep her name out of it, but it will be impossible to do so entirely. She was, you see, the motive.'

He ripped open the envelope that he held. An enclosure fell out. The covering letter was brief, and was from a firm of solicitors.

Dear Madam,
   The document you enclose is quite in order, and the fact of the marriage having taken place in a foreign country does not invalidate it in any way.

Yours truly, etc.

Poirot spread out the enclosure. It was a certificate of marriage between Donovan Bailey and Ernestine Grant, dated eight years ago.

'Oh, my God!' said Jimmy. 'Pat said she'd had a letter from the woman asking to see her, but she never dreamed it was anything important.'

Poirot nodded. 'Donovan knew – he went to see his wife this evening before going to the flat above – a strange irony, by the way, that led the unfortunate woman to come to this building where her rival lived – he murdered her in cold blood, and then went on to his evening's amusement. His wife must have told him that she had sent the marriage certificate to her solicitors and was expecting to hear from them. Doubtless he himself had tried to make her believe that there was a flaw in the marriage.'

'He seemed in quite good·spirits, too, all the evening. M. Poirot, you haven't let him escape?' Jimmy shuddered.

'There is no escape for him,' said Poirot gravely. 'You need not fear.'

'It's Pat I'm thinking about mostly,' said Jimmy. 'You don't think – she really cared.'

'*Mon ami*, that is your part,' said Poirot gently. 'To make her turn to you and forget. I do not think you will find it very difficult!'

THE ADVENTURE OF JOHNNIE WAVERLY

'You can understand the feelings of a mother,' said Mrs Waverly for perhaps the sixth time.

She looked appealingly at Poirot. My little friend, always sympathetic to motherhood in distress, gesticulated reassuringly.

'But yes, but yes, I comprehend perfectly. Have faith in Papa Poirot.'

'The police –' began Mr Waverly.

His wife waved the interruption aside. 'I won't have anything more to do with the police. We trusted to them and look what happened! But I'd heard so much of M. Poirot and the wonderful things he'd done, that I felt he might possibly be able to help us. A mother's feelings –'

Poirot hastily stemmed the reiteration with an eloquent gesture. Mrs Waverly's emotion was obviously genuine, but it assorted strangely with her shrewd, rather hard type of countenance. When I heard later that she was the daughter of a prominent steel manufacturer who had worked his way up in the world from an office boy to his present eminence, I realized that she had inherited many of the paternal qualities.

Mr Waverly was a big, florid, jovial-looking man. He stood with his legs straddled wide apart and looked the type of the country squire.

'I suppose you know all about this business, M. Poirot?'

The question was almost superfluous. For some days past the papers had been full of the sensational kidnapping of little Johnnie Waverly, the three-year-old son and heir of Marcus Waverly, Esq., of Waverly Court, Surrey, one of the oldest families in England.

'The main facts I know, of course, but recount to me the whole story, monsieur, I beg of you. And in detail if you please.'

'Well, I suppose the beginning of the whole thing was about ten days ago when I got an anonymous letter – beastly things, anyway – that I couldn't make head or tail of. The writer had the impudence to demand that I should pay him twenty-five thousand pounds – twenty-five thousand pounds, M. Poirot! Failing my agreement, he threatened to kidnap Johnnie. Of course I threw the thing into the wastepaper basket without more ado. Thought it was some silly joke. Five days later I got another letter. "Unless you pay, your son will be kidnapped on the twenty-ninth." That was on the twenty-seventh. Ada was worried, but I couldn't bring myself to treat the matter seriously. Damn it all, we're in England. Nobody goes about kidnapping children and holding them up to ransom.'

'It is not a common practice, certainly,' said Poirot. 'Proceed, monsieur.'

'Well, Ada gave me no peace, so – feeling a bit of a fool – I laid the matter before Scotland Yard. They didn't seem to take the thing very seriously – inclined to my view that it was some silly joke. On the twenty-eighth I got a third letter. "You have not paid. Your son will be taken from you at twelve o'clock noon tomorrow, the twenty-ninth. It will cost you fifty thousand pounds to recover him." Up I drove to Scotland Yard again. This time they were more impressed. They inclined to the view that the letters were written by a lunatic, and that in all probability an attempt of some kind would be made at the hour stated. They assured me that they would take all due precautions. Inspector NcNeil and a sufficient force would come down to Waverly on the morrow and take charge.

'I went home much relieved in mind. Yet we already had the feeling of being in a state of siege. I gave orders that no stranger was to be admitted, and that no one was to leave the house. The evening passed off without any untoward incident, but on the following morning my wife was seriously unwell. Alarmed by her condition, I sent for Doctor Dakers. Her symptoms appeared to puzzle him. While hesitating to suggest that she had been poisoned, I could see that that was what was in his mind. There was no danger, he assured me, but it would be a day or two before she would be able to get about again.

223

Returning to my own room, I was startled and amazed to find a note pinned to my pillow. It was in the same handwriting as the others and contained just three words: "At twelve o'clock".

'I admit, M. Poirot, that then I saw red! Someone in the house was in this – one of the servants. I had them all up, blackguarded them right and left. They never split on each other; it was Miss Collins, my wife's companion, who informed me that she had seen Johnnie's nurse slip down the drive early that morning. I taxed her with it, and she broke down. She had left the child with the nursery maid and stolen out to meet a friend of hers – a man! Pretty goings on! She denied having pinned the note to my pillow – she may have been speaking the truth, I don't know. I felt I couldn't take the risk of the child's own nurse being in the plot. One of the servants was implicated – of that I was sure. Finally I lost my temper and sacked the whole bunch, nurse and all. I gave them an hour to pack their boxes and get out of the house.'

Mr Waverly's face was quite two shades redder as he remembered his just wrath.

'Was not that a little injudicious, monsieur?' suggested Poirot. 'For all you know, you might have been playing into the enemy's hands.'

Mr Waverly stared at him. 'I don't see that. Send the whole lot packing, that was my idea. I wired to London for a fresh lot to be sent down that evening. In the meantime, there'd be only people I could trust in the house: my wife's secretary, Miss Collins, and Tredwell, the butler, who has been with me since I was a boy.'

'And this Miss Collins, how long has she been with you?'

'Just a year,' said Mrs Waverly. 'She has been invaluable to me as a secretary-companion, and is also a very efficient housekeeper.'

'The nurse?'

'She has been with me six months. She came to me with excellent references. All the same, I never really liked her, although Johnnie was quite devoted to her.'

'Still, I gather she had already left when the catastrophe

occurred. Perhaps, Monsieur Waverly, you will be so kind as to continue.'

Mr Waverly resumed his narrative.

'Inspector McNeil arrived about ten-thirty. The servants had all left by then. He declared himself quite satisfied with the internal arrangements. He had various men posted in the park outside, guarding all the approaches to the house, and he assured me that if the whole thing were not a hoax, we should undoubtedly catch my mysterious correspondent.

'I had Johnnie with me, and he and I and the inspector went together into the room we call the council chamber. The inspector locked the door. There is a big grandfather clock there, and as the hands drew near to twelve I don't mind confessing that I was as nervous as a cat. There was a whirring sound, and the clock began to strike. I clutched at Johnnie. I had a feeling a man might drop from the skies. The last stroke sounded, and as it did so, there was a great commotion outside – shouting and running. The inspector flung up the window, and a constable came running up.

'"We've got him sir," he panted. "He was sneaking up through the bushes. He's got a whole dope outfit on him."

'We hurried out on the terrace where two constables were holding a ruffianly-looking fellow in shabby clothes, who was twisting and turning in a vain endeavour to escape. One of the policemen held out an unrolled parcel which they had wrested from their captive. It contained a pad of cotton wool and a bottle of chloroform. It made my blood boil to see it. There was a note, too, addressed to me. I tore it open. It bore the following words: "You should have paid up. To ransom your son will now cost you fifty thousand. In spite of all your precautions he has been abducted on the twenty-ninth as I said."

'I gave a great laugh, the laugh of relief, but as I did so I heard the hum of a motor and a shout. I turned my head. Racing down the drive towards the south lodge at a furious speed was a low, long grey car. It was the man who drove it who shouted, but that was not what gave me a shock of horror. It was the sight of Johnnie's flaxen curls. The child was in the car beside him.

'The inspector ripped out an oath. "The child was here not a minute ago," he cried. His eyes swept over us. We were all there: myself, Tredwell, Miss Collins. "When did you last see him, Mr Waverly?"

'I cast my mind back, trying to remember. When the constable had called us, I had run out with the inspector, forgetting all about Johnnie.

'And then there came a sound that startled us, the chiming of a church clock from the village. With an exclamation the inspector pulled out his watch. It was exactly twelve o'clock. With one common accord we ran to the council chamber; the clock there marked the hour as ten minutes past. Someone must have deliberately tampered with it, for I have never known it gain or lose before. It is a perfect timekeeper.'

Mr Waverly paused. Poirot smiled to himself and straightened a little mat which the anxious father had pushed askew.

'A pleasing little problem, obscure and charming,' murmured Poirot. 'I will investigate it for you with pleasure. Truly it was planned *à merveille*.'

Mrs Waverly looked at him reproachfully. 'But my boy,' she wailed.

Poirot hastily composed his face and looked the picture of earnest sympathy again. 'He is safe, madame, he is unharmed. Rest assured, these miscreants will take the greatest care of him. Is he not to them the turkey – no, the goose – that lays the golden eggs?'

'M. Poirot, I'm sure there's only one thing to be done – pay up. I was all against it at first – but now! A mother's feelings – '

'But we have interrupted monsieur in his history,' cried Poirot hastily.

'I expect you know the rest pretty well from the papers,' said Mr Waverly. 'Of course, Inspector McNeil got on to the telephone immediately. A description of the car and the man was circulated all round, and it looked at first as though everything was going to turn out all right. A car, answering to the description, with a man and a small boy, had passed through various villages, apparently making for London. At one place they had stopped, and it was noticed that the child was crying and obviously afraid of his companion. When Inspector McNeil announced that the car had been stopped and the man and boy detained, I was almost ill with relief. You know the sequel. The boy was not Johnnie, and the man was an ardent motorist, fond of children, who had picked up a small child playing in the streets of Edenswell, a village about fifteen miles from us, and was kindly giving him a ride. Thanks to the cocksure blundering of the police, all traces have disappeared. Had they not persistently followed the wrong car, they might by now have found the boy.'

'Calm yourself, monsieur. The police are a brave and intelligent force of men. Their mistake was a very natural one. And altogether it was a clever scheme. As to the man they caught in the grounds, I understand that his defence has consisted all along of a persistent denial. He declared that the note and parcel were given to him to deliver at Waverly Court. The man who gave them to him handed him a ten-shilling note and promised him another if it were delivered at exactly ten minutes to twelve. He was to approach the house through the grounds and knock at the side door.'

'I don't believe a word of it,' declared Mrs Waverly hotly. 'It's all a parcel of lies.'

'*En verité*, it is a thin story,' said Poirot reflectively. 'But so far they have not shaken it. I understand, also, that he made a certain accusation?'

His glance interrogated Mr Waverly. The latter got rather red again.

'The fellow had the impertinence to pretend that he recognized in Tredwell the man who gave him the parcel. "Only the bloke has shaved off his moustache." Tredwell, who was born on the estate!'

Poirot smiled a little at the country gentleman's indignation. 'Yet you yourself suspect an inmate of the house to have been accessory to the abduction.'

'Yes, but not Tredwell.'

'And you, madame?' asked Poirot, suddenly turning to her.

'It could not have been Tredwell who gave this tramp the letter and parcel – if anybody ever did, which I don't believe.

It was given him at ten o'clock, he says. At ten o'clock Tredwell was with my husband in the smoking-room.'

'Were you able to see the face of the man in the car, monsieur? Did it resemble that of Tredwell in any way?'

'It was too far away for me to see his face.'

'Has Tredwell a brother, do you know?'

'He had several, but they are all dead. The last one was killed in the war.'

'I am not yet clear as to the grounds of Waverly Court. The car was heading for the south lodge. Is there another entrance?'

'Yes, what we call the east lodge. It can be seen from the other side of the house.'

'It seems to me strange that nobody saw the car entering the grounds.'

'There is a right of way through, and access to a small chapel. A good many cars pass through. The man must have stopped the car in a convenient place and run up to the house just as the alarm was given and attention attracted elsewhere.'

'Unless he was already inside the house,' mused Poirot. 'Is there any place where he could have hidden?'

'Well, we certainly didn't make a thorough search of the house beforehand. There seemed no need. I suppose he might have hidden himself somewhere, but who would have let him in?'

'We shall come to that later. One thing at a time – let us be methodical. There is no special hiding-place in the house? Waverly Court is an old place, and there are sometimes "priests' holes", as they call them.'

'By gad, there *is* a priest's hole. It opens from one of the panels in the hall.'

'Near the council chamber?'

'Just outside the door.'

'*Voilà!*'

'But nobody knows of its existence except my wife and myself.'

'Tredwell?'

'Well – he might have heard of it.'

'Miss Collins?'

228

'I have never mentioned it to her.'

Poirot reflected for a minute.

'Well, monsieur, the next thing is for me to come down to Waverly Court. If I arrive this afternoon, will it suit you?'

'Oh, as soon as possible, please, Monsieur Poirot!' cried Mrs Waverly. 'Read this once more.'

She thrust into his hands the last missive from the enemy which had reached the Waverlys that morning and which had sent her post-haste to Poirot. It gave clever and explicit directions for the paying over of the money, and ended with a threat that the boy's life would pay for any treachery. It was clear that a love of money warred with the essential mother love of Mrs Waverly, and that the latter was at last gaining the day.

Poirot detained Mrs Waverly for a minute behind her husband.

'Madame, the truth, if you please. Do you share your husband's faith in the butler, Tredwell?'

'I have nothing against him, Monsieur Poirot, I cannot see how he can have been concerned in this, but – well, I have never liked him – never!'

'One other thing, madame, can you give me the address of the child's nurse?'

'149 Netherall Road, Hammersmith. You don't imagine – '

'Never do I imagine. Only – I employ the little grey cells. And sometimes, just sometimes, I have a little idea.'

Poirot came back to me as the door closed.

'So madame has never liked the butler. It is interesting, that, eh, Hastings?'

I refused to be drawn. Poirot has deceived me so often that I now go warily. There is always a catch somewhere.

After completing an elaborate outdoor toilet, we set off for Netherall Road. We were fortunate enough to find Miss Jessie Withers at home. She was a pleasant-faced woman of thirty-five, capable and superior. I could not believe that she could be mixed up in the affair. She was bitterly resentful of the way she had been dismissed, but admitted that she had been in the wrong. She was engaged to be married to a painter and decorator who happened to be in the neighbourhood, and she had run out to meet him. The thing seemed natural enough. I could not quite understand Poirot. All his questions seemed to me quite irrelevant. They were concerned mainly with the daily routine of her life at Waverly Court. I was frankly bored and glad when Poirot took his departure.

'Kidnapping is an easy job, *mon ami*,' he observed, as he hailed a taxi in the Hammersmith Road and ordered it to drive to Waterloo. 'That child could have been abducted with the greatest ease any day for the last three years.'

'I don't see that that advances us much,' I remarked coldly.

'*Au contraire*, it advances us enormously, but enormously! If you must wear a tie pin, Hastings, at least let it be in the exact centre of your tie. At present it is at least a sixteenth of an inch too much to the right.'

Waverly Court was a fine old place and had recently been restored with taste and care. Mr Waverly showed us the council chamber, the terrace, and all the various spots connected with the case. Finally, at Poirot's request, he pressed a spring in the wall, a panel slid aside, and a short passage led us into the priest's hole.

'You see,' said Waverly. 'There is nothing here.'

The tiny room was bare enough, there was not even the mark of a footstep on the floor. I joined Poirot where he was bending attentively over a mark in the corner.

'What do you make of this, my friend?'

There were four imprints close together.

'A dog,' I cried.

'A very small dog, Hastings.'

'A Pom.'

'Smaller than a Pom.'

'A griffon?' I suggested doubtfully.

'Smaller even than a griffon. A species unknown to the Kennel Club.'

I looked at him. His face was alight with excitement and satisfaction.

'I was right,' he murmured. 'I knew I was right. Come, Hastings.'

As we stepped out into the hall and the panel closed behind

us, a young lady came out of a door farther down the passage. Mr Waverly presented her to us.

'Miss Collins.'

Miss Collins was about thirty years of age, brisk and alert in manner. She had fair, rather dull hair, and wore pince-nez.

At Poirot's request, we passed into a small morning-room, and he questioned her closely as to the servants and particularly as to Tredwell. She admitted that she did not like the butler.

'He gives himself airs,' she explained.

They then went into the question of the food eaten by Mrs Waverly on the night of the 28th. Miss Collins declared that she had partaken of the same dishes upstairs in her sitting-room and had felt no ill effects. As she was departing I nudged Poirot.

'The dog,' I whispered.

'Ah, yes, the dog!' He smiled broadly. 'Is there a dog kept here by any chance, mademoiselle?'

'There are two retrievers in the kennels outside.'

'No, I mean a small dog, a toy dog.'

'No – nothing of the kind.'

Poirot permitted her to depart. Then, pressing the bell, he remarked to me, 'She lies, that Mademoiselle Collins. Possibly I should, also, in her place. Now for the butler.'

Tredwell was a dignified individual. He told his story with perfect aplomb, and it was essentially the same as that of Mr Waverly. He admitted that he knew the secret of the priest's hole.

When he finally withdrew, pontifical to the last, I met Poirot's quizzical eyes.

'What do you make of it all, Hastings?'

'What do you?' I parried.

'How cautious you become. Never, never will the grey cells function unless you stimulate them. Ah, but I will not tease you! Let us make our deductions together. What points strike us specially as being difficult?'

'There is one thing that strikes me,' I said. 'Why did the man who kidnapped the child go out by the south lodge instead of by the east lodge where no one would see him?'

231

'That is a very good point, Hastings, an excellent one. I will match it with another. Why warn the Waverlys beforehand? Why not simply kidnap the child and hold him to ransom?'

'Because they hoped to get the money without being forced to action.'

'Surely it was very unlikely that the money would be paid on a mere threat?'

'Also they wanted to focus attention on twelve o'clock, so that when the tramp man was seized, the other could emerge from his hiding-place and get away with the child unnoticed.'

'That does not alter the fact that they were making a thing difficult that was perfectly easy. If they do not specify a time or date, nothing would be easier than to wait their chance, and carry off the child in a motor one day when he is out with his nurse.'

'Ye – e.,' I admitted doubtfully.

'In fact, there is a deliberate playing of the farce! Now let us approach the question from another side. Everything goes to show that there was an accomplice inside the house. Point number one, the mysterious poisoning of Mrs Waverly. Point number two, the letter pinned to the pillow. Point number three, the putting on of the clock ten minutes – all inside jobs. And an additional fact that you may not have noticed. There was no dust in the priest's hole. It had been swept out with a broom.

'Now then, we have four people in the house. We can exclude the nurse, since she could not have swept out the priest's hole, though she could have attended to the other three points. Four people, Mr and Mrs Waverly, Tredwell, the butler, and Miss Collins. We will take Miss Collins first. We have nothing much against her, except that we know very little about her, that she is obviously an intelligent young woman, and that she has only been here a year.'

'She lied about the dog, you said,' I reminded him.

'Ah, yes, the dog.' Poirot gave a peculiar smile. 'Now let us pass to Tredwell. There are several suspicious facts against him. For one thing, the tramp declares that it was Tredwell who gave him the parcel in the village.'

'But Tredwell can prove an alibi on that point.'

'Even then, he could have poisoned Mrs Waverly, pinned the note to the pillow, put on the clock, and swept out the priest's hole. On the other hand, he has been born and bred in the service of the Waverlys. It seems unlikely in the last degree that he should connive at the abduction of the son of the house. It is not in the picture!'

'Well, then?'

'We must proceed logically – however absurd it may seem. We will briefly consider Mrs Waverly. But she is rich, the money is hers. It is her money which has restored this impoverished estate. There would be no reason for her to kidnap her son and pay over her money to herself. The husband, no, is in a different position. He has a rich wife. It is not the same thing as being rich himself – in fact I have a little idea that the lady is not very fond of parting with her money, except on a very good pretext. But Mr Waverly, you can see at once, he is a *bon viveur*.'

'Impossible,' I spluttered.

'Not at all. Who sends away the servants? Mr Waverly. He can write the notes, drug his wife, put on the hands of the clock, and establish an excellent alibi for his faithful retainer Tredwell. Tredwell has never liked Mrs Waverly. He is devoted to his master and is willing to obey his orders implicitly. There were three of them in it. Waverly, Tredwell, and some friend of Waverly. That is the mistake the police made, they made no further inquiries about the man who drove the grey car with the wrong child in it. He was the third man. He picks up a child in a village near by, a boy with flaxen curls. He drives in through the east lodge and passes out through the south lodge just at the right moment, waving his hand and shouting. They cannot see his face or the number of the car, so obviously they cannot see the child's face, either. Then he lays a false trail to London. In the meantime, Tredwell has done his part in arranging for the parcel and note to be delivered by a rough-looking gentleman. His master can provide an alibi in the unlikely case of the man recognizing him, in spite of the false moustache he wore. As for Mr Waverly, as soon as the hullabaloo occurs outside, and the inspector rushes out, he quickly hides the child in the priest's hole, follows him out. Later in the day, when the inspector is gone and Miss Collins is out of the way, it will be easy enough to drive him off to some safe place in his own car.'

'But what about the dog?' I asked. 'And Miss Collins lying?'

'That was my little joke. I asked her if there were any toy dogs in the house, and she said no – but doubtless there are some – in the nursery! You see, Mr Waverly placed some toys in the priest's hole to keep Johnnie amused and quiet.'

'M. Poirot – ' Mr Waverly entered the room – 'have you discovered anything? Have you any clue to where the boy has been taken?'

Poirot handed him a piece of paper. 'Here is the address.'

'But this is a blank sheet.'

'Because I am waiting for you to write it down for me.'

'What the – ' Mr Waverly's face turned purple.

'I know everything, monsieur. I give you twenty-four hours to return the boy. Your ingenuity will be equal to the task of explaining his reappearance. Otherwise, Mrs Waverly will be informed of the exact sequence of events.'

Mr Waverly sank down in a chair and buried his face in his hands. 'He is with my old nurse, ten miles away. He is happy and well cared for.'

'I have no doubt of that. If I did not believe you to be a good father at heart, I should not be willing to give you another chance.'

'The scandal – '

'Exactly. Your name is an old and honoured one. Do not jeopardize it again. Good evening, Mr Waverly. Ah, by the way, one word of advice. Always sweep in the corners!'

THE KING OF CLUBS

'Truth,' I observed, laying aside the *Daily Newsmonger*, 'is stranger than fiction!'

The remark was not, perhaps, an original one. It appeared to incense my friend. Tilting his egg-shaped head on one side, the little man carefully flicked an imaginary fleck of dust from his carefully creased trousers, and observed: 'How profound! What a thinker is my friend Hastings!'

Without displaying any annoyance at this quite uncalled-for gibe, I tapped the sheet I had laid aside.

'You've read this morning's paper?'

'I have. And after reading it, I folded it anew symmetrically. I did not cast it on the floor as you have done, with your so lamentable absence of order and method.'

(That is the worst of Poirot. Order and Method are his gods. He goes so far as to attribute all his success to them.)

'Then you saw the account of the murder of Henry Reedburn, the impresario? It was that which prompted my remark. Not only is truth stranger than fiction – it is more dramatic. Think of that solid middle-class English family, the Oglanders. Father and mother, son and daughter, typical of thousands of families all over this country. The men of the family go to the city every day; the women look after the house. Their lives are perfectly peaceful, and utterly monotonous. Last night they were sitting in their neat suburban drawing-room at Daisymead, Streatham, playing bridge. Suddenly, without any warning, the french window bursts open, and a woman staggers into the room. Her grey satin frock is marked with a crimson stain. She utters one word, "Murder!" before she sinks to the ground insensible. It is possible that they recognize her from her pictures as Valerie Saintclair, the famous dancer who has lately take London by storm!'

'Is this your eloquence, or that of the *Daily Newsmonger*?' inquired Poirot.

'The *Daily Newsmonger* was in a hurry to go to press, and contented itself with bare facts. But the dramatic possibilities of the story struck me at once.'

Poirot nodded thoughtfully. 'Wherever there is human nature, there is drama. *But* – it is not always just where you think it is. Remember that. Still, I too am interested in the case, since it is likely that I shall be connected with it.'

'Indeed?'

'Yes. A gentleman rang me up this morning, and made an appointment with me on behalf of Prince Paul of Maurania.'

'But what has that to do with it?'

'You do not read your pretty little English scandal-papers. The ones with the funny stories, and "a little mouse has heard – " or "a little bird would like to know – " See here.'

I followed his short stubby finger along the paragraph: '– whether the foreign prince and the famous dancer are *really* affinities! And if the lady likes her new diamond ring!'

'And now to resume your so dramatic narrative,' said Poirot. 'Mademoiselle Saintclair had just fainted on the drawing-room carpet at Daisymead, you remember.'

I shrugged. 'As a result of Mademoiselle's first murmured words when she came round, the two male Oglanders stepped out, one to fetch a doctor to attend to the lady, who was evidently suffering terribly from shock, and the other to the police-station – whence after telling his story, he accompanied the police to Mon Désir, Mr Reedburn's magnificent villa, which is situated at no great distance from Daisymead. There they found the great man, who by the way suffers from a somewhat unsavoury reputation, lying in the library with the back of his head cracked open like an eggshell.'

'I have cramped your style,' said Poirot kindly. 'Forgive me, I pray ... Ah, here is M. le Prince!'

Our distinguished visitor was announced under the title of Count Feodor. He was a strange-looking youth, tall, eager, with a weak chin, the famous Mauranberg mouth, and the dark fiery eyes of a fanatic.

'M. Poirot?'

My friend bowed.

'Monsieur, I am in terrible trouble, greater than I can well express – '

Poirot waved his hand. 'I comprehend your anxiety. Mademoiselle Saintclair is a very dear friend, is it not so?'

The prince replied simply: 'I hope to make her my wife.'

Piorot sat up in his chair, and his eyes opened.

The prince continued: 'I should not be the first of my family to make a morganatic marriage. My brother Alexander has also defied the Emperor. We are living now in more enlightened days, free from the old caste-prejudice. Besides, Mademoiselle Saintclear, in actual fact, is quite my equal in rank. You have heard hints as to her history?'

'There are many romantic stories of her origin – not an uncommon thing with famous dancers. I have heard that she is the daughter of an Irish charwoman, also the story which makes her mother a Russian grand duchess.'

'The first story is, of course, nonsense,' said the young man. 'But the second is true. Valerie, though bound to secrecy, has let me guess as much. Besides, she proves it unconsciously in a thousand ways. I believe in heredity, M. Poirot.'

'I too believe in heredity,' said Poirot thoughtfully. 'I have seen some strange things in connection with it – *moi qui vous parle* ... But to business, M. le Prince. What do you want of me? What do you fear? I may speak freely, may I not? Is there anything to connect Mademoiselle Saintclair with the crime? She knew Reedburn of course?'

'Yes. He professed to be in love with her.'

'And she?'

'She would have nothing to say to him.'

Poirot looked at him keenly. 'Had she any reason to fear him?'

The young man hesitated. 'There was an incident. You know Zara, the clairvoyant?'

'No.'

'She is wonderful. You should consult her some time. Valerie and I went to see her last week. She read the cards for us. She spoke to Valerie of trouble – of gathering clouds; then she turned up the last card – the covering card, they call it. It was the king of clubs. She said to Valerie: "Beware. There is a man who holds you in his power. You fear him – you are in great danger through him. You know whom I mean?" Valerie was white to the lips. She nodded and said: "Yes, yes, I know." Shortly afterwards we left. Zara's last words to Valerie were: "Beware of the king of clubs. Danger threatens you!" I questioned Valerie. She would tell me nothing – assured me that all was well. But now, after last night, I am more sure than ever that in the king of clubs Valerie saw Reedburn, and that he was the man she feared.'

The Prince paused abruptly. 'Now you understand my agitation when I opened the paper this morning. Supposing Valerie, in a fit of madness – oh, it is impossible!'

Poirot rose from his seat, and patted the young man kindly on the shoulder. 'Do not distress yourself, I beg of you. Leave it in my hands.'

'You will go to Streatham? I gather she is still there, at Daisymead – prostrated by the shock.'

'I will go at once.'

'I have arranged matters – through the embassy. You will be allowed access everywhere.'

'Then we will depart – Hastings, you will accompany me? Au revoir, M. le Prince.'

Mon Désir was an exceptionally fine villa, thoroughly modern and comfortable. A short carriage-drive led up to it from the road, and beautiful gardens extended behind the house for some acres.

On mentioning Prince Paul's name, the butler who answered the door at once took us to the scene of the tragedy. The library was a magnificent room, running from back to front of the whole building, with a window at either end, one giving on the front carriage-drive, and the other on the garden. It was in the recess of the latter that the body had lain. It had been removed not long before, the police having concluded their examination.

'That is annoying,' I murmured to Poirot. 'Who knows what clues they may have destroyed?'

My little friend smiled. 'Eh – Eh! How often must I tell you that clues come from *within*? In the little grey cells of the brain lies the solution of every mystery.'

He turned to the butler. 'I suppose, except for the removal of the body, the room has not been touched?'

'No, sir. It's just as it was when the police came up last night.'

'These curtains, now. I see they pull right across the window recess. They are the same in the other window. Were they drawn last night?'

'Yes, sir, I draw them every night.'

'Then Reedburn must have drawn them back himself?'

'I suppose so, sir.'

'Did you know your master expected a visitor last night?'

'He did not say so, sir. But he gave orders he was not to be disturbed after dinner. You see, sir, there is a door leading out of the library on to the terrace at the side of the house. He could have admitted anyone that way.'

'Was he in the habit of doing that?'

The butler coughed discreetly. 'I believe so, sir.'

Poirot strode to the door in question. It was unlocked. He stepped through it on to the terrace which joined the drive on the right; on the left it led up to a red brick wall.

'The fruit garden, sir. There is a door leading into it farther along, but it was always locked at six o'clock.'

Poirot nodded, and re-entered the library, the butler following.

'Did you hear nothing of last night's events?'

'Well, sir, we heard voices in the library, a little before nine. But that wasn't unusual, especially being a lady's voice. But of course, once we were all in the servants' hall, right the other side, we didn't hear anything at all. And then, about eleven o'clock, the police came.'

'How many voices did you hear?'

'I couldn't say, sir. I only noticed the lady's.'

'Ah!'

239

'I beg pardon, sir, but Dr Ryan is still in the house, if you would care to see him.'

We jumped at the suggestion, and in a few minutes the doctor, a cheery, middle-aged man, joined us, and gave Poirot all the information he required. Reedburn had been lying near the window, his head by the marble window-seat. There were two wounds, one between the eyes, and the other, the fatal one, on the back of the head.

'He was lying on his back?'

'Yes. There is the mark.' He pointed to a small dark stain on the floor.

'Could not the blow on the back of the head have been caused by his striking the floor?'

'Impossible. Whatever the weapon was, it penetrated some distance into the skull.'

Poirot looked thoughtfully in front of him. In the embrasure of each window was a carved marble seat, the arms being fashioned in the form of a lion's head. A light came into Poirot's eyes. 'Supposing he had fallen backwards on this projecting lion's head, and slipped from there to the ground. Would not that cause a wound such as you describe?'

'Yes, it would. But the angle at which he was lying makes that theory impossible. And besides there could not fail to be traces of blood on the marble of the seat.'

'Unless they were washed away?'

The doctor shrugged his shoulders. 'That is hardly likely. It would be to no one's advantage to give an accident the appearance of murder.'

'Quite so,' acquiesced Poirot. 'Could either of the blows have been struck by a woman, do you think?'

'Oh, quite out of the question, I should say. You are thinking of Mademoiselle Saintclair, I suppose?'

'I think of no one in particular until I am sure,' said Poirot gently.

He turned his attention to the open french window, and the doctor continued:

'It is through here that Mademoiselle Saintclair fled. You can just catch a glimpse of Daisymead between the trees. Of course, there are many houses nearer to the front of the house on the road, but as it happens, Daisymead, though some distance away, is the only house visible this side.'

'Thank you for your amiability, Doctor,' said Poirot. 'Come, Hastings, we will follow the footsteps of Mademoiselle.'

Poirot led the way down through the garden, out through an iron gate, across a short stretch of green and in through the garden gate of Daisymead, which was an unpretentious little house in about half an acre of ground. There was a small flight of steps leading up to a french window. Poirot nodded in their direction.

'That is the way Mademoiselle Saintclair went. For us, who have not her urgency to plead, it will be better to go round to the front door.'

A maid admitted us and took us into the drawing-room, then went in search of Mrs Oglander. The room had evidently not been touched since the night before. The ashes were still in the grate, and the bridge-table was still in the centre of the room, with a dummy exposed, and the hands thrown down. The place was somewhat overloaded with gimcrack ornaments, and a good many family portraits of surpassing ugliness adorned the walls.

Poirot gazed at them more leniently than I did, and straightened one or two that were hanging a shade askew. '*La famille*, it is a strong tie, is it not? Sentiment, it takes the place of beauty.'

I agreed, my eyes being fixed on a family group comprising a gentleman with whiskers, a lady with a high 'front' of hair, a solid, thick-set boy, and two little girls tied up with a good many unnecessary bows of ribbon. I took this to be the Oglander family in earlier days, and studied it with interest.

The door opened, and a young woman came in. Her dark hair was neatly arranged, and she wore a drab-coloured sportscoat and a tweed skirt.

She looked at us inquiringly. Poirot stepped forward. 'Miss Oglander? I regret to derange you – especially after all you have been through. The whole affair must have been most disturbing.'

'It has been rather upsetting,' admitted the young lady cautiously. I began to think that the elements of drama were wasted on Miss Oglander, that her lack of imagination rose superior to any tragedy. I was confirmed in this belief as she continued: 'I must apologize for the state this room is in. Servants get so foolishly excited.'

'It was here that you were sitting last night, *n'est-ce pas*?'

'Yes, we were playing bridge after supper, when – '

'Excuse me – how long had you been playing?'

'Well – ' Miss Oglander considered. 'I really can't say. I suppose it must have been about ten o'clock. We had had several rubbers, I know.'

'And you yourself were sitting – where?'

'Facing the window. I was playing with my mother and had gone one no trump. Suddenly, without any warning, the window burst open, and Miss Saintclair staggered into the room.'

'You recognized her?'

'I had a vague idea her face was familiar.'

'She is still here, is she not?'

'Yes, but she refuses to see anyone. She is still quite prostrated.'

'I think she will see me. Will you tell her that I am here at the express request of Prince Paul of Maurania?'

I fancied that the mention of a royal prince rather shook Miss Oglander's imperturbable calm. But she left the room on her errand without any further remark, and returned almost immediately to say that Mademoiselle Saintclair would see us in her room.

We followed her upstairs, and into a fair-sized light bedroom. On a couch by the window a woman was lying who turned her head as we entered. The contrast between the two women struck me at once, the more so as in actual features and colouring they were not unalike – but oh, the difference! Not a look, not a gesture of Valerie Saintclair's but expressed drama. She seemed to exhale an atmosphere of romance. A scarlet flannel dressing-gown covered her feet – a homely garment in all conscience; but the charm of her personality invested it with an exotic flavour, and it seemed an Eastern robe of glowing colour.

Her large dark eyes fastened themselves on Poirot.

'You come from Paul?' Her voice matched her appearance – it was full and languid.

'Yes, mademoiselle. I am here to serve him – and you.'

'What do you want to know?'

'Everything that happened last night. *But everything*!'

She smiled rather wearily.

'Do you think I should lie? I am not stupid. I see well enough that there can be no concealment. He held a secret of mine, that man who is dead. He threatened me with it. For Paul's sake, I endeavoured to make terms with him. I could not risk losing Paul ... Now that he is dead, I am safe. But for all that, I did not kill him.'

Poirot shook his head with a smile. 'It is not necessary to tell me that, mademoiselle. Now recount to me what happened last night.'

'I offered him money. He appeared to be willing to treat with me. He appointed last night at nine o'clock. I was to go to Mon Désir. I knew the place; I had been there before. I was to go round to the side door into the library, so that the servants should not see me.

'Excuse me, mademoiselle, but were you not afraid to trust yourself alone there at night?'

Was it my fancy, or was there a momentary pause before she answered?

'Perhaps I was. But you see, there was no one I could ask to go with me. And I was desperate. Reedburn admitted me to the library. Oh, that man! I am glad he is dead! He played with me, as a cat does with a mouse. He taunted me. I begged and implored him on my knees. I offered him every jewel I have. All in vain! Then he named his own terms. Perhaps you can guess what they were. I refused. I told him what I thought of him. I raved at him. He remained calmly smiling. And then, as I fell to silence at last, there was a sound – from behind the curtain in the window ... He heard it too. He strode to the curtains and flung them wide apart. There was a man there, hiding – a dreadful-looking man, a sort of tramp. He struck at Mr Reedburn – then he struck again, and he went down. The tramp clutched at me with his bloodstained hand. I tore myself free, slipped through the window, and ran for my life. Then I perceived the lights in this house, and made for them. The blinds were up, and I saw some people playing bridge. I almost fell into the room. I just managed to gasp out "Murder!" and then everything went black – '

'Thank you, Mademoiselle. It must have been a great shock to your nervous system. As to this tramp, could you describe him? Do you remember what he was wearing?'

'No – it was all so quick. But I should know the man anywhere. His face is burnt in on my brain.'

'Just one more question, mademoiselle. The curtains of the *other* window, the one giving on the drive, were they drawn?'

For the first time a puzzled expression crept over the dancer's face. She seemed to be trying to remember.

'*Eh bien, mademoiselle?*'

'I think – I am almost sure – yes, quite sure! They were *not* drawn.'

'That is curious, since the other ones were. No matter. It is, I dare say, of no great importance. You are remaining here long, mademoiselle?'

'The doctor thinks I shall be fit to return to town tomorrow.' She looked round the room. Miss Oglander had gone out. 'These people, they are very kind – but they are not of my world. I shock them! And to me – well, I am not fond of the *bourgeoisie*!'

A faint note of bitterness underlay her words.

Poirot nodded. 'I understand. I hope I have not fatigued you unduly with my questions?'

'Not at all, monsieur. I am only too anxious Paul should know all as soon as possible.'

'Then I will wish you good day, mademoiselle.'

As Poirot was leaving the room, he paused, and pounced on a pair of patent-leather slippers. 'Yours, mademoiselle?'

'Yes, monsieur. They have just been cleaned and brought up.'

'Ah!' said Poirot, as we descended the stairs. 'It seems that the domestics are not too excited to clean shoes, though they forget a grate. Well, *mon ami*, at first there appeared to be one or two points of interest, but I fear, I very much fear, that we must regard the case as finished. It all seems straightforward enough.'

'And the murderer?'

'Hercule Poirot does not hunt down tramps,' replied my friend grandiloquently.

Miss Oglander met us in the hall. 'If you will wait in the drawing-room a minute, Mamma would like to speak to you.'

The room was still untouched, and Poirot idly gathered up the cards, shuffling them with his tiny, fastidiously groomed hands.

'Do you know what I think, my friend?'

'No?' I said eagerly.

'I think that Miss Oglander made a mistake in going one no trump. She should have gone three spades.'

'Poirot! You are the limit.'

'*Mon Dieu*, I cannot always be talking blood and thunder!'

Suddenly he stiffened: 'Hastings – *Hastings*. See! The king of clubs is missing from the pack!'

'Zara!' I cried.

'Eh?' he did not seem to understand my allusion. Mechanically he stacked the cards and put them away in their cases. His face was very grave.

'Hastings,' he said at last, 'I, Hercule Poirot, have come near to making a big mistake – a very big mistake.'

I gazed at him, impressed, but utterly uncomprehending.

'We must begin again, Hastings. Yes, we must begin again. But this time we shall not err.'

He was interrupted by the entrance of a handsome middle-aged lady. She carried some household books in her hand. Poirot bowed to her.

'Do I understand, sir, that you are a friend of – er – Miss Saintclair's?'

'I come from a friend of hers, madame.'

'Oh, I see. I thought perhaps –'

Poirot suddenly waved brusquely at the window.

'Your blinds were not pulled down last night?'

'No – I suppose that is why Miss Saintclair saw the light so plainly.'

'There was moonlight last night. I wonder that you did not see Mademoiselle Saintclair from your seat here facing the windows?'

'I suppose we were engrossed with our game. Nothing like this has ever happened before to us.'

'I can quite believe that, madame. And I will put your mind at rest. Mademoiselle Saintclair is leaving tomorrow.'

'Oh!' The good lady's face cleared.

'And I will wish you good morning, madame.'

A servant was cleaning the steps as we went out of the front door. Poirot addressed her.

'Was it you who cleaned the shoes of the young lady upstairs?'

The maid shook her head. 'No, sir. I don't think they've been cleaned.'

'Who cleaned them, then?' I inquired of Poirot, as we walked down the road.

'Nobody. They did not need cleaning.'

'I grant that walking on the road or path on a fine night would not soil them. But surely after going through the long grass of the garden, they would have been soiled and stained.'

'Yes,' said Poirot with a curious smile. 'In that case, I agree, they would have been stained.'

'But –'

'Have patience a little half-hour, my friend. We are going back to Mon Désir.'

The butler looked surprised at our reappearance, but offered no objection to our returning to the library.

'Hi, that's the wrong window, Poirot,' I cried as he made for the one overlooking the carriage-drive.

'I think not, my friend. See here.' He pointed to the marble lion's head. On it was a faint discoloured smear. He shifted his finger and pointed to a similar stain on the polished floor.

'Someone struck Reedburn a blow with his clenched fist betwen the eyes. He fell backward on this projecting bit of marble, then slipped to the floor. Afterwards, he was dragged across the floor to the other window, and laid there instead, but not quite at the same angle, as the Doctor's evidence told us.'

'But why? It seems utterly unnecessary.'

'On the contrary, it was essential. Also, it is the key to the murderer's identity – though, by the way, he had no intention of killing Reedburn, and so it is hardly permissible to call him a murderer. He must be a very strong man!'

'Because of having dragged the body across the floor?'

'Not altogether. It has been an interesting case. I nearly made an imbecile of myself, though.'

'Do you mean to say it is over, that you know everything?'

'Yes.'

A remembrance smote me. 'No,' I cried. 'There is one thing you do *not* know!'

'And that?'

'You do not know where the missing king of clubs is!'

'Eh? Oh, that is droll! That is very droll, my friend.'

'Why?'

'*Because it is in my pocket!*' He drew it forth with a flourish.

'Oh!' I said, rather crestfallen. 'Where did you find it? Here?'

'There was nothing sensational about it. It had simply not been taken out with the other cards. It was in the box.'

'H'm! All the same, it gave you an idea, didn't it?'

'Yes, my friend. I present my respects to His Majesty.'

'And to Madame Zara!'

'Ah, yes – to the lady also.'

'Well, what are we going to do now?'

'We are going to return to town. But I must have a few words with a certain lady at Daisymead first.'

The same little maid opened the door to us.

'They're all at lunch now, sir – unless it's Miss Saintclair you want to see, and she's resting.'

'It will do if I can see Mrs Oglander for a few minutes. Will you tell her?'

We were led into the drawing-room to wait. I had a glimpse of the family in the dining-room as we passed, now reinforced by the presence of two heavy, solid-looking men, one with a moustache, the other with a beard also.

In a few minutes Mrs Oglander came into the room, looking inquiringly at Poirot, who bowed.

'Madame, we, in our country, have a great tenderness, a great respect for the mother. The *mère de famille*, she is everything!'

Mrs Oglander looked rather astonished at this opening.

'It is for that reason that I have come – to allay a mother's anxiety. The murderer of Mr Reedburn will not be discovered. Have no fear. I, Hercule Poirot, tell you so. I am right, am I not? Or is it a wife that I must reassure?'

There was a moment's pause. Mrs Oglander seemed searching Poirot with her eyes. At last she said quietly: 'I don't know how you know – but yes, you are right.'

Poirot nodded gravely. 'That is all, madame. But do not be uneasy. Your English policemen have not the eyes of Hercule Poirot.' He tapped the family portrait on the wall with his fingernail.

'You had another daughter once. She is dead, madame?'

Again there was a pause, as she searched him with her eyes. Then she answered: 'Yes, she is dead.'

'Ah!' said Poirot briskly. 'Well, we must return to town. You permit that I return the king of clubs to the pack? It was your only slip. You understand, to have played bridge for an hour or so, with only fifty-one cards – well, no one who knows anything of the game would credit it for a minute! *Bonjour*!'

'And now, my friend,' said Poirot as we stepped towards the station, 'you see it all!'

'I see nothing! Who killed Reedburn?'

'John Oglander, Junior. I was not quite sure if it was the

248

father or the son, but I fixed on the son as being the stronger and younger of the two. It had to be one of them, because of the window.'

'Why?'

'There were four exits from the library – two doors, two windows; but evidently only one would do. Three exits gave on the front, directly or indirectly. The tragedy had to occur in the back window in order to make it appear that Valerie Saintclair came to Daisymead by chance. Really, of course, she fainted, and John Oglander carried her across over his shoulders. That is why I said he must be a strong man.'

'Did they go there together, then?'

'Yes. You remember Valerie's hesitation when I asked her if she was not afraid to go alone? John Oglander went with her – which didn't improve Reedburn's temper, I fancy. They quarrelled, and it was probably some insult levelled at Valerie that made Oglander hit him. The rest, you know.'

'But why the bridge?'

'Bridge presupposes four players. A simple thing like that carries a lot of conviction. Who would have supposed that there had been only three people in that room all the evening?'

I was still puzzled.

'There's one thing I don't understand. What have the Oglanders to do with the dancer Valerie Saintclair?'

'Ah, that I wonder you did not see. And yet you looked long enough at that picture on the wall – longer than I did. Mrs Oglander's other daughter may be dead to her family, but the world knows her as Valerie Saintclair!'

'*What*?'

'Did you not see the resemblance the moment you saw the two sisters together?'

'No,' I confessed. 'I only thought how extraordinarily dissimilar they were.'

'That is because your mind is so open to external romantic impressions, my dear Hastings. The features are almost identical. So is the colouring. The interesting thing is that Valerie is ashamed of her family, and her family is ashamed of her. Nevertheless, in a moment of peril, she turned to her brother for help, and when things went wrong, they all hung together in a remarkable way. Family strength is a marvellous thing. They can all act, that family. That is where Valerie gets her histrionic talent from. I, like Prince Paul, believe in heredity! They deceived *me*! But for a lucky accident, and test question to Mrs Oglander by which I got her to contradict her daughter's account of how they were sitting, the Oglander family would have put a defeat on Hercule Poirot.'

'What shall you tell the Prince?'

'That Valerie could not possibly have committed the crime, and that I doubt if that tramp will ever be found. Also, to convey my compliments to Zara. A curious coincidence, that! I think I shall call this little affair the Adventure of the King of Clubs. What do you think, my friend?'

THE ADVENTURE OF THE CLAPHAM COOK

At the time that I was sharing rooms with my friend Hercule Poirot, it was my custom to read aloud to him the headlines in the morning newspaper, the *Daily Blare*.

The *Daily Blare* was a paper that made the most of any opportunity for sensationalism. Robberies and murders did not lurk obscurely in its back pages. Instead they hit you in the eye in large type on the front page.

ABSCONDING BANK CLERK DISAPPEARS WITH FIFTY THOU-SAND POUNDS' WORTH OF NEGOTIABLE SECURITIES, I read.

HUSBAND PUTS HIS HEAD IN GAS-OVEN. UNHAPPY HOME LIFE. MISSING TYPIST. PRETTY GIRL OF TWENTY-ONE. WHERE IS EDNA FIELD?

'There you are, Poirot, plenty to choose from. An absconding bank clerk, a mysterious suicide, a missing typist – which will you have?'

My friend was in a placid mood. He quietly shook his head.

'I am not greatly attracted to any of them, *mon ami*. Today I feel inclined for the life of ease. It would have to be a very interesting problem to tempt me from my chair. See you, I have affairs of importance of my own to attend to.'

'Such as?'

'My wardrobe, Hastings. If I mistake not, there is on my new grey suit the spot of grease – only the unique spot, but it is sufficient to trouble me. Then there is my winter overcoat – I must lay him aside in the powder of Keatings. And I think – yes, I think – the moment is ripe for the trimmings of my moustaches – and afterwards I must apply the pomade.'

'Well,' I said, strolling to the window, 'I doubt if you'll be able to carry out this delirious programme. That was a ring at the bell. You have a client.'

'Unless the affair is one of national importance, I touch it not,' declared Poirot with dignity.

A moment later our privacy was invaded by a stout redfaced lady who panted audibly as a result of her rapid ascent of the stairs.

'You're M. Poirot?' she demanded, as she sank into a chair.

'I am Hercule Poirot, yes, madame.'

'You're not a bit like what I thought you'd be,' said the lady, eyeing him with some disfavour. 'Did you pay for the bit in the paper saying what a clever detective you were, or did they put it in themselves?'

'Madame!' said Poirot, drawing himself up.

'I'm sorry, I'm sure, but you know what these papers are nowadays. You begin reading a nice article "What a bride said to her plain unmarried friend", and it's all about a simple thing you buy at the chemist's and shampoo your hair with. Nothing but puff. But no offence taken, I hope? I'll tell you what I want you to do for me. I want you to find my cook.'

Poirot stared at her; for once his ready tongue failed him. I turned aside to hide the broadening smile I could not control.

'It's all this wicked dole,' continued the lady. 'Putting ideas into servants' heads, wanting to be typists and what nots. Stop the dole, that's what I say. I'd like to know what *my* servants have to complain of – afternoon and evening off a week, alternate Sundays, washing put out, same food as we have – and never a bit of margarine in the house, nothing but the very best butter.'

She paused for want of breath and Poirot seized his opportunity. He spoke in his haughtiest manner, rising to his feet as he did so.

'I fear you are making a mistake, madame. I am not holding an inquiry into the conditions of domestic service. I am a private detective.'

'I know that,' said our visitor. 'Didn't I tell you I wanted you to find my cook for me? Walked out of the house on Wednesday, without so much as a word to me, and never came back.'

'I am sorry, madame, but I do not touch this particular kind of business. I wish you good morning.'

Our visitor snorted with indignation.

'That's it, is it, my fine fellow? Too proud, eh? Only deal with Government secrets and countesses' jewels? Let me tell you a servant's every bit as important as a tiara to a woman in my position. We can't all be fine ladies going out in our motors with our diamonds and our pearls. A good cook's a good cook – and when you lose her, it's as much to you as her pearls are to some fine lady.'

For a moment or two it appeared to be a toss up between Poirot's dignity and his sense of humour. Finally he laughed and sat down again.

'Madame, you are in the right, and I am in the wrong. Your remarks are just and intelligent. This case will be a novelty. Never yet have I hunted a missing domestic. Truly here is the problem of national importance that I was demanding of fate just before your arrival. *En avant*! You say this jewel of a cook went out on Wednesday and did not return. That is the day before yesterday.'

'Yes, it was her day out.'

'But probably, madame, she has met with some accident. Have you inquired at any of the hospitals?'

'That's exactly what I thought yesterday, but this morning, if you please, she sent for her box. And not so much as a line to me! If I'd been at home, I'd not have let it go – treating me like that! But I'd just stepped out to the butcher.'

'Will you describe her to me?'

'She was middle-aged, stout, black hair turning grey – most respectable. She'd been ten years in her last place. Eliza Dunn, her name was.'

'And you had had – no disagreement with her on the Wednesday?'

'None whatsoever. That's what makes it all so queer.'

'How many servants do you keep, madame?'

'Two. The house-parlourmaid, Annie, is a very nice girl. A bit forgetful and her head full of young men, but a good servant if you keep her up to her work.'

'Did she and the cook get on well together?'

'They had their ups and downs, of course – but on the whole, very well.'

'And the girl can throw no light on the mystery?'

'She says not – but you know what servants are – they all hang together.'

'Well, well, we must look into this. Where did you say you resided, madame?'

'At Clapham; 88 Prince Albert Road.'

'*Bien*, madame, I will wish you good morning, and you may count upon seeing me at your residence during the course of the day.'

Mrs Todd, for such was our new friend's name, then took her departure. Poirot looked at me somewhat ruefully.

'Well, well, Hastings, this is a novel affair that we have here. The Disappearance of the Clapham Cook! Never, *never*, must our friend Inspector Japp get to hear of this!'

He then proceeded to heat an iron and carefully removed the grease spot from his grey suit by means of a piece of blotting-paper. His moustaches he regretfully postponed to another day, and we set out for Clapham.

Prince Albert Road proved to be a street of small prim houses, all exactly alike, with neat lace curtains veiling the windows, and well-polished brass knockers on the doors.

We rang the bell at No. 88, and the door was opened by a neat maid with a pretty face. Mrs Todd came out in the hall to greet us.

'Don't go, Annie,' she cried. 'This gentleman's a detective and he'll want to ask you some questions.'

Annie's face displayed a struggle between alarm and a pleasurable excitement.

'I thank you, madame,' said Poirot bowing. 'I would like to question your maid now – and to see her alone, if I may.'

We were shown into a small drawing-room, and when Mrs Todd, with obvious reluctance, had left the room, Poirot commenced his cross-examination.

'*Voyons, Mademoiselle Annie*, all that you shall tell us will be of the greatest importance. You alone can shed any light on the case. Without your assistance I can do nothing.'

The alarm vanished from the girl's face and the pleasurable excitement became more strongly marked.

'I'm sure, sir,' she said, 'I'll tell you anything I can.'

'That is good.' Poirot beamed approval on her. 'Now, first of all what is your own idea? You are a girl of remarkable intelligence. That can be seen at once! What is your own explanation of Eliza's disappearance?'

Thus encouraged, Annie fairly flowed into excited speech.

'White slavers, sir, I've said so all along! Cook was always warning me against them. "Don't you sniff no scent, or eat any sweets – no matter how gentlemanly the fellow!" Those were her words to me. And now they've got her! I'm sure of it. As likely as not, she's been shipped to Turkey or one of them Eastern places where I've heard they like them fat!'

Poirot preserved an admirable gravity.

'But in that case – and it is indeed an idea! – would she have sent for her trunk?'

'Well, I don't know, sir. She'd want her things – even in those foreign places.'

'Who came for the trunk – a man?'

'It was Carter Paterson, sir.'

'Did you pack it?'

'No, sir, it was already packed and corded.'

'Ah! That's interesting. That shows that when she left the house on Wednesday, she had already determined not to return. You see that, do you not?'

'Yes, sir.' Annie looked slightly taken aback. 'I hadn't thought of that. But it might still have been white slavers, mightn't it, sir? she added wistfully.

'Undoubtedly!' said Poirot gravely. He went on: 'Did you both occupy the same bedroom?'

'No, sir, we had separate rooms.'

'And had Eliza expressed any dissatisfaction with her present post to you at all? Were you both happy here?'

'She'd never mentioned leaving. The place is all right – ' The girl hesitated.

'Speak freely,' said Poirot kindly. 'I shall not tell your mistress.'

'Well, of course, sir, she's a caution, Missus is. But the food's good. Plenty of it, and no stinting. Something hot for supper, good outings, and as much frying-fat as you like. And anyway, if Eliza did want to make a change, she'd never have gone off this way, I'm sure. She'd have stayed her month. Why, Missus could have a month's wages out of her for doing this!'

'And the work, it is not too hard?'

'Well, she's particular – always poking round in corners and looking for dust. And then there's the lodger, or paying guest as he's always called. But that's only breakfast and dinner, same as Master. They're out all day in the City.'

'You like your master?'

'He's all right – very quiet and a bit on the stingy side.'

'You can't remember, I suppose, the last thing Eliza said before she went out?'

'Yes, I can. "If there's any stewed peaches over from the dining-room," she says, "we'll have them for supper, and a bit of bacon and some fried potatoes." Mad over stewed peaches, she was. I shouldn't wonder if they didn't get her that way.'

'Was Wednesday her regular day out?'

'Yes, she had Wednesdays and I had Thursdays.'

Poirot asked a few more questions, then declared himself satisfied. Annie departed, and Mrs Todd hurried in, her face alight with curiosity. She had, I felt certain, bitterly resented her exclusion from the room during our conversation with Annie. Poirot, however, was careful to soothe her feelings tactfully.

'It is difficult,' he explained, 'for a woman of exceptional intelligence such as yourself, madame, to bear patiently the roundabout methods we poor detectives are forced to use. To have patience with stupidity is difficult for the quick-witted.'

Having thus charmed away any little resentment on Mrs Todd's part, he brought the conversation round to her husband and elicited the information that he worked with a firm in the City and would not be home until after six.

'Doubtless he is very disturbed and worried by this unaccountable business, eh? Is it not so?'

'He's never worried,' declared Mrs Todd. ' "Well, well, get another, my dear." That's all *he* said! He's so calm that it drives me to distraction sometimes. "An ungrateful woman," he said. "We are well rid of her." '

'What about the other inmates of the house, madame?'

'You mean Mr Simpson, our paying guest? Well, as long as he gets his breakfast and his evening meal all right, *he* doesn't worry.'

'What is his profession, madame?'

'He works in a bank.' She mentioned its name, and I started slightly, remembering my perusal of the *Daily Blare*.

'A young man?'

'Twenty-eight, I believe. Nice quiet young fellow.'

'I should like to have a few words with him, and also with your husband, if I may. I will return for that purpose this evening. I venture to suggest that you should repose yourself a little, madame, you look fatigued.'

'I should just think I am! First the worry about Eliza, and then I was at the sales practically all yesterday, and you know what *that* is, M. Poirot, and what with one thing and another and a lot to do in the house, because of course Annie can't do it all – and very likely she'll give notice anyway, being unsettled in this way – well, what with it all, I'm tired out!'

Poirot murmured sympathetically, and we took our leave.

'It's a curious coincidence,' I said, 'but that absconding clerk, Davis, was from the same bank as Simpson. Can there be any connection, do you think?'

Poirot smiled.

'At the one end, a defaulting clerk, at the other a vanishing cook. It is hard to see any relation between the two, unless possibly Davis visited Simpson, fell in love with the cook, and persuaded her to accompany him on his flight!'

I laughed. But Poirot remained grave.

'He might have done worse,' he said reprovingly. 'Remember, Hastings, if you are going into exile, a good cook may be of more comfort than a pretty face!' He paused for a moment and then went on. 'It is a curious case, full of contradictory features. I am interested – yes, I am distinctly interested.'

That evening we returned to 88 Prince Albert Road and interviewed both Todd and Simpson. The former was a melancholy lantern-jawed man of forty-odd.

'Oh! Yes, yes,' he said vaguely. 'Eliza. Yes. A good cook, I believe. And economical. I make a strong point of economy.'

'Can you imagine any reason for her leaving you so suddenly?'

'Oh, well,' said Mr Todd vaguely. 'Servants, you know. My wife worries too much. Worn out from always worrying. The whole problem's quite simple really. "Get another, my dear," I say. "Get another." That's all there is to it. No good crying over spilt milk.'

Mr Simpson was equally unhelpful. He was a quiet inconspicuous young man with spectacles.

'I must have seen her, I suppose,' he said. 'Elderly woman, wasn't she? Of course, it's the other one I see always, Annie. Nice girl. Very obliging.'

'Were those two on good terms with each other?'

Mr Simpson said he couldn't say, he was sure. He supposed so.

'Well, we get nothing of interest there, *mon ami*,' said Poirot as we left the house. Our departure had been delayed by a burst of vociferous repetition from Mrs Todd, who repeated everything she had said that morning at rather greater length.

'Are you disappointed?' I asked. 'Did you expect to hear something?'

Poirot shook his head.

'There was a possibility, of course,' he said. 'But I hardly thought it likely.'

The next development was a letter which Poirot received on the following morning. He read it, turned purple with indignation, and handed it to me.

Mrs Todd regrets that after all she will not avail herself

of Mr Poirot's services. After talking the matter over with her husband she sees that it is foolish to call in a detective about a purely domestic affair. Mrs Todd encloses a guinea for consultation fee.

'Aha!' cried Poirot angrily. 'And they think to get rid of Hercule Poirot like that! As a favour – a great favour – I consent to investigate their miserable little twopenny-halfpenny affair – and they dismiss me *comme ça*! Here, I mistake not, is the hand of Mr Todd. But I say no! – thirty-six times no! I will spend my own guineas, thirty-six hundred of them if need be, but I will get to the bottom of this matter!'

'Yes,' I said. 'But how?'

Poirot calmed down a little.

'*D'abord*,' he said, 'we will advertise in the papers. Let me see – yes – something like this: "If Eliza Dunn will communicate with this address, she will hear of something to her advantage.' Put it in all the papers you can think of, Hastings. Then I will make some little inquiries of my own. Go, go – all must be done as quickly as possible!'

I did not see him again until the evening, when he condescended to tell me what he had been doing.

'I have made inquiries at the firm of Mr Todd. He was not absent on Wednesday, and he bears a good character – so much for him. Then Simpson, on Thursday he was ill and did not come to the bank, but he was there on Wednesday. He was moderately friendly with Davis. Nothing out of the common. There does not seem to be anything there. No. We must place our reliance on the advertisement.'

The advertisement duly appeared in all the principal daily papers. By Poirot's orders it was to be continued every day for a week. His eagerness over this uninteresting matter of a defaulting cook was extraordinary, but I realized that he considered it a point of honour to persevere until he finally succeeded. Several extremely interesting cases were brought to him about this time, but he declined them all. Every morning he would rush at his letters, scrutinize them earnestly and then lay them down with a sigh.

But our patience was rewarded at last. On the Wednesday following Mrs Todd's visit, our landlady informed us that a person of the name of Eliza Dunn had called.

'*Enfin!*' cried Poirot. 'But make her mount then! At once. Immediately.'

Thus admonished, our landlady hurried out and returned a moment or two later, ushering in Miss Dunn. Our quarry was much as described: tall, stout, and eminently respectable.

'I came in answer to the advertisement,' she explained. 'I thought there must be some muddle or other, and that perhaps you didn't know I'd already got my legacy.'

Poirot was studying her attentively. He drew forward a chair with a flourish.

'The truth of the matter is,' he explained, 'that your late mistress, Mrs Todd, was much concerned about you. She feared some accident might have befallen you.'

Eliza Dunn seemed very much surprised.

'Didn't she get my letter then?'

'She got no word of any kind.' He paused, and then said persuasively: 'Recount to me the whole story, will you not?'

Eliza Dunn needed no encouragement. She plunged at once into a lengthy narrative.

'I was just coming home on Wednesday night and had nearly got to the house, when a gentleman stopped me. A tall gentleman he was, with a beard and a big hat. "Miss Eliza Dunn?" he said. "Yes," I said. "I've been inquiring for you at No. 88," he said. "They told me I might meet you coming along here. Miss Dunn, I have come from Australia specially to find you. Do you happen to know the maiden name of your maternal grandmother?" "Jane Emmott," I said. "Exactly," he said. "Now, Miss Dunn, although you may never have heard of the fact, your grandmother had a great friend, Eliza Leech. This friend went to Australia where she married a very wealthy settler. Her two children died in infancy, and she inherited all her husband's property. She died a few months ago, and by her will you inherit a house in this country and a considerable sum of money."

'You could have knocked me down with a feather,' continued Miss Dunn. 'For a minute, I was suspicious, and he must have seen it, for he smiled. "Quite right to be on your guard, Miss Dunn," he said. "Here are my credentials." He handed me a letter from some lawyers in Melbourne, Hurst and Crotchet, and a card. He was Mr Crotchet. "There are one or two conditions," he said. "Our client was a little eccentric, you know. The bequest is conditional on your taking possession of the house (it is in Cumberland) before twelve o'clock tomorrow. The other condition is of no importance – it is merely a stipulation that you should not be in domestic service." My face fell. "Oh, Mr Crotchet," I said. "I'm a cook. Didn't they tell you at the house?" "Dear, dear," he said. "I had no idea of such a thing. I thought you might possibly be a companion or governess there. This is very unfortunate – very unfortunate indeed."

' "Shall I have to lose all the money?" I said, anxious like. He thought for a minute or two. "There are always ways of getting round the law, Miss Dunn," he said at last. "We as lawyers know that. The way out here is for you to have left your employment this afternoon." "But my month?" I said. "My dear Miss Dunn," he said with a smile. "You can leave an employer any minute by forfeiting a month's wages. Your mistress will understand in view of the circumstances. The difficulty is *time*! It is imperative that you should catch the 11.5 from King's Cross to the north. I can advance you ten pounds or so for the fare, and you can write a note at the station to your employer. I will take it to her myself and explain the whole circumstances." I agreed, of course, and an hour later I was in the train, so flustered that I didn't know whether I was on my head or heels. Indeed by the time I got to Carlisle, I was half inclined to think the whole thing was one of those confidence tricks you read about. But I went to the address he had given me – solicitors they were, and it was all right. A nice little house, and an income of three hundred a year. These lawyers knew very little, they'd just got a letter from a gentleman in London instructing them to hand over the house to me and £150 for the first six months. Mr Crotchet sent up my things to me, but there was no word from Missus. I supposed she was angry and grudged me my bit of luck. She kept back my box too, and sent my clothes in paper parcels. But there, of course if she never had my letter, she might think it a bit cool of me.'

Poirot had listened attentively to this long history. Now he nodded his head as though completely satisfied.

'Thank you, mademoiselle. There had been, as you say, a little muddle. Permit me to recompense you for your trouble.' He handed her an envelope. 'You return to Cumberland immediately? A little word in your ear. *Do not forget how to cook*. It is always useful to have something to fall back upon in case things go wrong.'

'Credulous,' he murmured, as our visitor departed, 'but perhaps not more than most of her class.' His face grew grave. 'Come, Hastings, there is no time to be lost. Get a taxi while I write a note to Japp.'

Poirot was waiting on the doorstep when I returned with the taxi.

'Where are we going?' I asked anxiously.

'First, to despatch this note by special messenger.'

This was done, and re-entering the taxi Poirot gave the address to the driver.

'Eighty-eight Prince Albert Road, Clapham.'

'So we are going there?'

'*Mais oui*. Though frankly I fear we shall be too late. Our bird will have flown, Hastings.'

'Who is our bird?'

Poirot smiled.

'The inconspicuous Mr Simpson.'

'What?' I exclaimed.

'Oh, come now, Hastings, do not tell me that all is not clear to you now!'

'The cook was got out of the way, I realize that,' I said, slightly piqued. 'But why? *Why* should Simpson wish to get her out of the house? Did she know something about him?'

'Nothing whatever.'

'Well, then – '

'But he wanted something that she had.'

'Money? The Australian legacy?'

'No, my friend – something quite different.' He paused a moment and then said gravely: '*A battered tin trunk . . .*'

I looked sideways at him. His statement seemed so fantastic that I suspected him of pulling my leg, but he was perfectly grave and serious.

'Surely he could buy a trunk if he wanted one,' I cried.

'He did not want a new trunk. He wanted a trunk of pedigree. A trunk of assured respectability.'

'Look here, Poirot,' I cried, 'this really is a bit thick. You're pulling my leg.'

He looked at me.

'You lack the brains and the imagination of Mr Simpson, Hastings. See here: On Wednesday evening, Simpson decoys away the cook. A printed card and a printed sheet of notepaper are simple matters to obtain, and he is willing to pay £150 and a year's house rent to assure the success of his plan. Miss Dunn does not recognize him – the beard and the hat and the slight colonial accent completely deceive her. That is the end of Wednesday – except for the trifling fact that Simpson has helped himself to fifty thousand pounds' worth of negotiable securities.'

'*Simpson* – but it was *Davis* –'

'If you will kindly permit me to continue, Hastings! Simpson knows that the theft will be discovered on Thursday afternoon. He does not go to the bank on Thursday, but he lies in wait for Davis when he comes out to lunch. Perhaps he admits the theft and tells Davis he will return the securities to him – anyhow he succeeds in getting Davis to come to Clapham with him. It is the maid's day out, and Mrs Todd was at the sales, so there is no one in the house. When the theft is discovered and Davis is missing, the implication will be overwhelming. Davis is the thief! Mr Simpson will be perfectly safe, and can return to work on the morrow like the honest clerk they think him.'

'And Davis?'

Poirot made an expressive gesture, and slowly shook his head.

'It seems too cold-blooded to be believed, and yet what other explanation can there be, *mon ami*. The one difficulty for a murderer is the disposal of the body – and Simpson had planned that out beforehand. I was struck at once by the fact that although Eliza Dunn obviously meant to return that night when she went out (witness her remark about the stewed peaches) *yet her trunk was all ready packed when they came for it*. It was Simpson who sent word to Carter Paterson to call on Friday and it was Simpson who corded up the box on Thursday afternoon. What suspicion could possibly arise? A maid leaves and sends for her box, it is labelled and addressed ready in her name, probably to a railway station within easy reach of London. On Saturday afternoon, Simpson, in his Australian disguise, claims it, he affixes a new label and address and redespatches it somewhere else, again "to be left till called for". When the authorities get suspicious, for excellent reasons, and open it, all that can be elicited will be that a bearded colonial despatched it from some junction near London. There will be nothing to connect it with 88 Prince Albert Road. Ah! Here we are.'

Poirot's prognostications had been correct. Simpson had left days previously. But he was not to escape the consequences of his crime. By the aid of wireless, he was discovered on the *Olympia*, en route to America.

A tin trunk, addressed to Mr Henry Wintergreen, attracted the attention of railway officials at Glasgow. It was opened and found to contain the body of the unfortunate Davis.

Mrs Todd's cheque for a guinea was never cashed. Instead Poirot had it framed and hung on the wall of our sitting-room.

'It is to me a little reminder, Hastings. Never to despise the trivial – the undignified. A disappearing domestic at one end – a cold-blooded murder at the other. To me, one of the most interesting of my cases.'

Murder in Mesopotamia

Nurse Amy Leatheran had a most unusual patient. Louise, according to her husband, celebrated archaeologist Dr Leidner, suffered from 'nervous terror'. Her fantasies were vivid and horrifying: a disembodied hand, a yellow, dead face pressed against the window. Who or what did she fear?

At the site of a dig in the Iraqi desert, surely she was safe from danger. Most of the expedition were old colleagues and friends. Yet they seemed an unnaturally formal group – there was tension, uneasiness even, in the air. Something very sinister was going on, and it involved ... murder.

Ordeal by Innocence

The verdict is murder...

And while serving a life sentence for killing his mother, Jacko Argyle dies. Two years later, a stranger shatters the peace of the Argyle household. Can Arthur Calgary provide the missing link in Jacko's defence? Was Jacko sentenced for a murder he didn't commit?

And if Jacko didn't murder his mother ... *who did*?

The ABC Murders

A is for Andover – and Mrs Ascher battered to death.
B is for Bexhill – and Betty Barnard is strangled.
C is for Sir Carmichael Clarke clubbed and killed.

Beside each body lay a copy of the ABC Railway Guide – open at the relevant page. The police were baffled. But the murderer had already made a grave mistake. He had challenged Hercule Poirot to unmask him…

'The acknowledged queen of detective fiction.'
OBSERVER

Taken at
the Flood

Gordon Cloade is killed in an air-raid on London. He has left no will and his vast fortune passes to his young wife, Rosaleen.

But five other people have been promised a share in that fortune – five people who desperately need the money. Now it can only become theirs if Rosaleen should happen to die before them.

There are five people with a strong motive for murder and violent murder is committed.

But Rosaleen is not the victim.

'Miss Christie is a master of the art of the cosy murder story told briskly, vivaciously, and with ever-fertile imagination.'
MANCHESTER EVENING NEWS

ALSO BY AGATHA CHRISTIE

Elephants Can Remember

Hercule Poirot stood on the cliff overlooking the rocks below and the sea breaking against them. Here, where he stood, the bodies of a husband and wife had been found. Here, three weeks before that, a woman had walked in her sleep and fallen to her death.

Why had these things happened ...?

'A classic example of the ingenious three-card trick that she has been playing on us for so many years.'
SUNDAY EXPRESS

'Splendid ... she tells us all we want to know and nothing that is irrelevant.'
THE TIMES

ALSO BY AGATHA CHRISTIE

The Seven
Dials Mystery

Seven clocks ticking ominously in a suicide's room
and a dying friend whose last words are 'seven dials'
lead dapper Jimmy Thesiger and his irrepressible
girlfriend to a Soho club.

There they learn of the Seven Dials Society: seven
masked conspirators who meet in a secret room to
talk about stealing scientific secrets – and plan the
next murder...

'Her gift is pure genius.'
OBSERVER

Fontana

The Christie Collection

all titles £3.99 each

You can buy Fontana paperbacks at your local bookshop or newsagent. Or you can order them from Fontana Paperbacks, Cash Sales Department, Box 29, Douglas, Isle of Man. Please send a cheque, postal or money order (not currency) worth the purchase price plus 22p per book for postage (maximum postage required is £3.00 for orders within the UK).

NAME (Block letters)_____

ADDRESS_____

_____

TITLES_____

_____